Dedication

To my friend, Artist extraordinaire, Sheila Howell. Thank you

Table of Contents

When the Curtain Fell

Lanie took the letter secretary and good friend Blake Nelson handed her, already feeling a sinking in her stomach just from the expression on his face. She wasn't wrong. It was from Tim Frawley, her old English teacher, and drama coach. God, so long ago since she had even heard his name. But she'd thought of him. She pictured him, tall and slim, glasses perched on his aquiline nose, moving around the stage like a cat as he called out notes and made constructive comments. He had so much enthusiasm for his subject, his dramatic instinct impeccable.

The familiar logo at the top of the letter, intertwined in red and silver ribbon -- Port Ainsley High School -- the school she'd run away from, the town she'd escaped, nearly fifteen years ago.

Mr. Frawley had heaped high praise on her in the letter, saying how proud they all were of her, complimenting her on her accomplishments over the years. "You know I always told you you were a fine actress," he'd written. "And now everyone knows."

How she'd wanted to please Mr. Frawley. How she adored him. And in the end, she'd let him down. Nancy Cole, her understudy had saved the day after she'd fled the building. The show must go on. She wanted to hate Nancy, too, but no one could hate Nancy. Perhaps she could be forgiven for not being overly happy for her.

While it warmed her to read Mr. Frawley's kind words, at the same time they took her to a place from which she couldn't seem to escape. She went back there now, an image of her mother rising to the screen of her mind. She was asleep on the living room sofa, snoring softly. The blanket Lanie (Jenny then) had draped over earlier her mother now covered her face, showing only the top of her head, the mass of black, curly hair. Her mother had beautiful hair. Lanie's was straight and light brown, like her father's.

The smell of alcohol wafted up to her, a little less potent than when her mom came stumbling in just after 3:00 am.

Ever since Daddy left and moved in with his new girlfriend three months ago, Mom had sunk deeper and deeper into a dark depression coupled with wild mood swings. She'd go from cursing her, bellowing things like, 'You're just like your goddamn father' to she didn't know what she'd do without her. Sometimes she just sat staring into space, tears streaming down her face. And then the string of sleazy men came into their lives. It made Lanie feel ashamed. Especially the way a couple of them had looked at her, like they were stripping her clothes off with their eyes, sneakily of course. She felt sorry for her mother, and at other times she just felt contempt for her. Why couldn't she just pull herself together? Accept what happened and move forward in her life. Where did my sweet, funny, loving mother go? Daddy sent her away, she thought. He broke her heart. He broke her spirit.

"Where did you go, Lanie?"

Blake's voice brought her back to the present, to her apartment, softly scented with cut flowers and herbs from her window boxes. The oak floors gleamed and her eggshell walls were hung with her favorite paintings, a few nice prints, and some fine originals done by local artists. She reminded herself how very blessed she was.

She handed Blake back the letter in which her old teacher had invited her to return to play the role of Susy Hendrix in After Dark, a terrific thriller Audrey Hepburn had starred in on-screen. She'd played a recently blinded woman terrorized by a trio of thugs as they search for a heroin-stuffed doll they believe is in her apartment. This production was to be a fundraiser for renovations, including new, 'badly needed', stage curtains. They were needed even when she was there. "If you could see your way clear, Ms. Nichols, we'd be so honored... " They would stage it on dates to accommodate her busy career.

Ms. Nichols. She smiled almost sadly. He'd always called her Jenny. Her real name

- Jenny Beddow. The name sounded strange to her as if it belonged to someone else. She was getting enough work now that she'd probably been recognized by a smattering of people in her hometown. She was on Facebook and fan letters were being forwarded through her agent. It was no doubt how Mr. Frawley found her.

Sweet man, she thought. Mr. Frawley, always in her corner. He'd come to the house that night while she was packing to make her escape. He'd knocked several times and called to her through the door, but she didn't answer. Hard to answer when you're choking on tears of shame and disappointment. After a while, she heard his footsteps retreating down the stairs.

Landing the role of Shakespeare's Juliet had been a dream come true. Not that it came as a huge surprise to read her name - Jennifer Beddow - on the cast list taped on the classroom door. She'd felt good about her audition. You usually knew when you fell short. That hadn't changed. She was by nature a shy person. Yet she was at home on stage. She came alive on stage.

"It's an opportunity to finally put this behind you," Blake said, reluctantly taking the letter from her outstretched hand and setting it atop the growing pile of fan letters. Blake was younger than Lanie by eight years, boyishly handsome, and gay. He was not only her guy Friday, but her best friend and housemate had been for five years now. He'd come to Paul's Restaurant one afternoon where she waitressed and asked if he could put up an ad. She'd been here since she landed in Toronto; Paul Madison had a soft spot for actors and scheduled her hours around her auditions.

Blake had been looking for office work. He had a diploma in communications and time management, a course he took online. It turned out he had a natural ability to organize and people liked him. He'd been living in his car back then. Later, she learned he'd recently broken up with a long-time boyfriend and was also a struggling playwright. She knew about struggling. She looked at the ad for several days, then a few days later called him.

As for her, there'd been a couple of promising romances along the way, one that saw an impressive diamond ring on her finger, but her friendship with Blake was the only one that endured. Blake still dated, but nothing serious. He was spending most evenings with his dad who was in a nursing home and sadly, no longer knew his son. "He never did know me," he told Lanie. "Didn't want to."

"Lanie," he said now," bringing her back to the issue at hand. "You didn't let what happened back then stop you from pursuing your dream to become an actress. Face your demons once and for all. You can do this; you should do this."

"I know you think so. But no. Please, just make my excuses. Send a generous donation on my behalf."

"Give it some thought at least. Sleep on it."

"No. There's nothing to think about. I can't go back there. And I definitely can't perform on that stage. Enough, okay, Blake."

But he wasn't ready to let it go. "You know, what happened wouldn't be that big a deal today. Times have changed. People share the most intimate things about themselves, especially over the Internet. Hell, I was still in the closet back when you were in high school."

She smiled and touched his cheek with her fingertips. He had suffered too. "I'm going to bed now. I've got an audition in the morning, remember?" She was reading for a role in a new TV comedy. "Goodnight, sweet friend."

She slipped under the cool sheets, but sleep evaded her. Her thoughts returned to Port Ainsley, like the needle slipping into the familiar groove of an old phonograph record.

She was on stage and had just spoken from the balcony, the familiar line: "Romeo, Romeo, wherefore art thou, Romeo?" She was in the zone, encompassing all of Juliet within herself. Mr. Frawley had said she was perfect with her willowy frame, and her long, fair hair. She, Lanie was Juliet.

And then it happened. From some part of her consciousness, she heard the commotion at the back of the theatre, tried to block it out, staying in character. Until the moment when she recognized the sound of her mother's voice, jolting her from the dream of Juliet. Horror impaled her very soul, striking her immovable. And then was looking at her mother stagger and lurch down the aisle toward the stage. "Thazz my daughter," she told them all, slurring her words amidst craning necks and whispers, her words thick and slurred. "Momma's here, my beautiful Jenny."

It couldn't be; it was some kind of nightmare. I must be asleep, dreaming.

But she was awake. She heard the gasps from the audience. Isolated snickers found their way to her ears. Her mother continued to make her way unsteadily up the aisle to the front of the auditorium, once nearly falling into the audience, coming nearer to her. Nearer. Grinning like a monster.

Galvanized from her frozen stance, Lanie ran off the stage, raced from the building, and later that night, the town. She ended up here, in Toronto.

Even now, lying in the bed staring at the ceiling, that same scalding shame flooded through her, withering her heart. How she had hated her mother at that moment. She'd wanted her dead, a wish that was to be granted just two weeks later when she was struck and killed by a car. A hit-and-run, the paper said. She was crossing the street in front of her building. She never regained consciousness. She'd been drinking. There were no witnesses. Lanie didn't go to the funeral.

She turned in the bed and switched on the lamp, a sense of panic washing over her. Her body felt clammy and she couldn't get a full breath. Stop it. It was a long time ago. Take deep breaths, she told herself. Soon, she was breathing calmly. She didn't hate her mother anymore. She never did. She'd always loved her, though it took some time to forgive her. With the passing of those same years, she began to realize how betrayed her mother must have felt. First by Lanie's father, and then by Lanie herself. Her husband and daughter. Betrayed and abandoned by them both. She hadn't deserved that. Her mother was a sensitive woman, emotionally fragile. She'd found comfort in a bottle, in the attentions of men who could only hurt her. She'd needed help. Maybe if I'd been older, Lanie thought, by way of justification. Too late now, of course. You can't go back and change a damn thing.

The woman her dad had left her mother for was long out of the picture, and Evan Beddow now lived alone in a rooming house. In a weak moment, she called him one night, and they both cried on the phone. He'd made a mistake. A terrible mistake, he said. "I'm so sorry." He'd sounded old, and tired. He'd not only gone to her mother's funeral, but he also took care of the arrangements. Somehow she knew he would. "I looked for you, Jenny, honey," he said hoarsely. "I didn't know where you'd gone."

No one had. How could she have done that? Yet, the longer she'd stayed away, the more impossible it seemed to change the course of her journey. She didn't like to think it was in part vengeance. But maybe it was.

She promised she'd see him soon, and she meant to. We forget sometimes that our parents aren't perfect beings. They are human, just like us. They mess up. They fall apart. We don't know that when we're kids. We think they're omniscient, like God. She'd given little thought to how devastated they both must have been when she disappeared, never knowing where she'd gone. Not even if she was alive.

I can see Dad if I go home, she thought. I'll also visit Mom's grave, so long overdue. And didn't she owe something to Mr. Frawley? He'd championed her, made her believe in her ability to succeed as an actress. If not for him, who knew what her life might have been like right now?

Blake was right; it was time to face her demons.

Lanie hesitated as she faced the opaque glass door with the word OFFICE stenciled on it. The rest of the cast had been rehearsing for a while now, and she had some catching up to do, although she'd been over the script every chance she got. It was a great role and thankfully she was a quick study.

"Lanie, how are you doing?" Blake said softly at her shoulder.

"Fine. At least I think I am."

He lay an encouraging hand on her shoulder. "Remember, you're Elaine Nichols, a successful actor. All that crap happened years ago. People forget. They're too busy worrying about their own lives. And it wasn't your fault, anyway. You were just a little girl."

Not so little, she thought. Putting a smile on her face, she rapped lightly on the door and opened it. The woman at the desk, tall and dark-haired, looking like she was cast in a movie as the secretary, shot to her feet, clearly flustered. Oh, Ms. Nichols, I'm so pleased to meet you, she said, extending her hand. Mr. Frawley is so looking forward to seeing you again. They're all in the rehearsal hall right now. The whole cast is very excited that you're doing this. Thank you so much. I'm a big fan."

Lanie was touched and found herself relaxing. The woman asked about their flight, which had been smooth and non-eventful.

"Flowers and cards have already started arriving; I've forwarded them on to your hotel suite. Tickets are going like wildfire."

"That's great." Both excitement and fear rippled through her.

"I'm Irene Hemmings, by the way. "

"Hi, Irene. And please call me Lanie for Elaine.   My middle name, for my grandmother."   She introduced Blake and they all headed for the rehearsal hall, the sound of their combined footsteps echoing on the hardwood floor, bringing back old memories.

Tim Frawley must have heard them because he met them halfway down the hall. "Oh, Jenn... Ms. Nichols... " He was smiling, but with a shyness she couldn't recall, and which she found endearing. He put out a hand in greeting. She ignored it and hugged him. "Jen's fine. Though I go by Lanie now."

"You can't know how happy I am to see you," he said.

"Me too, Tim. I'm looking forward to working with you again."   He looked the same but for a smattering of grey in his hair and a few lines at the corners of his eyes. He introduced her to the rest of the cast, who welcomed her warmly.

They chatted for a half-hour or so, then he said, "We'll let you get settled into your hotel. Same time tomorrow?"

Back at the hotel, Blake took a call from the senior's home to be told his dad had fallen into a coma and was not expected to live. He booked a flight. "I'll come back for opening night if I possibly can," he told her. "Maybe sooner."

"I'm fine. Take all the time you need. You know I'd be with you if I could. I plan to go see Mom's grave while I'm here, and since Saturday is the last show night, I'll go in the afternoon and fly back on Sunday."

"Sounds like a plan. You have a good show. Break a leg."

"I'll do my best."

In the morning, she accompanied him down on the elevator and waved goodbye when he got in the cab. Minutes later, the cab disappeared around the next corner, leaving her feeling oddly alone and filled with a strange sense of dread. Why couldn't she shake this feeling that something terrible awaited her?

Finally, it was opening night. It seemed to come up so quickly. Before she was ready. Lanie was more nervous than when she'd played at the Royal Alexander or Stratford in Toronto. She could hear the audience down in the auditorium, talking, laughing, settling in their seats. Her heart was racing like a trip hammer in her chest.

Would they remember? This was a new generation. How silly she was. Of course, they'd remember. Maybe not from personal experience, but they would have heard the story, and no doubt many of their parents were probably out there.   Let it go, Lanie! Let it go! She slid her damp hands down the sides of her vintage skirt, then gripped the cane the prop girl handed her, smiling.

The house lights dimmed and the curtains whispered open with just the slightest creaking. Only up close could you see the light shining through the heavy but threadbare red velvet fabric.

The auditorium silenced and the suspenseful piano theme rose from the orchestra pit, just the softest of percussion, building, now fading out...

The curtains opened, evoking a smattering of applause, rightly so, she thought. Carl Branden was a wonderful set designer. He did the sets when she was here.

This is a mistake. Too late to back out now. Take deep, slow breaths. You are Suzy Hendricks, a blind woman. Suzy is strong. She has courage.

Picking up her cue, Lanie unlocked the door that led onto the stair landing that descended into Suzy's apartment. The applause was immediate. It quickly swelled then faded to silence. Holding tight to the handrail, she took each step carefully, white cane tapping tentatively as she went.

At the bottom, she cocked her head slightly, listening, called out: "Sam.

From that moment, the character of Suzy, and the more than competent cast, carried her through, Beyond the footlights, the audience was riveted. She could feel it. With the final word, applause broke out and they were given a standing ovation and three curtain calls.

After they'd taken their final bows, and the last straggler had left the auditorium, she was swarmed by the cast and crew who showered her with with praise and she, in turn, returned their affection and appreciation. Many members of the audience had come backstage to congratulate them, some she remembered, all seemed delighted to meet her – for the first time, or again. She was exhausted and at the same time, she was flying.

The cast, everyone, had been so wonderful to work with, far more capable than their amateur status would suggest. Hard-working thespians, everyone. And nothing terrible had happened. It was all in her mind. She silently thanked Blake for pushing her to do this. She felt a measure of freedom she had not realized she'd lost. As if a mountain of sludge had slid off her shoulders.

"You were amazing," Tim told her as she was getting into her coat. "But then that comes as no surprise to me."

"Thanks. I loved every minute of it." She gave a self-conscious chuckle. "Well, there were a few minutes there that haunted me. Thanks so much for thinking of me for this part, Tim."

"Who else? You were perfect. Perfect. Are you heading back to the hotel or is Blake picking you up?"

"Taking a cab. Blake's in Toronto. His dad passed away yesterday."

"I'm sorry."

"Yeah. It's complicated. I'm going to fly back on Monday."

He nodded. "If you have no other plans, I'd love to take you to dinner tomorrow. Or maybe lunch if you'd prefer that. I want to hear all about everything you've been doing these past long years."

"I'm planning on visiting my mother's grave tomorrow. I never have. So dinner sounds great."

"Wonderful, Jen...Lanie. I'll drive you to the airport Monday if that's okay."

"Oh, Tim, thanks, but I can just grab a cab. I..."

"Please. I'd like to."

"Well, if you're sure. It would be greatly appreciated."

Was this more than just a mentor interest? Could that be possible? She'd never thought of him that way. She respected him, sure; she was grateful to him. But more than that?

Sunday dawned cool and grey with rolling dark clouds moving in. Seeing Tim's dark blue Toyota pull up at the curb, she hurried out the lobby doors. He got out and opened the door for her. "Hi. You okay?"

He was wearing slacks and a navy blazer. His usually messy hair from school was neatly combed. He'd dressed up. She wasn't sure if that was true or if she was altogether okay. But she would be. She'd bought silk flowers in the hotel gift shop to lay on the grave. They would last awhile. Unlike Lanie, her mother had never liked plants or flowers she had to take care of. "I'm good. Thanks."

"You're even more beautiful than I remember."

"Thank you," she smiled. "You're looking pretty dapper yourself."

They were quiet on the rest of the drive. The way he'd looked at her when she was coming out of the hotel lobby let her know she hadn't imagined a romantic interest in her and had to admit, she didn't find him unattractive. Had he always had a thing for her? Funny, she hadn't ever considered him in that light, though she knew some of the girls at school had had crushes.

"I miss her," she blurted, surprising herself.

He touched her hand but said nothing. He returned it to the wheel as he turned into the cemetery and they drove up the narrow, path, gravel crunching softly beneath the tires. Glancing at the paper with the directions her father had given her, she said, "It's just to your left."

He stopped the car and Lanie got out and walked a few feet ahead. There it was. Just behind a small upright gravestone embedded with angels, where a 7-year-old child name Molly Banks was buried, was her mother's grave, her name spelled out; Ellen Mary Beddow, and the dates marking her life.

Lanie knelt on the hard ground, her eyes filling with tears despite her promise not to cry and make her old teacher feel the need to comfort her. She laid the flowers on the grave and place her palm flat on the small stone, which her father had arranged. Despite the chill in the air, a warmth emitted from the stone. She hadn't even known if someone was taking care of the arrangements. She hadn't called to ask. How could she be so callous? So uncaring. You just assumed your father would take care of things, she told herself. Had she?

"I'm sorry, Mom," she whispered, tears running down her face.

She felt the weight of Tim's hand on her shoulder. "I'm sorry, too, Jennie. But it was a terrible thing she did. You mustn't beat up on yourself."

She turned and looked up at him. "What?"

"I was broken up when you sent me away that night, Jenny – the night you left town. I knocked and knocked on your door...I could hear you crying."

"I know. I heard you." What is he saying? "I loved my mother."

A small gust of wind came up, blowing her hair across her face. She clawed it back as she rose to her feet.

"That's because you're a loving person, Jenny. She didn't deserve your love. She didn't care about you. She destroyed our play."

It was just a play. A damn play.

"I knew that wherever you went, she would follow you through your life. She would just hurt you again and again. You looked so beautiful standing on that stage. God, I wanted you. But you were my student. I looked for you everywhere, you know. Searched the internet for your name, but of course, you'd changed it. And then one day I was watching television, and there you were. That was cruel of you, Jenny."

A trickling of ice slid down her spinal column. She couldn't breathe. Couldn't reconcile what she was hearing from this man she'd known for so long. The man she admired and respected. Crazy. Crazy.

"I was getting ready to drive away when I saw her come out of your building. Oddly, I was surprised to see her. I thought I would just go home again, keep vigil another time, as I had the night before and the night before that. She was a small woman, wasn't she?" He looked somewhere past Lanie as if seeing her mother in some other dimension. His attention returned to her. "I waited until she was halfway across the street. It was just past dusk, not a soul around."

There was a buzzing around her head, a roaring in her ears.

"I stepped on the gas," he told her. "For a split second, we made eye contact. She looked surprised. Confused, maybe. The impact made just the slightest sound. Only a gentle bump. He drew his coat more tightly about him. "We should leave now. It's getting chilly. Why are you looking at me like that, Jenny? I did it for you."

His eyes had changed and he was someone she didn't know. No longer the kind, warm Mr. Frawley, not Tim, as he'd asked her to call him, but something else. Something dark and dangerous. A wisp of cloud drifted past the sliver of moon, and a chill gripped her. She stood in shock, her heart a frantic weight in her chest, keenly aware that she was alone in a cemetery with a killer.

And then a voice spoke to her. Her mother's voice. "You're an actress, Jen. Act. Save yourself." A warm, caring voice, as it had been before her father left. A voice not inside Jen's head, not in her imagination, but right here, just at her left shoulder.

No deep breath. Smooth. Meet him where he is. "I'm just so surprised, Tim. That you would avenge me like that. That you cared about me that much."

She saw him relax visibly, and the smile tug at the corners of his mouth. "Of course I did. I told you."

"I think I've always loved you, Tim. I just didn't know it." An involuntary shiver went through her that had nothing to do with the chill air. "You're right, it is getting cold. Shall we go?"

She kept up a light chatter in the car, mostly about the play, until he drew up at the curb in front of the hotel. She knew she couldn't carry this through dinner with him.

"Tim, I'm awfully tired. Would you mind if
we skipped dinner and instead you pick me
up for breakfast in the morning?"

He leaned over and kissed her. "Of
course not You get a good night's sleep. I
promise I won't rush you, Jenny. I know you
need time to get used to the idea of a life with
your old acting coach."

"Ever sensitive, Tim. Thank you." She
got out of the car, a soft smile on her face, not
rushing. No hurry.

Inside her room with the door locked,
she sagged against it and waited for her heart
to settle down, for her gag reflexes to calm.
Then, her hand shaking, she phoned the
desk.

"This is Lanie Nichols, room 707. Please
connect to me the Port Ainsley police
department."

The End

Dark Reunion

Laurie arrived at the reunion alone. David had begged off, saying he didn't even plan on going to his own reunion but encouraging her to go and have a good time. "Those things can dredge up a lot of adolescent garbage," he'd said. Later, his words would come back to haunt her.

When she was dressed, she did a little whirl in front of him and was rewarded with a whistle. "Hey, I'm not so sure I should let you go alone. You look too damn good."

"You don't think it's too short."

"Yeah, actually I do. Why don't you wear your old plaid nightshirt over it? It's in your drawer. I'll get it."

She laughed and kissed him goodbye.

It was an hour's flight from Halifax to Saint John. She took a cab from her mother's. And now that she was here, she wasn't sure why. She'd never been in the clique, part of the "in-crowd." Still, there were a few people she was looking forward to seeing again. Dodie, her best friend, wouldn't be here; she'd gotten her nursing degree and moved to the States.

The gym was bright and noisy, festive with red and blue balloons (the school colors), streamers, and flowers. A mingling of perfumes and good food wafted to her as she scanned the crowd for a familiar face. She spotted Harold Thomas across the room, doing a slow move to the beat of Barry Manilow's Mandy blaring from the sound system. He held a glass of punch in his hand, and his eyes were closed. Laurie smiled, remembering. Short and squat, Harold was never much to look at, but he was a terrific dancer. The girls had stood in line to dance with him. "Me next, Harold. You promised." She'd seen his picture in the paper a few times over the years. He'd made a success of himself in the insurance business. He didn't look any different, just older.

She turned to see a woman in a purple pantsuit rushing toward her, smiling hugely, finally wrapping her in a warm Chanel fragrant embrace. "My God, Laurie Stevens, dark and adorable as ever. You look the same as you did in high school." She held her at arm's length. "You have no idea who in the hell I am, do you?"

Well, I..." Laurie wracked her brain.

"Can't blame you. I've put on a few pounds. I'm..."

"Alice Moore," Laurie jumped in, grateful to have remembered. "Of course I do. It's great to see you again," she said, meaning it. "How are you?"

"Not so bad. The name's Dowling now. Divorced," she added with an apologetic shrug.

Alice had always been a warm, friendly person, but fiercely competitive, especially in sports. Both women turned as a male voice greeted them. Laurie recognized that sexy, boyish grin at once. She'd had such a crush on Aaron Hamilton, while all he could see was blond, popular Jillian Thorne. He was still tall and good-looking, but his thick sandy hair was a thing of the past. He got in a couple of bald jokes before anyone else could. Other people joined them,

and at some point they all gravitated toward the buffet table, in particular, the punch bowl. Someone said it was generously laced.

Aaron related the story of the time when meek, soft-spoken Miss Ruth Bell grabbed Derek Speight (a foot taller than her) by the front of his shirt and slammed him up against the blackboard. Derek was always cutting up in class, but for some reason on this particular Monday morning, he'd pressed her wrong (or right, depending on how you looked at it) buttons. He'd put up a hand to defend himself, and Miss Bell said, in an unintentional Clint Eastwood impression, "I know karate. Don't fool with me, boy."

A howl of laughter went up around the table. Aaron always could tell a story. Back then, of course, they'd dared only a few nervous giggles behind their books. And Eastwood wasn't yet a household name.

Someone said Derek died of a heart attack last year, and the laughter trickled off.

Laurie had just bitten a cube of cheddar off a toothpick when she saw Jillian Thorne heading in their direction, looking like something out of vogue in a yellow strapless number, her handsome doctor husband in tow. The local paper did a big spread when she married heart surgeon, Doctor Eric Wilson. Laurie thought he looked uncomfortable. The way David would have looked if he'd come.

Within minutes Jillian grabbed center stage, just like in the old days. She kept touching Aaron's arm while she talked animatedly. Laurie felt herself go quiet inside, just like she used to when Jillian was anywhere near her. You're a grown woman with two grown children, she reminded herself. It didn't help. David was right. There was something slightly masochistic about these things. She drifted off with her glass of punch, a half-smile on her face. I'll give it an hour. Then I'm out of here.

"Hello, Laurie."

Laurie turned to see a stunning woman in a caramel silk suit dress, the skirt coming nearly to her ankles, the shirt loose and flowing, smiling tentatively at her. Straight auburn hair ending just below her ears gleamed like satin under the lights. "Elegant" was the word that came to mind. Laurie stared hard, but nothing clicked in.

"I'm sorry, I ...it's my eyes. I don't see as well as..."

The woman smiled and put out a hand. "You always were so nice. Always caring of other people's feelings."

Now that they were standing face to face, Laurie sensed something familiar about the woman. She has beautiful eyes, clear as crystal pools.

"You probably don't remember me. I'm Margaret Dross."

For a moment, Laurie couldn't answer. "Margaret," she said at last, trying not to look as stunned as she felt. "Of course - I remember you. You look fabulous. What are you doing now? Are you married? Is your husband with you?" My God, I can't believe this woman is the same girl who sat at the back of the room, with the stringy hair and glasses and those tiny eyes behind them practically lost in all that flesh. So painfully shy, far worse than I ever was. And that mother - always coming to the school to make sure she came directly home, ranting at her within everyone's hearing. Someone told her Mrs. Dross was a religious fanatic.

"No to both your questions," Margaret said. "I still live with my mother on Douglas Avenue. She's not so well these days. I work as a bookkeeper with Howe and Rivers, a law firm. I have my own office in the back. A cubbyhole, actually, but I like it."

That's great, Margaret. You were always a whiz at math."

"I like the way I can make things come out even in the end," she smiled.

Laurie had a flash memory of Margaret walking alone down the school corridor, shoulders hunched forward, shoelaces clicking on the polished floor.

A peal of laughter drifted from the buffet table. "I can use a little more of that punch, Margaret. How about you?" She touched a hand to the woman's shoulder. "Makes things more tolerable. Come on. I bet you haven't eaten anything, either."

Margaret drew back, a trace of fear coming into her face. "No, it's okay. I'm not really hungry. You go ahead, though. I think I'll just walk around a little." She smiled again as she moved away. "You look really pretty, Laurie. That color of blue matches your eyes."

Laurie understood her reluctance to go into the lion's den. School couldn't have been much fun for Margaret. She was always alone. Sometimes Laurie would seek her out, and share her sandwich. So why is she here, Laurie wondered, if not to show off how great she looks now? Damn, I really want Jillian to see her. I want Jillian's husband to see her. Nasty, Laurie. Nasty.

When she returned to the table to refill her glass, the good doctor was just pocketing his pager, apologizing for having to rush off, leaving Jillian with a long-suffering smile on her face. Laurie thought he looked secretly relieved, and wondered if maybe he hadn't arranged to be called away.

You have such a devious mind, Laurie Stevens Dobson.

Laurie didn't see Margaret again until she was leaving. A few taxis were lined up in front of the building. Margaret caught up with her as she was going down the wide cement steps.

"Hi, Laurie. I have my car here. Can I give you a ride?" "Well, thanks, but I don't know if it's on your way..."

"It doesn't matter. I don't have anywhere special to go. I guess you're staying with your mom while you're here, huh? Is she still on Visart?"

"Yes, I'm surprised you remem..."

"I remember a lot of things, Laurie. It's that blue station wagon right there." She unlocked and opened the door. "Hop in."

"Well, thanks, Margaret, this is great." Laurie slid into the passenger seat. The car smelled faintly of dry cleaning, leather, and Vick's cough drops. "This is sweet of you. I appreciate it. And it will give us a chance to get caught up."

"You have two boys," Margaret said, smiling, surprising Laurie yet again. "Your husband's into computers." She switched on the ignition, and the car purred to life. "I never did find Mr. Right. What with the job and taking care of Mom there hasn't been much time for socializing."

"Oh," Laurie said, nodding, wondering why they were just sitting here with the motor running. When she felt something hard pressing into her ribs, she looked down, thinking it was probably the buckle of an errant seatbelt. Seeing the gun in Margaret's hand, she felt only bewilderment. And then she thought maybe it was some kind of weird "reunion" joke. Until she looked up, into Margaret's eyes. "Margaret, what are...?"

"Just be calm, Laurie. It's not you I want to hurt. You were always nice to me. I didn't know quite how I was going to manage to get Jillian into the car, but it's all worked out well. Her husband being called away like that was a stroke of luck. Yes, there she is now, just coming out of the building. Call her, Laurie. Tell her we'll give her a ride wherever she's going."

"Margaret, don't do this. This is crazy..."

"Call her, Laurie." The gun jabbed her ribs, making her wince. "Call her before she gets into that taxi or you'll be sorry."

Past the tightness in her throat, Laurie called to Jillian out the passenger window. The smell of the Atlantic and the oil refinery east of the city came in the window on the warm May air. Say no, Jillian. Be the snooty bitch you always were and say no. But she didn't say no. In fact, after peering in the window she smiled her cheerleader smile and hopped into the back seat. "This is great. Thanks a million. I thought I'd be able to get a lift with Aaron, but he's got someone coming to pick him up. His wife. Hey, it's still early, ladies. Why don't we all go for a drink? I know a place that has a terrific little jazz band."

Jillian sounded as if she'd already dipped into the punch bowl a time too many. "That sounds like a fun idea, doesn't it, Margaret?"

Margaret shot her a look. Laurie fell silent.

"Margaret?" Jillian leaned over the back seat to closer scrutinize her driver. "I can't remember any Margaret in our class except for .." She let out a small chuckle and Laurie's stomach sank. "But she's obviously not you, dear. Whose class were you in?"

The car bolted forward, nearly striking the taxi in front; the driver made an obscene gesture at them. Margaret didn't slow down until they were halfway up Main Street, then she made a sharp right, pulling into an alley between a barber shop and the Army Surplus. She turned in her seat, trained the gun on Jillian.

"You get in the passenger seat, Jillian. Laurie, you drive. I'll get in the back."

"What is this?" Jillian said, indignant. "Is this some kind of sick jo..." Before she could complete the sentence, Margaret struck out with the gun. At the sickening crack, Laurie instinctively made a grab for the weapon. And in the next instant found herself staring down the barrel.

"Don't be stupid, Laurie."

"Okay," Laurie whispered, drawing back. She glanced behind her to see Jillian sitting with her hand pressed against her cheek, weeping softly. A rivulet of dark blood ran down between her fingers. "Why?" she whimpered. "Who are you?"

"I'm getting out now," Margaret said, with deadly softness. "You get in the passenger seat, Jillian like I told you."

The alley was so narrow there was barely room for them to squeeze through the doors, but at last they were all in their assigned places.

Jillian sat beside her, still clutching her face, but she had stopped crying. The clock on the dash said 10:55 p.m. Laurie told her mom she'd be home by eleven, or call if she just happened to be having too good a time. Right.

Back it out slow," Margaret said in her ear. Laurie felt the heat of the gun on the back of her head.

Five minutes later they were turning into a paved drive on Douglas Avenue. You couldn't see the colour of the house at night, but Laurie knew it was white, Victorian-style, fronted by a high cedar hedge, ancient elms, like sentinels, on either side. She'd passed it many times on her way to the museum, though she never knew that Margaret lived here.

Margaret ushered them into the foyer. Even before she switched on the light, Laurie could smell the dark mustiness of the house, the oppressiveness. The smell of Vick's was in the air. And something else - something dark, deeper, that Laurie couldn't discern.

Limp, yellowing doilies caressed the backs and arms of overstuffed furniture. A dust-covered piano stood against the far wall. The rug Laurie stood on was Oriental, its design barely visible. A grandfather clock stood in the corner beneath the staircase, its pendulum still.

Margaret reached for their coats as pleasantly as if this were a social call she and Jillian were making, and Margaret was the welcoming hostess. She's mad, Laurie thought. Margaret is stark, raving mad. As she began to unbutton her beige trench coat she considered whipping it at Margaret in an attempt to knock the gun from her hand. But what if she missed? The gun in her old classmate's hand was as steady as those contact-lens emerald eyes. The moment when Laurie might have done something came and went. She would wait for a better opportunity, catch her off-guard, she thought, as Margaret paraded them at gunpoint through a small hallway into the kitchen.

She shoved Jillian into a hard-back chair near an old-fashioned wood-burning stove that took up most of one wall. David had an avid interest in antiques; he would have loved this stove

- this house.

Margaret handed Laurie a length of white cord from the table which stood in front of the window. A green window blind shut out the world. "Tie her up."

A light bulb hung from the ceiling by a chain, casting the kitchen in greasy light. Laurie saw the narrow back door; it was bolted. She wondered how long it would take her to release the bolt. What was out there? A shed? Another locked door? Booby traps?

Dishes were piled in a chipped enamel sink. The place smelled.

"She was always a lazy, demanding woman," Margaret said as if reading Laurie's thoughts. "She made me do all the housework when I was in school, and even after I went out to work. You can see I've become quite slovenly of late. I apologize for that. But I've grown to hate this house so much, I can't bear to put a dustcloth to it...I said tight, Laurie," Margaret grabbed the cord from Laurie's hands, gave it a hard yank that made Jillian cry out. "Use a little elbow grease, as my dear Momma use to say." Margaret giggled, and the sound sent chills along Laurie's spine.

With silent apology, averting her eyes from Jillian's, Laurie drew the rope taut around those pale, thin wrists.

"Good. Now wind the cord around those two back middle rungs, and knot it double. Then do her ankles."

Jillian was trying for her old arrogant expression and failing miserably. You could see she was terrified. She isn't the only one, Laurie thought. Blood seeped from the cut on Jillian's cheekbone. Smears of it had dried on the front of her yellow dress. For the first time ever, Laurie felt sorry for Jillian.

As Laurie was making the final knot, Margaret suddenly stepped forward and grabbed a handful of Jillian's hair, and snapped her head back. 'How does it feel? How does it feel to be trapped, Jillian? To feel yourself at someone else's mercy? But you had no mercy, did you, Jillian?"

Blood pounded hot in Laurie's own ears at the sound of Jillian's sobs and pleas. "Please, I have money. My husband will..."

"Shut up!"

The room was silent, waiting.

I have to do something. That "just right moment" wasn't going to present itself just for her convenience. If there was to be any opportunity for escape, she would have to create it. Though Margaret's attention was on Jillian, she also kept a wary eye on Laurie. Laurie wondered if she could overtake her. It wasn't likely. Margaret was bigger, certainly taller, and probably a hell of a lot stronger, much of her strength born of rage. Maybe if Jillian hadn't been tied up, the two of them together...

This is a nightmare, isn't it? Any second now I'll wake up and Mom and I will laugh about this dream I'm having. You read about this sort of thing. You saw it played out on the movie screen while you filled your face with popcorn. But it never happened to you, or to anyone connected with you.

Laurie steeled herself. "Margaret, I have to go to the bathroom. All that punch, you know..." She tried to smile.

"Sure, Laurie." She waved the gun in the direction of the living room. "Upstairs, second door on the left."

"It's okay then if..." "Of course."

Taken aback at having had her request so readily granted, she mumbled her thanks and went through the hallway with tentative steps, half thinking that it was a trick and that any second a bullet would slam into her back. She didn't let out her breath until she was out of Margaret's view.

The front door seemed a mile away as if she were looking at it through the wrong end of a telescope. She was sure Margaret hadn't locked it.

Her coat was draped over the sofa back with Jillian's. She tiptoed toward it, grateful for the silent carpet beneath her feet. She wouldn't stop running until she got to the hotel, then she'd call the police. She reached for her coat.

"I'll kill her the minute you close the door after you, Laurie," Margaret called out, as calmly as if she were asking her to pick up a loaf of bread on the way. For one shameful instant, Laurie asked herself what Jillian had ever done for her that she should leave her own life in danger. Then she turned and resignedly went up the stairs.

Laurie quickly checked the two bedrooms on the right. The second room smelled more strongly of Vick's and just faintly of rosewater. An open Bible lay on the night table. Beside it, nearly hidden by wads of Kleenex, was a phone. Heart racing, Laurie eased the receiver from its cradle and put it to her ear. There was a kind of "whooshing" sound like you heard when you listened into a seashell. Laurie pressed the button a couple of times, trying to get a dial tone. She'd call her mom. It was the only number she could recall at the moment.

Suddenly, the "whooshing" stopped, replaced by the terrifying sound of Margaret's voice. "Hang it up, Laurie."

Laurie's heart shot into her throat. "Margaret. I was just calling my mom. She'll be worr..."

"Hang it up. Now. You've got two minutes to get down here. You really disappoint me, Laurie. I thought you understood." The phone clicked off.

A green enameled clawfoot tub dominated the bathroom. A plastic curtain was drawn across it. After the shock of hearing Margaret's voice on the phone, Laurie really did have to go. Seated there, listening to the slow drip, drip, drip of water into the tub, something - something, made her reach out and take an edge of the curtain in her hand and draw it back - slowly, very slowly, as if in some part of her mind she already knew what she would find.

The woman's splayed feet were revealed to her first. They were swollen, with dark bluish toenails that badly needed cutting. Her mottled flesh was white as bread dough. Laurie did not remember her being such a large woman. Mrs. Dross would not have fit in Laurie's small apartment-sized tub. Pale eyes stared up at her from beneath a skim of water. Her mouth was slightly open, to reveal loose dentures. Tendrils of wispy grey hair floated about her face.

She managed to draw the curtains across. In the hallway, she closed her eyes and sagged against the wall. The image of the corpse remained behind her lids. She fought to keep from passing out. Bile rose bitter in her throat. She had to get hold of herself. Margaret mustn't know I saw her. Oh, my God, she murdered her mother.

Jillian was sitting docilely in the chair, watching Laurie enter the kitchen. She was drawn, and so pale Laurie could see the scars at the corner of her eyes from her eyelift. The tears had washed away the makeup. The cut on her cheekbone was swollen and discolored.

I have to do something.

"Could we have tea - or coffee?" Laurie asked, forcing a smile at their captor. "You've been terribly hurt, Margaret. We need to talk about it."

"Talking won't make the dreams go away. You don't know what she did to me, Laurie." "I think I do."

"Did you know she took pictures of me in the gym shower and showed them around the school?"

Laurie had a vague recollection of talk surrounding the incident. She wouldn't have been one of the people shown the pictures. She shook her head.

"People whispered and laughed behind my back. The boys said ugly, horrible things to me, right out. I told my mother, but she just said I must have done something to deserve it. She said it was punishment from God...No, no tea or coffee, Laurie. Sorry. There won't be time."

"I didn't mean any harm, Margaret," Jillian said in a small voice. "It was all in fun. We were kids. I never even thought of it again."

Whatever she had to drink, she's sober now. "Fun for you, maybe," Laurie said, turning on a startled Jillian. "You were always one who liked having a laugh at someone else's expense. You need to understand what you did. You need to atone." Please, please let this work.

Jillian twisted in the chair. The tears came again. "Why are you ganging up with her?" "Why not? You always traveled with your little gang." Laurie glanced at the owl clock

on the wall. Mom will be looking for me by now. She'll be putting on water for tea, wanting to hear all about the evening. Would she get to tell her?

"One thing I did always wonder about," Margaret said, lowering the gun a little. "Why me, Jillian? Why were you so cruel? What did I ever do to make you hate me so much?"

"Nothing. I didn't hate you. I didn't..."

Laurie thought that was probably true. Margaret had meant nothing to Jillian. She was as insignificant as a fly on the windowsill, except as a target, an amusement.

"Do you remember daring Jason Belding to ask me to the school dance, Jillian?" "No," she whispered.

"I thought he liked me. Oh, at first I couldn't believe he wanted to take me out, but he was really nice. He said he couldn't pick me up because he had to work late, but that he'd meet me at the dance. I spent all my babysitting money on a new dress. It was the first time I dared to wear lipstick. I had to sneak out of the house. When I got there, he was with someone else, one of your friends. He looked kind of embarrassed like he felt bad. You had this smirk on your face, so I knew right away you pushed him to do it. Everyone always wanted to please you, Jillian. You had it all. Everything your way."

"You're wrong, Margaret," Jillian said. "You..."

"Do you remember following me one day?" Margaret went on. "Chanting 'here pig here pig, oink, oink'," Margaret hunched over, crossed the floor and back, as she mimicked the ugly

words that would never leave her. For an instant, looking at her, Laurie was reminded of Sally Fields in the role of Sybil. "Do you remember that?" Margaret asked, stopping.

Jillian shifted her eyes.

She remembered. As did Laurie. She'd tried to make them stop, but they wouldn't. She could still hear the stomp, stomp, stomp of those feet following behind Margaret's, marking time with the hateful chant. The momentum and volume seemed to take on a life of its own. It was horrible. And then Margaret lost her rhythm, stumbled, and fell on the broken sidewalk. She was crawling around, sobbing, feeling about for her glasses. Laurie picked them up out of the gutter and helped her up. Her knees and hands were bleeding. Jillian and her pals had gone off, laughing.

"It was twenty years ago, for God's sake, Margaret," Jillian said, to Laurie's utter amazement. "You should be over it by now."

"Over it?" Margaret said quietly.

Jillian strained against the ropes. "Do it then," she cried. "Just go ahead and get it over with. Maybe it will make you feel better to know my life is crap these days. My 15-year-old daughter ran away six months ago because she hates me, and I have no idea where the hell she is. My husband is divorcing me to marry some little slut nurse at the hospital. And I'm well on my way to becoming a full-fledged alcoholic. So if you want to kill me, Margaret, then please, please, just do it. The truth be known, you'd be doing me a favor."

The confusion came into Margaret's face. Who would have thought Jillian Thorne's life could be anything but perfect?

"You would punish her more by letting her live. Margaret, you don't want to hurt anyone. You'd be no better than your tormentors, then. You'd be no better than Jillian. Don't you see that? Please, give me the gun."

"She was all I had. She's gone now."

She's talking about her mother. She knows I saw her. "What happened, Margaret? What made you...?"

Margaret looked momentarily bewildered then her eyes widened in surprise. "I didn't do anything, Laurie. I wouldn't hurt my mother. I love her. She had a heart attack. I - found her when I got home from work today. The doctor kept telling her she needed to lose weight, but she wouldn't listen."

It hadn't occurred to Laurie she'd died of natural causes. Relieved, she said, "We should call an ambulance."

"Don't you think it's a little late for that?"

"They'd take her to the morgue. Or we could call the police."

"Not yet. I'm dead too, you know. So she has to die. Because of her I have nothing. No one."

"Margaret, you're not dead. You were a victim of childish cruelty, but it's over now. You could have your pick of men. Take a look at yourself in the mirror, girl. You could be a model." Margaret smiled thinly. "It's a costume."

Her words hung in the air.

"I'm sorry, Margaret," Jillian said. "I didn't know..." "Sure you did." She raised the gun.

It was now or never. Not daring to give it further thought, Laurie went into a crouch, and dived at Margaret, pulling off a tackle Joe Namath would have been proud of. The gun flew out

of Margaret's hand and slid across the linoleum floor under the table. Laurie rolled off Margaret, scrambled after it, banged her knee on the table leg.

Margaret's hand clamped around her ankle, and tried to drag her back, but too late. Flinging herself on her back, Laurie gripped the gun with both hands and aimed it squarely at Margaret.

Margaret's eyes filled. "I thought you were my friend, Laurie."

"I am," she gasped, removing one hand from the gun to rub the fire from her knee. "Believe me, I am."

It was after two in the morning when she arrived at her mother's in a taxi. Officer Jason Belding had offered to have someone drive her, but she knew it would frighten her mother to see her pull up in a police car. Jason had assured her that Margaret wouldn't serve any jail time, since no one was interested in pressing charges. True to form, once Jillian knew she was safe she was ready to throw Margaret to the wolves, but Laurie convinced her she owed her a break.

Margaret would get the help she needed and deserved. Jason thought she would be allowed to attend her mom's funeral, escorted of course. Laurie planned to be there, too. She would call David in the morning and explain.

"You really must have had a great time," her mother said, busying herself with the teapot and cups, despite the hour. "Tell me everything."

Laurie smelled freshly baked chocolate chip cookies. Her favorite. There but for the grace of God -- and Mom.

"You wouldn't believe it. You just wouldn't believe it."

The End

Freeing Henry

Lila shot up in bed, gasping for breath, Henry's voice still following her into waking. The terrible dream echoed in her small room and inside her head. Henry was calling to her, anguish in his plaintive cry, throat raspy from so much weeping.

When her racing heart slowed, she slipped out of bed, shed the damp nightshirt, and stood in front of the vanity mirror. She wasn't muscular in the way a couple of the body-building women at the gym were, but you could easily see the definition of her biceps, triceps, her pectorals. Definitions that didn't show under her usual loose clothing. She gazed approvingly at her reflection, though not out of vanity. She felt she was ready.

Yes, it was time.

Henry's voice had grown fainter, though still deep and resonant. Like James Earl Jones. She loved Henry's voice. Though she hadn't missed the accusing note in his railing. She didn't blame him.

"You promised, Lila."

Yes. And she meant to keep that promise. Such a long time you've waited. Such cruelty you've endured.

Soon now.

Gathering up what she would need to accomplish her goal, Lila slipped the items into a leather tote bag.

She grabbed her terrycloth robe, padded across the hall to the bathroom. She turned the faucets on full and stepped beneath the shower.

It was a hot and humid Saturday in July. She pulled a blue cotton dress from her closet and skimmed her dark hair into a French roll to stay cool; she would brush it out before she got there. It was crucial that grandfather not send her away. Not until she'd set Henry free. Her grandfather might well be furious that she would dare to darken his doorway after running away as she had.

The cream-colored Honda was new to her and purred with good health as it took her back to the house where she'd lived with grandfather until she was fourteen.

Before that, her father lived there with them. But he was killed when a truck carrying a load of lumber crashed into his car, leaving it to explode and burn up on the side of the road. A few days after it happened, her grandfather took her to the site. She could still smell the gasoline and boiled paint and rubber. Bits of wood were scattered along the shoulder of the road.

Bad Omen

Dean L. Hovey

- with-

John Wisdomkeeper

Print ISBNs

Amazon Print 9780228627531
Ingram Spark 9780228627548
Barnes & Noble 9780228627555
BWL Print 9780228627562

"I'm all you have now, Lila," her grandfather said, taking her hand in his.

As the little car swallowed up the miles of pavement, Lila's thoughts returned to Henry. He'd been her best friend. They shared secrets and laments. Memories flooded, tightening Lila's mouth, bringing a strange expression into her blue eyes. Catching a glimpse of herself in the rearview mirror, she relaxed her face, her body. She was just worried about Henry, that was all.

Finally, she saw the old sign just ahead on the left: Ebsen's Mill. The only evidence of the old mill that closed down in the early thirties. People moved away; houses were abandoned, torn down. A few summer camps had gone up in their stead, hunting lodges.

She recognized the sway-backed red-roofed barn. Higher up on the hill, the white Baptist church came into view. Soon the car hit the dirt road which ran about three miles. Lila pulled off onto the side of the road and let her hair down and gave it a quick brush.

Too soon she was turning into the familiar driveway.

She exited the car and shut the door, the sound amplified in the stillness. But not all was still. She could hear the murmur of the stream behind the house where frogs croaked and insects whined. She'd swum in that stream as a child which was surprisingly deep in places. Her father was alive then.

She started up the stone walk, near hidden now by tall grasses that appeared to have gone unmowed since her father's passing. Sensing someone watching her, she looked up. The limp curtain on the upstairs window dropped back into place.

He would keep her waiting.

So often a place where you once lived can seem smaller when you see it again through adult eyes. Not so with this house; With its gingerbread trim and long windows, it towered above her. Abram Parson and grandmother Lilias (for whom Lila was named) had lived here for more than half a century. Abram himself grew up in this house.

Lila came here as a baby, her father told her. He'd lost his job and times were hard. It was meant to be temporary. Her mother cooked and kept house. Daddy fixed what needed fixing. He lost himself when her mother died of heart failure. Lila had no memory of that time.

Lila was wary of Abram Parson and tried to stay out of his way. Daddy kept promising they would get their own place soon, and it made her happy to think of it, though deep down she didn't believe they would. Daddy was a good man, kind and loving, but he wasn't strong enough for the world. She could always sense Abram's contempt for him and knew that Daddy felt it too. He would slip into the black place in his mind and disappear for days, lose the latest job. She would watch out the window for him.

And then one day he would show up in the doorway beaming a smile at her and it was like the sun came out. He would pick her up in his arms, ruffle her hair and they would both be happy again. He'd always have a little treat for her: a doll, ribbons for her hair, a chocolate bar. If Abram wasn't home, he'd get out the guitar and they'd sing songs. Or she'd place her small feet over his and he'd dance around the room with her and make her laugh.

After the accident, she cried herself to sleep every night. She felt so alone. One night Abram came to her room. 'Our little secret', he said. She was seven.

On another day a woman came to the house and said Lila had to go to school. The school bus would pick her up, which kind of excited her, but grandfather said there'd be no need; he would drive her to and from school.

A fat drop of rain slid beneath her collar on spider legs as she ascended the wide cement steps. Lifting the brass knocker she brought it against the oak door – and again. The sound reverberated throughout the house.

Soon she heard the slow shuffling footsteps on the old wood floor. They stopped on the other side of the door. A click of the lock and the door opened.

The six years since she'd seen him had bent his back; he carried a cane now. His face was drawn, almost cadaver-like. His milky grey eyes held a smile. Or maybe a sneer. He looked smaller. He had seemed like a giant to her when she was a child.

"I've had a mild stroke," he said, reading her expression.

"Oh. I'm sorry."

"It's okay. I'm fine now." He patted her shoulder, and she resisted shrinking from his touch. "Come in, child. Such a lovely young woman you turned out to be. Of course, you were always a pretty little thing. I wish your grandmother could see you. You favor her, you know. She was a fine figure of a woman, was Lilias. Do you have luggage?"

"I'm not staying long. I have just this one suitcase."

"It's been a long time, Lila. Please, come inside."

Lightning flashed followed by a low rumble of thunder. "I think we're in for a downpour. "You don't want your old grandpa catching pneumonia."

Playing on her sympathy, making her feel guilty, ungrateful. Blaming her... she shook the thought away. I'm here for one reason. To free Henry.

"Very well." At least, he wasn't going to send her away.

"My dear, you must be tired after the long drive."

"No. It's a lovely drive."

"You must have a husband now? Children? Yes?"

"No. I have a job. A nice place to live. No one bothers me."

He nodded, eyes narrowing. "You were young when you left here. But you got on."

"Yes. I found a temporary live-in job as a mother's helper." The woman had broken her arm and needed help with her two little boys. When her arm healed, she helped Lila enroll in the new school.

"I work as a bookkeeper now." She liked working with numbers; she was good at it. She liked the way she could make things come out right in the end.

She looked around. Little had been done to the place. Just as if she had never left. Perhaps an added layer of neglect. This had always been a dark house. Heavy antique furniture, stuffed chairs. Thick musty drapes he kept closed. The heaviness weighed on her even now.

She saw Henry from the corner of her eye but didn't let herself look at him fully. She could sense his joy at seeing her, all anger at her forgotten. Bless him.

His eyes followed her as she left the room. Dear Henry. He had seen her through so much. Cried with her. She with him.

Abram Parson was an avid hunter in his day and had shot the moose. Shot Henry. He was proud of his trophy. It had not been enough to merely take his life, to stand over his dying body posed with his gun, a prideful grin on his face. In a final act of humiliation, he'd cut off his head and nailed it (though he'd used screws) to the wall.

But Henry was alive and as handsome as ever, even if there was a sadness in his eyes, a weariness that went beyond sadness. But his spirit soared just now. His handsomeness glowed. She glimpsed again the massive head, the magnificent spread of antlers, like open hands, the dark intelligent eyes that, though replaced, embodied his spirit. Some said the moose was an ugly animal. That simply wasn't true; Henry was beautiful All animals were beautiful in their own way. But Henry most especially.

Lila asked Abram if she might go upstairs and look around. "Nostalgia, I suppose," she smiled.

"Yes, yes," he said eagerly, you know this house is your home, Lila. For as long as you like. Explore away."

She could tell he was relieved that she wasn't angry with him, hadn't brought a police officer with her. No need for that. Let bygones be bygones. Lila had forgiven him. He was an old man now. Harmless.

Later, she made a supper of potato scallop and biscuits, his favorite, while rain lashed the windows with sudden fury.

"You're still a great little cook." He picked up his mug of tea and slurped it. Her eyes were drawn to the movement of his mouth. She could almost feel it on her little girl's lips, wet, searching, tongue thrusting inside like a venomous snake. "C'mon, baby, give old Abram a kiss."

Her eye was drawn to his trembling hand that brought the fork of food to his mouth. The same hand that had slid under the blanket, forced her legs apart while she cried and begged him to stop. Lila flicked the memories away, like turning off a light. No point in harboring old wounds.

She cleared the dishes. Outside the window, the woods were becoming one with the coming night. The rain had eased up.

"I'm glad you enjoyed the meal, Grandfather. Shall we have our tea in the living room?" Henry would be lonely in there by himself. He'd be wondering. But he'd already proven himself a patient soul.

"It's good that you're feeling better, grandfather," Lila said, setting the tray on which she'd placed two mugs of tea, on the rough-hewn coffee table. She poured a little milk into Abram's the way he liked it. Smiled over the rim of her mug. He reached out with his trembling hand and lay it over hers.

She did not move her hand for a moment, then slid it discretely away. The pills that she had ground into powder were already starting to do their job. His eyes were growing heavy. A thread of drool seeped from the corner of his mouth. But she needed to be sure he wouldn't wake up while she freed. Henry understood and waited with her.

Abram's head dropped suddenly jolting him awake. He rose unsteadily from his chair. "I'm very tired now, Lila so I'm going upstairs to bed. You just make yourself at home."

"I will. Do you need help getting up the stairs?"

"Oh, no. I climb them every night."

He clutched the railing, holding his cane with the other hand, and made his way up the stairs like a drunk trying to appear sober. When he disappeared beyond the landing she turned to Henry and smiled. Henry smiled back.

"He'll sleep for a long time," Lila said.

"Did you remember to bring a screwdriver?" Henry said, in that glorious James Earl Jones voice.

"Of course I did, you silly." She produced it from the tote bag.

Years before, she'd tried to set Henry free, more than once, but she was always too little, never strong enough. And she'd been afraid that even if she was successful in getting all the screws out of the board that held him to the wall, she would drop Henry and perhaps break off some part of his handsome rack of antlers: They were seventy inches across, she remembered her grandfather saying. He was proud of his trophy.

Lila felt the power in her arms and shoulders today though and knew it would be fine. With the removal of the last screw, she felt his head beginning to slip in her arms.

"Careful, Lila."

"Don't worry, Henry. I've got you." And then she was easing Henry down off the wall and setting him on a sofa with great care. An enormous sigh escaped him, like the rush of an ocean wave to the shore. "Thank you, dear Lila. Thank you."

"You're welcome."

"You're my best friend, Lila. You've always been there for me."

"I love you, Henry."

A heavyweight came over her then. Never before had she been so tired, so drained in both body and soul, as if someone had attached a hose to her and was siphoning the last drop of energy. "I'm going to lie down here on the floor, Henry," she said. "I need to rest for just a little while." She removed the faded patchwork quilt from the back of the sofa, smoothed it out on the floor and curled into a fetal position. Within seconds, she slept. In sleep, she dreamed.

When Lila woke, morning light filtered through the drapes, spilling a pale swath of sunlight across the faded rug; dust motes floated in the air. She'd slept straight through the night. Yet it seemed only moments had passed. She'd had a terrible dream but couldn't remember the details? Something to do with Henry.

Yes. I saw his antlers climbing the stairs, splashed high in silhouette against the wall. like black fire. I must have followed him.

She sat up and looked at the sofa where she'd deposited Henry. As she knew he would be, he was gone. The dream returned to her now. And with it her grandfather's scream of terror as the antlers stabbed him again and again, slicing and gouging. I must have been standing in the doorway, watching. Rise and fall, rise and fall. Such terrible rage. Even madness. Henry, Henry, what have you done? Lila raced up the stairs, already knowing what she would find.

The old man lay on his back gazing up at her out of unfocused rheumy eyes. Blood trickled from his nose and mouth as he moaned weakly. He seemed to understand it all as his thin aged body shivered and the final light left his eyes. He stared blankly past the tines of Henry's antlers embedded in his chest.

She switched on a lamp throwing shadows onto the eerie scene and wrapped her arms around Henry's broad neck and pulled. There was the slightest sucking sound as the antlers left his body. The release was sudden and Lila stumbled backward but caught herself before she could fall.

"Thanks," Henry breathed.

"Why did you do...?"

"He deserved it," Henry said simply.

No point in chastising him. No point at all. She found a rag under the bathroom sink and ran water over it, squeezed out the excess. As she turned to leave the bathroom, she caught her reflection in the mirror; her blue dress was dotted and streaked with blood. She cleaned it with the cold water as best she could. She washed the blood from her face. Her upper arms felt raw and burning. Henry was heavier than she'd thought.

How pale she looked in the mirror. Absently massaging her aching arms and shoulders, a strange calm settled over her. Of course, she was sorry this had happened. A terrible act of vengeance her friend had committed. She had pardoned grandfather of all sins, long ago.

Back in her grandfather's bedroom, she cleaned the blood from each of the tines of Henry's antlers. Looking into his staring eyes she saw no shred of remorse and could only shake her head in dismay.

"I'll drop you off in the woods on my way home, Henry. You'll be fine. You're free now."

He would roam the woods again the way he was meant to. He'd nibble grass, water-Lilies, munch birch, and willow. Drink cool water from the stream. Unassaulted. Unafraid. She was sure the Lord would allow him that. Henry had suffered so. Surely the Lord would forgive him.

As she had forgiven Abram Parson, her grandfather. Lila was a forgiving soul.

But Henry. Well, Henry knew how to carry a grudge.

The End

The House at the End of the Street

Feeling a thrill of both recognition and surprise, Nancy double-checked the address she'd scribbled on the scrap of paper she held in her hand. But there was no doubt; this was the same beautiful white two-story house, with its black shutters and gingerbread trim, she'd passed to and from school for much of her young life, and that she'd so often fantasized about. She had imagined how it would look inside: chandeliers, oriental rugs, a sweeping staircase leading to beautiful bedrooms. A house fit for a movie star. Set back from the street, the manicured lawn rolled down to the ornamental wrought-iron gate parallel to the street. There were a few well-placed white birch trees, one of which had a cozy bench beneath it. Nancy had never seen anyone sitting there.

She was here to be interviewed for the job of companion to an elderly woman. Light housekeeping and meal preparation included, the ad said. No problem.

Looking up at the house a moment longer, she then opened the gate that swung inward easily and went up the stone walk flanked by colorful flowers, that gave off a wonderful fragrance. Taking a deep breath, she rang the bell.

At once, a tall man perhaps in his somewhere in his forties wearing black-rimmed glasses opened the door and smiled at her. He had a nice face and deep blue eyes. "Hello. You must be Nancy. Meadows. I'm Richard Preston, Mrs. Worth's lawyer, and friend of many years. Mrs. Worth is waiting for you in the library slash bedroom since the stairs have become too much for her." He gestured to the partially open French doors. "You may go right in,"

The house was even grander than she had imagined as a little girl. The staircase curved upward in the center of the large room, leading to the landing that she assumed branched off to opulent bedrooms. An enormous crystal chandelier hung from the high ceiling completing the Hollywood ambiance. She could almost see the legendary Norma Desmond descending the stairs in Sunset Boulevard. "I'm ready for my close-up, Mr. DeMille."

On entering the library, a wall of bookshelves held many leather-bound books. There was a small fireplace, and Nancy envisioned a crackling fire to warm chill winter nights. Knowing she might never come here again, she tried to burn every detail to memory.

Mrs. Worth sat like a queen on a luxurious sofa, a crocheted shawl draped across her knees. Beneath silvery, upswept hair, her face, with its classic bone structure, was pale and too thin. But the light blue eyes that scrutinized Nancy, held an unmistakable sparkle.

"I can see you're impressed with the place. Proves you have good taste. It will go to my niece when I'm gone; no doubt she'll make the place unrecognizable. But I suppose most young people would prefer it more modern, open concept as they say, lots of granite and stainless steel. Still, makes me sad. Come closer, my dear. My eyes aren't as sharp as they used to be. Sit, please."

A chair angled toward Mrs. Worth and Nancy sat, horrified at the thought of someone changing anything about this house, let alone tearing down walls.

She'd worn her navy linen suit and pearls. The pearls had belonged to her mother when she was alive. They weren't real of course, and Mrs. Worth would know that. But she thought they looked nice.

"Well, Nancy Meadows, you look like a sensible young woman. Are you?"

"I am, yes, ma'am."

"Always?"

"I think so. Yes."

"Really. How boring for you. I was a bit of cut-up myself at your age. So what do you do for fun?"

Nancy tried to hide her surprise at the woman's candor. "I like to read. Take walks. I love old movies."

"Aw, an old soul. You're not the type to take off with my best jewelry, are you?"

"Oh, no. Ma'am. I would never..."

"Please, quit calling me Ma'am. Makes me feel like an old woman. Oh, hell I am an old woman."

Nancy couldn't suppress a grin and Mrs. Worth held hers, barely. She was engaging in a little tease. "You may call me Delia. That's if I decide to hire you."

"Of course."

"I assume you have references."

She had two. Mrs. Worth scanned them. "Fred Belding, Poor Freddy. You were his caretaker, then. He speaks highly of you."

"I didn't know he'd written that letter. His sister found it in his papers. You knew him?"

"In another time. So tell me. Why is a lovely-looking, smart girl like yourself wanting to be a companion to an old lady? Surely you can find something -- more suitable. Or perhaps you should be in university. What are you? Eighteen?"

"Twenty-two. I've never been terribly comfortable with people my own age. After the death of my parents during the pandemic, I was raised by an elderly aunt who is also gone now. She loved the old movies too; we would watch them together. I enjoyed her company and that of her friends. And I like to help people who may not be as physically strong and agile as they once were."

"Is there a boyfriend?"

"No. I find boys my own age rather silly."

Delia Worth grew thoughtful, then reached for her cane beside her, transferred the shawl from her knees to her shoulders, and rose shakily to her feet. Nancy had a natural urge to help, but feared being thought presumptuous."

"Richard," Mrs. Worth called into the other room. "I don't think we need look further."

Nancy's heartbeat kicked up a notch. Was it possible? Did she have the job? Was going to live in this beautiful house -- the house she'd dreamed of as a child -- and be a companion to this elegant lady. She felt like she was floating a few feet above the carpet.

The lawyer stood in the doorway, his smile including them both. "You've obviously made an impression, Miss Meadows." He turned his attention to Mrs. Worth. "Your niece is here, Delia," he said softly.

A woman strode into the room with barely a glance at Nancy. She kissed her aunt's cheek lightly. Nancy took in the taupe linen dress, the highlighted hair. Sea green Gucci sandals and bag, (the brass double G's visible) completed the ensemble. Nancy felt drab by comparison; the pearls didn't seem quite so smart.

"Who are you bringing into the house now, dear Auntie? You're quite vulnerable, you know, and they're all kinds of lowlife out there, willing to scam an old lady. "No offense," she said to Nancy, whose face had caught fire.

"I'm sorry, Nancy," Mrs. Worth said. "Bethany, that was unkind even for you. "Nancy, you may begin tomorrow," she said, smiling apologetically. "Molly, my cleaning lady will be here in the morning and she'll show you around. If that's acceptable to you."

Yes, yes. Very acceptable. Thank you, Mrs. Worth."

"Delia. Remember?"

"Thank you ...Delia."

On her way out, Nancy heard Mrs. Worth chastise gently, "Who I bring into this house is my affair, Bethany, dear. I've been handling my affairs for a lifetime now. I'm sure I'll be fine. Now, to what do I owe the pleasure, darling? Haven't seen you in a while."

"Can't I check up on my favorite aunt without being suspect? I had my Tarot cards read yesterday and she said I'm coming into a lot of money."

"Really? So when am I to die?"

"Oh, Aunt Delia, you're terrible." She trilled a laugh that scraped along Nancy's nerves.

Early the next morning Nancy arrived with two suitcases and was met at the door by a jolly-faced woman wiping her hands on a dishtowel. "You're Nancy," she smiled. "Ma'am said I was to put the coffee on, so help yourself. There are eggs or cereal, whatever..."

"I've already eaten, thank you."

She put out a rough, reddened hand, the one not holding the dishtowel. "I'm Molly, by the by. Molly Inman. I come twice a week to clean. When you've finished your coffee, I'll give you the grand tour."

Her bedroom was upstairs, third on the right.   It was a spacious room, flooded with light pouring in through the tall window facing onto the lawn. The room had its own small fireplace and a bed the size of a raft. Feeling like she had tumbled into a fairytale, she unpacked her few things and went down into the well-equipped kitchen.

Having prepared a vegetable soup for lunch and a light salad, and apple strudel for dessert. She carried the tray to her new employer, who removed her glasses and set down the book she'd been reading and drew the folding table close to her.

"Ah," she said, smiling her approval. "I could smell the hot apple and cinnamon from the kitchen. My favorite. But you don't have to go to such trouble, dear. I've always been a light eater, conscious of my weight, you see. A piece of toast and tea is generally what I take for lunch. Not that it matters now, but eating light has kept me trim and reasonably healthy at ninety-two. Along with dancing."

"You were a dancer?”

Delia Worth brightened. "Once a dancer, always a dancer, my dear. I was dancing right up until my 90th birthday, for myself only, of course. Until I slipped on the icy step outside and broke my hip.”

“I'm so sorry.”

“Me too.”

“You look like a dancer. You're still beautiful.”

"You're very kind, Nancy. Though I must confess I was paid a similar compliment by a count once, and also a prince, as I recall. He had terrible table manners. But he was very rich. He bought me expensive gifts and perfume. Chanel No. 5. It's still my favorite. I was quite a dish back then."

"Yes, I can see that. You're regal, yet earthy." She took the tray away and it pleased her to see nothing left.

"You have a way with words, Nancy Meadows."

"I read a lot.”

"We have that in common. Although I didn't take to books until I was much older.”

"Would it be rude of me to ask if you're – husband's passed?" Nancy asked timidly.

“Or if I'm divorced? Yes, it would, but I'll answer. I only ever loved one man and I married him. His name was Stephen – Stephen Crane, like the man who wrote The

Red Badge of Courage. Ironically, he died in the war."

"I'm sorry. I didn't mean to pry."

"It's fine. A long time ago. What about you? Despite finding boys your age silly, I'm sure you've dated at some point?"

"I did. Briefly. It didn't work out.”

"Relationships often don't. Better to think of your future on your own terms. Along with Ricard's investment brilliance, I have my career as a dancer to thank for the comfortable life I have at my advanced age. For this house."

“Really?”

“Yes. Exotic dancing. I wanted to be on the legitimate stage, but it was not to be. It was the depression, you see, times were tough. A lot of the girls I worked with had other dreams - actresses, singers, even ballerinas - but you made do. If you wanted to eat.” She laughed and Nancy heard a bitter note in the laugh that told her all Delia's memories weren't so great.

"Not everyone called it exotic dancing," she said, a little defensively. "I was also called a stripper, as my niece likes to remind me. As did my brother when he was alive. But we were never cheap or vulgar, not like the girls now. We were ladies. Always well spoken, well turned out. It's all about stirring the imagination of your audience, not baring it all. There's no mystery there. I never did the bump-and-grind routine. The good ones didn't have to. You must have heard of Gypsy Rose Lee."

"Yes, of course."

"She and I were good friends at one time. She died young. 59, seems very young to me now. She was so vital. I learned a lot from Gyp. As no doubt, you did from your aunt and her friends. Different things, of course."

Nancy found herself sitting beside her employer on the divan, without being aware of making the move. "Very different, I'm sure. She must have been really something."

"Gypsy? Yes, she was. Her real name was Rose Louise Hovic. She was witty and smart. I didn't have her gift of gab, but I did all right. Those were the times; we partied with famous actors like Spencer Tracy, big-name politicians, art dealers. I met Artie Shaw. He was a big celebrity bandleader. He was married for a time to Betty Grable. He treated her lousy, we all knew about it. At least we heard about it. Do you like to dance, Nancy?"

"I love it. Though I haven't danced much, mainly in my bedroom with no one watching."

"You have wonderful posture and you move like a dancer. I used to take a lot of the new girls under my wing: I could teach you. Would you like that?"

"I – don't know. I don't think..."

"It could be fun. And a great way to stay in shape. Give it some thought. Would you like to see some photos – of that time..."

"Oh, yes, please. I'd be honored."

"They're in the studio, in the closet. Right through there. She gestured to the other set of French doors, which Nancy had assumed led to Delia's private washroom. "Don't be confused by the wall mirrors and ballet barre in there. At one time, I planned to teach dance, but it never came to fruition. I took tap and ballet as a child, you know. There's an old record player and a few LP's in there as well, dear."

She was met with an expanse of gleaming hardwood floors, their golden hue reflected in the wall of mirrors at the back and side of the room. She crossed to the dressing room which was complete with a walk-in closet, makeup mirror with lights, and washroom facilities including a large shower. All seemed to be waiting to fulfill their intended purpose.

Over the next couple of weeks, Nancy entered into an alternate world as she perused the many photos in album after album. The early ones in black and white, later in vivid color, with a running commentary from Delia. Newspaper clippings and posters celebrated the stunning and steamy, 'Delilah', Delia's stage name.

Through her imagination, Nancy lost herself in smoky rooms filled with throbbing, thumping music, enthusiastic audiences.

Delia taught her some basic moves in exotic dancing. And as they grew closer, the stories never lost their thrill for her, though some of her stories grew darker.

"It wasn't all good times and glamour," she told her once and Nancy knew the admission didn't come easy. She spoke of nights when some man would hurl ugly insults or reach for her like she was a piece of meat on a hook. "There was one club manager, Minsky's I think it was, who decided he didn't want to pay me. A short, fat little creep named Fritz. I don't remember his last name. I threatened to have the place closed down if he didn't give me my money. It got ugly. You absorb a lot and some you block out. But it seeps through..You oughta know about that too. But I guess I needn't worry about painting too rosy a picture for you; it's not like you're going to tread my path. Burlesque is dead and gone."

"It's different, to be sure. She'd been sheltered but she wasn't stupid. "They were nasty men and I'm sorry you experienced that. But I love hearing these stories, Delia, the good and the not-so-good. It all made you the person you are now, which is pretty wonderful, in my opinion. You look tired, Delia. Let's get you over to your chair and I'll make up your bed."

"You're sweet. Anyway, no one ever wants to hear these old tales so it's nice to have someone to tell them to."

Settled beneath the blankets, Delia asked, "What about you, Nancy? What is your dream?"

"I'm living it." She fluffed a pillow, cupped Delia's head, and slid it under. "Being here, being your companion, it's everything." She picked up a loose photo that had fallen out of the album and admired it. "You were so gorgeous, Delia."

Delia smiled, looking at the photo in Nancy's hand. "Actually, you remind me a little of myself back then. Willowy. Long dark hair, those blue bedroom eyes. Take a look in the closet and pick yourself out a couple of my old gowns."

"Oh, no I couldn't..."

"Of course, you can. I'll be your tutor, your muse. I'll dance vicariously through you. Would you refuse an old lady the pleasure?"

Nancy knew it was emotional blackmail, and Delia's grin told her she wasn't oblivious either.

* * *

The black silk gown flowed over Nancy's skin like cool water and Delilah's dance shoes fit like Cinderella's glass slippers. She smiled at her fanciful self in the mirror. Her aunt, who'd been very religious and thought dance was the devil's work, would have been shocked to see her now.

Delia was most complimentary. "You look stunning, dear. " Then added in almost a whisper. "Bethany must never know about this."

Her niece visited often. She was always pleasant, but Nancy didn't trust the smile that didn't quite reach her eyes and would make herself scarce when she was around.

Once, passing the door, she overheard Delia say, her voice lowered. "I don't know what you have against Nancy, Bethany. We get on well. She's a lovely young woman and she plays a mean game of scrabble. Unlike you," she half-teased, "who looks like she's having teeth pulled to sit through a game. And then you throw the game just to get it over with."

"I might sue for alienation of affection." Bethany chuckled to show she was kidding, but it left Nancy with an uneasy feeling.

When the door closed behind her, Nancy got ready for her dance lesson.

"Put the album on, darling. It was "The Entertainer," Nancy said and Delia's face lit up as the music began to play. Nancy swayed to the rhythm.

At first, she felt awkward and self-conscious, but she gradually lost herself to the music.

"Yes, that's it. Feel the beat enter your body, give yourself to it. You own the stage. Not so fast," she directed. "Slower, subtle, giving just a hint of your mystery. Strike an

attitude. A little naughty, a little haughty. ..
ah, yes, much better.”

* * *

It was 1940, the room is smoke-filled,
and there's laughter, applause. Glasses
tinkling -- and the music... the photographs
in the album came alive in her alternate
world.

"Enough. Turn it off. "

Nancy had been caught up in the
moment, and now stood frozen, worried she
had somehow displeased Delia. And then
Delia cried, "Oh, these legs, these useless
legs."

The next night Delia insisted she put on
the gold lame. "I'm going to show you some
great new moves."

"Delia, are you sure? I don't..."

"Yes, I'm sure. Forget last night. I was
wallowing in self-pity. Yearning for my
misspent youth.”

Nancy danced for Delia most every
evening, taking in all her instruction and
advice, but gradually putting her own stamp
on the routines Delia taught her, perhaps
more Lopez than Delilah. Delia told her she
was wonderful. "My family was
embarrassed by what I did for a living. But
my parents are gone long ago, my brother
more recently, and I don't give a damn what
my niece thinks. I supposed I've spoiled her,
to my detriment. I often see the disdain on

her face when I refer to my dancing days. You know it's hard not to mention it ever: dancing was my whole life. And I was damn good at it."

"I know," Nancy said.

"You don't know anything," she gently contradicted. "You're a baby."

"But I do. I almost feel like I went through it with you."

"As much as I hate to say it, you're getting to be damn near as good as I was. Damn near, I said." She smiled. "I see you're developing a style of your own. You were born to dance, Nancy. We'll have a glass of very fine wine later to celebrate your progress."

As the music began to play, the beat and throb of it filled the room, once more entering her body. She sashayed across the floor in Delia's high heels, shoulders back, proud, the way Delia and shown her.

One evening, in the midst of her performance, Richard came into the room. Nancy faltered, but Delia motioned her to continue, and after an awkward beat or two, she did. When she finished, they both applauded. Before leaving, Richard apologized to her for his intrusion, but Delia had invited him and told him to say nothing, and would not listen to his arguments against it. Nancy felt mildly betrayed, but it didn't last. She was proud of her skills and knew her dancing had pleased him. More important, she had felt safe under his gaze, admired but not leered at. She liked Richard Preston. Liked his quiet strength, and the warmth and intelligence in his eyes.

Later, alone in her room, the music continued to play in her head and Nancy twirled in front of the long mirror, revealing a long, shapely leg in the net stockings Delia had given her. Despite the 70 years that lie between them, Nancy and Delia had become best friends. They'd crossed generations to a deeper place inside both of them.

One afternoon during a visit from Bethany, Nancy heard her on the telephone. "I don't think that old lady is ever going to kick the bucket," she half-whispered. "It's like she's got a new lease on life. The money is going to pay to keep her old bones alive. I love my aunt, but damn, Gerald, we could do so much with it."

Nancy, stunned by what she'd heard, slipped out of sight. She knew she couldn't tell Delia; she'd be devastated. Or think I was just jealous. What about Richard? But what proof did she have? Only what she'd heard on the phone, and it wasn't as if they'd been planning her murder. And she'd said she loved Delia. Maybe I'm making too much of it.

On a snowy Monday morning just before Christmas, Nancy had been out doing some last-minute shopping for Delia and upon returning, was met at the door by Bethany which surprised her, since Delia's niece generally visited in the afternoon. She'd been crying.

"My aunt passed away a short time ago, Nancy, while you were out – somewhere. We'll have no more need of your services."

Nancy stood outside the door, stunned at the news, unable to take in that Delia was dead. Gone from the world. That couldn't be. "But she was fine when I left her," she stammered, the tears coming despite her efforts to retain her dignity. "She asked me to get -- I can't believe it. When? Where's Molly? What happened?" In shock, she was barely able to put a coherent sentence together. But she remembered the phone call. Had Bethany done something to Delia?

Taking the bags from Nancy, she handed her an envelope. "We've paid you a month's severance. Though I can't justify a letter of reference. I must admit you worked very hard to gain my aunt's trust. Things are missing, some jewelry, but we'll just let that go unless you force my hand. I knew what you were the minute I laid eyes on you." She reached behind her and brought out Nancy's suitcases.

Nancy swallowed hard. "I'm not a thief. And I don't require a reference from you, Bethany. It would mean nothing. She picked up her suitcases and turned to leave, hearing the door close behind her.

Blinded by tears, she practically stumbled into Richard coming up the snow-covered walk.

"Nancy, I just got the call. I knew you'd be devastated, I am myself, dear. Let's go back inside..."

"No. Bethany just gave me my severance pay and told me I'm no longer needed. When did Delia die? She was fine when I left this morning. Molly was with her. How did everything happen -- so fast, Richard." She broke into sobs and Richard held her until they subsided.

"She had a massive stroke, dear. Let's be glad it took her. She wouldn't have wanted to spend whatever time she had left, unable to speak, perhaps even to think." He glared at the front door, anger in those warm eyes. "I'm sorry about Bethany. She's a spoiled, selfish woman. But not to worry, Between us, Delia left her amazing dancing student well taken care of. Wipe your eyes. It'll all be fine."

He removed a crisp white handkerchief from his suit jacket breast pocket and took her suitcases from her. "Let's go sit on the bench over there for a minute or two." He brushed the snow off the seat with his sleeve. "When we leave here, we'll book you into a hotel room for the time being."

"Delia was one of the kindest people I ever knew. She's already given me so much." She glanced over her shoulder. "She loved that house, Richard. She was proud of it. I can't bear the thought of its being torn apart and changed. It would lose its own heart."

"I'm sorry. She wanted to leave you the house, you know, but Bethany would have fought you in court for it and won. You were with Delia less than a year, merely an employee, as far as the law is concerned. Delia's considerable bequest to you will assuredly irk, but I don't think she'll complain too loudly. She's already fixing to move into the home. But you'll have enough money to buy yourself a place of your own if you choose, perhaps in a similar style..."

I want to keep the house for Delia.

The following day, at the reading of the Will, Molly Inman sat sniffing and wiping her tears. She wouldn't need to clean anyone's house for the rest of her life, unless she wanted to, which was unlikely.

Delia's wealth went far beyond what Nancy could have conceived of. As far as Bethany harming her aunt, Molly said she and Bethany were together in the kitchen when they both heard the thump and ran to see Delia on the floor, unconscious, and called 911.

Bethany had not looked at Nancy during the entire proceedings, but Nancy felt her fury from across the room. Her husband sat beside her, a seemingly amused expression on his face. Nancy thought there was something smarmy about him.

Later that day, sitting across from Richard in a small cafe, she asked, already knowing the answer, "Do I have enough money to buy the house from Bethany?"

"Yes. But she wouldn't sell it to you, Nancy. You know that."

She doesn't love the house as I do, Nancy thought. The house was like a friend that someone was threatening to disfigure. She needed to let go, but how could she?

Richard reached across the table and thumbed an errant tear from her cheek. For some time Nancy had sensed his attraction to her and it surprised her how much she liked and trusted him. Perhaps in part because Delia did. But she knew it was more than that.

"I do know that Bethany's planning to come to the house on Tuesday night and staying over," Richard said. "She wants to get the feel of the place. I'm guessing the dance studio will be the first to go."

The very thought of its destruction brought a wrenching, almost physical pain to her heart.

"I still can't believe she's gone, Richard. Without any warning at all."

"She was old, Nancy."

No, she wasn't. She was the youngest person I ever knew."

"She was 92, darling, soon to be 93. We don't get to live forever. Nancy, you've given her more in these last months than you realize. You let her live again. Truly live."

"I hope so."

"It's true. She'd come to love you like a daughter. Perhaps that's why she sent you on those errands. She didn't want you to be the one to find her. As for Bethany's eagerness to dismantle the dance studio, it's almost as if it offends her," Richard said, more to himself than to Nancy.

There had to be a way to save it.

* * *

It was well after midnight as she lay in a bed in a hotel room that a vague idea began to take shape in her mind. By morning, the plan was solidified. It might not work, but she had little to lose.

* * *

On Tuesday night, long before Bethany arrived at the house, Nancy used the key Delia had given her to let herself inside. Going straight to the dance studio, she placed candles strategically around the room, creating an eerie ambiance in the otherwise darkened space. But she was counting on Bethany's own imagination to supply the crucial ingredient. She recalled the Tarot cards Bethany believed in. Wiping clammy hands on her jeans, she changed into the gold lame dress still hanging in Delia's closet. She checked her make-up which she'd applied with great care, and her hair.

Everything ready, she waited, pacing, double-checking that she had thought of everything. It was coming onto darkness when she finally heard the key in the lock and the front door open.

* * *

Please let this work. She stepped back into the deepening shadows.

Bethany's heels clicked on the stretches of hardwood between the carpets, growing sharper as she entered the library, then fell silent. Nancy let out a breath and dropped the needle into the familiar groove of the old record player. The music began to play. She'd chosen The Stripper by David Rose, slightly tinny from wear, played ever so softly, as if coming through a rent in time... the beat of the drums, the blare of horns work their magic...Bwaaa na naaaaa, bwaaa na naaaaa...

Bwaaa na naaaaa, BWAA NA NAAAAA Naaa...

The dancer began to sway ...

The French doors flew open, causing the candle flames to flicker in the sudden draft, multiplying themselves in the mirrored walls. The fiery circle embraced the ghostly dancer in her shimmery dress, throwing the rest of the room into darkness.

* * *

Bethany stood frozen in the doorway, eyes wide, her face cast in horror at the sight of her Aunt Delia in her younger days

85

moving barely perceptibly. The dancer smiled at the paralyzed spectator, and reached out to her with pale spectral hands.

A blood-curdling scream broke from Bethany as she whirled and fled the room, and seconds later, the house, the front door slamming against the wall in her wake.

Richard showed only mild surprise when Bethany phoned him the following day and directed him to put the house on the market, that she'd changed her mind. Nancy was elated and Richard set up the sale of the house so that Bethany would never know the real name of the purchaser. Only three months later, she and Richard were quietly married and Nancy had never been happier.

It was the last time she saw Delia's niece until today as she'd been coming down the walkway on her way to her dance lesson. Bethany was driving past the house and seeing her, suddenly braked. Nancy hesitated on the walkway. Their eyes met for a long moment before Bethany sped off. Nancy continued on to her lesson.

She'd been taking modern dance at the Dance Academy across town for the last several months and loved every minute. Even the exhausting work of striving for excellence. Come next fall she would have her certification to teach young people in her own home. A degree in dance was also in her plans. She had no taste for performance except for her own pleasure, and to illustrate routines for her students.

She would carry on Delia's dream, while also making it her own.

They were in the library and Richard was working on a brief. Nancy sensed Delia's presence in the room, she could almost smell her perfume. Chanel No. 5.

"Bethany looked like she saw a ghost," she told Richard, who knew nothing about her little ruse. Or so she thought until he looked up from his laptop and said quietly: "Strange how it all worked out, isn't it? Delia always said you were a smart girl. "Almost as if Delia herself had planned it," he said, with a trace of a smile.

The End

A Long Dark Road

Elsie Heming had spent the afternoon visiting with her oldest and dearest friend, Nora Rivers, who was recuperating from a gall bladder operation. Elsie had picked up several containers of Chinese food for dinner, Nora's favorite. Finished cleaning up, she was folding the red and white checked dish towel over the towel-holder by the stove, when a darkness descended over the kitchen, like a bad omen. Glancing out Nora's kitchen window, it surprised her at how dark it had gotten. A small rush of dread went through her, thinking of the drive home. She hated night driving. The nights came so early now.

"I didn't realize it was so late, Nora, so I'm going to take off," she said," shrugging into her coat. "Will you be okay?"

"I'm pioneer stock, I'll be fine," she said, pushing back a few strands of hair that had escaped the thick braid coiled around her head. "I'm sorry, Elsie, I should have reminded you, I know how much you dislike driving at night."

Dislike was an understatement. Elsie wished her friend would move back to the city but Nora loved it out here in the boonies, unlike Elsie who liked the hustle and bustle of the city, the rumble of trucks, car horns, and people laughing and talking as they walked past her window. The pulse of life.

They'd been sitting at Nora's scarred and battered old wood table, but strong as the oak it was made of, passed down from generations of Rivers, all afternoon. Elsie remembered it well, having spent a good deal of time at Nora's house when they were kids. Nora was a retired teacher, a widow like herself. Elsie had worked in the school office. So much water under the bridge. So many memories.

"I didn't plan to stay so long," Elsie said. "But you're such great company I never want to leave."

"We have lots to reminisce about, you and I. You do me good, my friend. Best I've felt in days. "I'd insist you stay the night, but I know you don't like to leave Molly alone." They both were cat ladies. They hugged like the old friends they were. Very different in many ways, yet connected at a deeper level. Nora had been her maid-of-honor when she and John were married. And was there for his funeral and Elsie's plunge into despair in the months following.

As Elsie draped her teal blue scarf about her neck, she admired the portrait propped on the sideboard. Nora followed her gaze. "And I really do love this painting, Nora. Wish I had your talent."

"I kind of like it myself," Nora smiled. "Ginger is a good subject, aren't you, sweet girl." The aptly named cat had awakened from her nap and was presently circling Nora's ankles, purring loudly. "It's a great pastime. And it makes me happy."

Elsie hitched her leather bag over her shoulder. "I know. And I'm glad. But don't overdo. Take care of yourself. Let your body heal."

"Don't worry about me," Nora said, walking her to the door. "I must say I like your hair. I wasn't sure when you said you were going to stop coloring it. But it looks great; pearl-white in that youthful cut. You remind me a little of Helen Mirren. Call me when you get home, okay?"

"I will. And thanks." Elsie felt a glow from Nora's compliment. The truth was the chemicals had been making her hair thin enough to see her scalp. "Glad you like it. Looks like a storm on the way," Elsie said as they stood in the open doorway gazing up at the roiling black clouds. A low rumble of thunder sounded, not far off. The leaves on the trees shivered.

Ginger added her own complaint and Nora scooped the cat up in her arms.

"It was nice out when I left home," Elsie said. "Didn't think to check the weather, not that it matters."

"If you didn't check the weather then you probably don't have an umbrella in the car."

"Oh, Well, I don't think I'll need..."

"Take this one," she said before Elsie could protest further, retrieving it from the small closet. "I've got several. You'll still have to get from your parking spot to your building."

Settling into the driver's seat, Elsie gave Nora a departing wave and pulled out of the driveway, past Nora's jeep, taking a mental snapshot of her friend standing in the doorway lit by the night-light, cradling her beloved Ginger in her arms. That would have made a great painting, too, Elsie mused as she picked up speed and headed down the Old Post Road. She'd enjoyed the drive on the way up. The leaves had turned color and were glorious in their golds, copper, and scarlets. But now the woods were dark against an angry sky. She couldn't wait to get home to her apartment, get into her fuzzy white robe and find a good thriller to watch on Netflix. Simple pleasures.

But she couldn't complain and mostly she was grateful. She was in good health and took care of herself, did her daily exercises, and walked the streets of her little city, always finding something to stir her interest, a historical building, a view of the bay. When the weather didn't cooperate she opted for her treadmill. Of course, she had her share of issues that aging brought to everyone, some neurological damage to her feet, arthritis, and so on. But nothing serious enough to slow her down and she mostly tried to ignore it. She wasn't that old. Seventy-three wasn't the seventy-three of her childhood. Several months back, she'd even taken some well-intended advice and dated a very nice-looking, pleasant man for a short time, but she didn't fit right in his arms. When she was with him she felt like she was cheating on John.

John would be gone five years this December. They'd been watching an old black and white noir movie on the Turner Channel. Something with Barbara Stanwick. He'd gone to make coffee and minutes later, she heard the thud of his falling and raced into the kitchen to find him on the floor. Just like that, he was gone. His eyes were open, though no longer seeing. There'd been no history of heart problems, no warning of a massive coronary. He'd had a full checkup only a couple of months earlier and received a good bill of health. Her life was changed forever.

For a long time after he died, she wandered around like the victim of a bomb blast. Cried till there were no tears left, and her eyes felt like they were scraped with sandpaper. Unconsciously, in the night, she would reach for him across the empty space in the bed. Sometimes a wall of grief would wash over her like a tidal wave, taking her breath, threatening to drown her. But we all suffer terrible losses. And more so as we age. At some point, you just have to get on with it.

They'd had no children, though they tried. "Stop trying so hard and it will happen," the doctor said. But it never did, so they became everything to one another, and they'd been happy. She was kind of a happy camper by nature anyway, adaptable, John said. You're the kind of woman who, if the door won't open, you'll carve out a new one. She smiled at the memory and hoped she was that woman he described. But she missed him every day, his wry sense of humor, his touch. He was her safe place.

A light rain began to patter against the windshield and Elsie turned on the wipers. She tuned in to the station that played music of the forties and fifties: a little Glenn Miller at the moment that sweet song. Honeysuckle Rose. God, that was an old one.

The Old Post Road was long, a narrow tunnel hemmed in by dark woods, and seemed even longer tonight. Most drivers used the new main highway now. She passed only a couple of cars along the way. Lulled by the rhythm of the wipers blended with the music, and the hum of the wheels on rough pavement, Elsie's heart leaped when the car dropped suddenly with a bone-jarring thump that reverberated through her body, followed by a jerky vibrating ride as the car took her further down the road. Whump! whump! whump! She eased off on the gas and brought the car to a crawling stop on the shoulder. Sat unmoving until her heartbeat settled down. Oh, no, please not here. But it was here; in the dark and the cold, and the rain. She had a flat, she was sure of it. Damn.

She got out of the car long enough to feel the cold rain on her face and confirm that the flat was on the front passenger side.

Even as she dug the cellphone out of her bag to call triple-A, she knew with a sickening sureness that the thing would be dead. She'd purchased it for emergencies like this one and didn't miss the irony of that. She was always forgetting to charge it. John took care of mechanical issues or else she'd be fortunate enough to be near a service station if something went wrong with the car. Not this time.

Right again; the cellphone was dead. No pulse, zero, zip.

Hazard lights flashing, she sat and contemplated her situation. She seemed to recall seeing a spare tire in the trunk. After a moment, she got out of the car and hurried around to the front passenger side. A wet chill crept inside her coat collar and she turned it up, tucking the scarf inside her coat as a bolt of lightning flashed very low in the sky followed by a deafening crack of thunder.

She opened the trunk. The spare tire was there, but no jack, not that she'd know how to use it though she'd watched John change a tire often enough. She should have paid more attention. Her car was just a few months old, used but in excellent shape and she'd given the trunk only a cursory check.

Hearing a distant car motor, Elsie's spirits lifted. As the headlights grew brighter, she stood at the edge of the road waving her arms frantically, hoping to flag it down, but the car sped on by, leaving her to stare after it until the taillights disappeared around a bend in the road. Thanks a lot.

Someone else will come along, she told herself.

forcing herself to remain calm, she remembered passing a store and small service station a few miles back; she could walk there if she had to. She was a good walker. She knew there was a flashlight in the glove compartment because she'd put it there herself. God knew, there was no place darker than a country road at night unless it was the grave. The lights were sparse along this road, but Elsie hadn't given it much thought since she'd expected to be home long before now. She clicked the button on the flashlight, and hope dimmed along with the faint, almost non-existent light. When was the last time you changed the batteries? she chastised herself. A further search in the glove compartment turned up no extras. So what now? The rain was coming down in earnest now, drumming on the roof. Well, nothing to be done for it.

Exiting the car again, she peered through the darkness and the driving rain hoping for a glimpse of headlights, willing them to appear. Standing there in the driving rain, she had never felt so alone or so stupid in her life. Might as well get back in the car. She'd be able to see any approaching headlights in the rearview mirror. She was cold now, wet and uncomfortable. Surely someone was bound to come along. The roar of the rain sounded faintly like applause in the dark confines of the front seat, as if mocking her.

She'd been sitting there for maybe ten minutes when she started at a sudden rapping on her driver's window, sending her heart into her throat. She turned to see a man smiling in at her, releasing a flood of relief through her. She lowered the window. He was a nice-looking man in a black raincoat with the hood drawn up. He held his flashlight off to the side. He was maybe in his mid-forties. The older she got the harder it was to tell people's ages. A policeman?

"Looks like you're having a problem, Ma'am," he said, almost shouting over the rain. Where had he come from? Glancing in the rearview mirror, she saw the van parked behind her car. She'd neither heard nor seen it drive up. She must have looked away from the rearview mirror for a moment.

"An understatement, to say the least. I've never been so happy to see anyone in my life. Thank you so much for stopping. I have a flat tire and nothing to change it with, not that I could anyway. There's a spare tire in the trunk but I wouldn't think of asking you to change it in this downpour. If you could just call Triple-A for me that would be great. I'm afraid my cellphone is quite dead."

"I expect they're pretty busy on a night like this. Heaven knows when they'd get here and it's not safe for you alone on this road. But it's no problem changing the tire. It'll just take a few minutes. I've got a tarp in the van. Give me your keys and I'll get the tire out of the trunk. You just stay in the car so you don't get any wetter than you already are. Ma'am." Elsie handed him the keys and told him her name.

"Hi. Name's Ed. Ed Jones. I had a favorite aunt named Elsie."

Clutching the keys in his large hand, he smiled at her and disappeared behind the car; a second later the trunk lid went up. Elsie watched in the rearview mirror as he lifted out the tire and laid it down beside the flat tire on her passenger side, then went back to the van to get the tarp, she assumed. Rain hammered on the roof. He's going to get drenched, she thought, despite the hooded raincoat.

She was surprised when the door of the van opened and two more men climbed out. Something in the way they moved seemed almost predatory. and Elsie's earlier sense of unease shot up a notch.

The dark rainy night and all. That's all it is. That, and your imagination. Trying to quell her nerves, she turned up the music on the radio and was about to withdraw her hand when the music was interrupted by a news bulletin: "Police are on the hunt for three men who went on a crime spree earlier tonight robbing several businesses in Granville. One man was fatally shot and a young woman was rushed to hospital with life-threatening injuries from ..."

It was as if an anvil had dropped on her heart. Her hand trembled as she switched off the radio, her throat tightening. Had they heard the bulletin? Still looking in the rearview mirror, she thought they seemed nervous. What were they in deep conversation about? They couldn't have heard anything over the rain. Could they? Almost in sync, as if they'd read her thoughts, the two abandoned their discussion and looked in her direction. She looked away.

Elsie's heart raced, every cell in her body on alert. She could smell the rush of adrenaline that told us to fight or run. She wasn't much of a fighter. She would dare to drive away right now, flat or no flat, but she knew they'd be on her in a minute. And then she remembered that Ed Jones, if that was his real name which she now doubted, had her car keys, so driving away wasn't an option. He was clearly their leader. Her rescuer was no rescuer at all, but a con, a charmer. The other two were younger, rougher around the edges, and looked like what they were: criminals. Thugs.

Was she jumping to conclusions? Maybe they weren't the same men, at all? She knew she was grasping at straws. As if to confirm what she already knew, the taller and slighter of the two men grasped his arm, as if nursing a wound, his face twisted in pain. He'd been injured.

She might be forgetful but she wasn't stupid. She watched crime shows on TV. and knew exactly what was going on. These men weren't doing her any favors; they needed to switch vehicles, the only reason they'd stopped. They were desperate. They wanted her car. You're in big trouble, Elsie Heming. She had seen their faces; she could identify them. They had already battered at least one woman tonight and shot someone else; they wouldn't think twice about getting rid of her. You didn't need to be a genius to know how this would end for her. Elsie felt like the proverbial sitting duck.

"Get out! Run," she could almost hear John say. "Run into the woods, my darling. Hide."

Stricken with terror, but determined to fight for her life, she eased her door open an inch and waited. Remembering Nora's umbrella on the seat beside her, she gripped it in her hand. Not much of a weapon, but something.

Thunder rumbled and clapped and growled a short distance off. A steak of blue-white Lightning snaked across the black sky, turning night into day. Once the tire is on, I will disappear. They will lose the van. And they would lose me. She let out a long, shaky breath, counted in her head, visualizing a clean leap from the car. One. Two. Three.

NOW!

Elsie was out of the car and running down a brief stretch of road and into the woods, turning her ankle in a dip in the shoulder, not quite a ditch. The heels of her shoes sunk into the soft, wet earth, pain stabbing her ankle with every step. But she trudged on.

* * *

The three turned in surprise. The one who'd introduced himself to Elsie as Ed Jones chuckled. "Fast for an old girl. Get her, Ham," he said. "Throw her in the van and ditch them both."

Ham, a bull of a man, short, with sheared hair, guided by his flashlight, took off after her.

Jake watched Ham disappear into the woods. Then, tightening the final lug nut, he slipped into the driver's seat. The wounded man climbed gingerly into the back seat and lay back. "I'm bleedin' bad, man."

"Quit bellyachin'. Make a tourniquet out of your tee-shirt, or something. "

A short distance into the woods, Elsie ducked behind a tree and remained there, not moving, not daring to breathe as she watched the man run through the woods after her, thrashing and slipping as he went, once falling on all fours, cursing her in vile terms.

Elsie tried to make herself part of the tree, feeling the rough, wet bark against her

100

cheek, aware of the sharp smell of pine and resin. Thunder boomed straight above her, and the rain came down with a new fury, pounding her bent head. Water ran from her hair, drenching her through her clothes within seconds and plastering her hair to her head like a tight cap. Close behind her, she heard his angry curses, his boots lurching through the woods as the circle of bright light darted here and there, seeking her out.

"Where are you, bitch?" came an angry bellow close by.

This could not be. She'd been chatting and sipping tea with her old friend just an eye-blink ago, it seemed, and now here she was; trapped in a nightmare, hiding in the woods from a madman who was intent on killing her.

She could see him now, a silhouette behind the flashlight he held and she clung to the tree like a second skin, quieting her gasps. The storm is your friend, she told herself, as she tried to relax her trembling body. Her sodden coat hung on her like a heavy blanket. She watched the circle of light dart here and there through the woods, spot-lighting patches of rain-battered trees, as in a stage setting. She could hear his stomping boots, his grumbling, and curses as he searched out his prey. Suddenly, the light flashed in her eyes and she blinked but didn't move. When he came at her, she drove the point of the umbrella into his throat with all the strength that was in her, and then she ran as fast as she could, hobbling on the ankle, hearing his howls behind her. Twigs and branches and twigs clawed her face, drawing blood that blended with the rain.

After a few minutes, she heard him say to himself, "To hell with this', and the halo of light from the flashlight was moving away from her, gradually growing smaller, returning the night to darkness.

The rain was easing up. the storm calming, leaving the woods silent. Elsie remained still as a posed mannequin behind a different tree. But the tune of safety was a siren's song. She didn't trust it. Had he really left? Given up? It might be a trick. After what felt like an hour, she allowed herself to release her grip on the tree and let out a long, slow breath. She was soaked through, shivering uncontrollably against the cold that had burrowed into her aging bones. Her heart was fluttering wildly. Finally, she stepped out from the tree. Had taken one wobbly step when the blaze of light revealed the patch of woods before her and realized he'd come up behind her. The flashlight arched through the darkness and in the instant before it came down, she heard the rumble of a motor starting up and visualized her bag with all her information, in the back seat. And then saw nothing at all as pain exploded inside her head, sending shards of lightning bolts through her skull. Elsie sagged to the ground, the thick blackness wrapping around her like a great shroud.

Far away, the faint wail of a siren sounded.

* * *

"Mrs. Heming... Elsie... can you open your eyes?"

A woman's voice, soft, concerned.

Her lids fluttered open long enough to see a blurred vision of the nurse in white standing over her. White walls behind her. Medicinal smells under the stronger aroma of coffee permeated the air. Opening her eyes made her headache worse so she closed them again. "My head hurts," she managed, her voice raspy. " Her mouth felt dry as chalk and tasted of chemicals. The doctor came to see her and then the nurse brought her tea. She slept then and woke feeling much better.

It was a shock to find out I'd been in a coma for four days. She learned she wouldn't be alive if not for Nora, who became concerned when Elsie didn't call her, as promised. "So I called you," Nora said. When I got no answer and knew you'd had plenty of time to get home, I grew worried. I turned on the radio just for the company while I paced and that's when I heard the news bulletin about the police trying to track three men in a van and called the police."

Elsie got the whole story piecemeal over the next couple of days, mainly from Nora. They'd found her leather bag in the ditch, relieved of a small amount of cash, and credit

103

cards which the police had already reported stolen.

It wasn't until the next day when police spotted Elsie's car parked around the back of a rundown motel, that the three of them were rounded up and dragged off to jail in handcuffs. Two had to be taken to hospital, one with a bullet in his arm, the other with a puncture wound to the throat, serious but neither life-threatening. "I owe you a new umbrella," Elsie said.

"Oh, yes, I'm very concerned about that umbrella," Nora teased. "By the way, Molly says to tell you she misses you."

"Thanks for taking care of her."

"She's a joy. She and Ginger are already fast friends."

"Good. Why am I not surprised."

"When I think of what could have happened... you wouldn't have lasted the night out there with your injuries. Maybe even without them." She'd had some swelling, resulting from a brain bleed, along with severe hypothermia, various cuts, scrapes, and bruises. "It was pretty dicey for a while," Nora said. "You're no spring chicken, you know."

Elsie tried not to laugh. "I know."

"Anyway, I'm glad you're back."

"Me too." She saw out her window the enamel blue sky, not a cloud anywhere, the top of the church steeple. A seagull high up. "Well, maybe not entirely back," she said. I don't remember anything about what happened to me. The last thing I recall is seeing you standing in her doorway with Ginger in your arms."

Though that wasn't entirely true. She vaguely remembered the kindly face of a man with snow-white hair, and a deep, reassuring voice telling her that she'd be fine as she floated through the darkness to someplace warm and dry. The ambulance probably, she thought now. They'd no doubt removed her wet clothes and wrapped her in blankets.

"Your rescuer has been calling every day," the dark-eyed, very sweet nurse told her later that day. She was turning her pillows, straightening and smoothing her top sheet and blanket. "Those lovely roses are from him. Nice gentleman. Not hard on the eyes, either." She winked.

He arrived in the evening, during visiting hours. He was tall with thick, white hair as she remembered, dressed casually in jeans and a leather jacket. "Hello, Elsie. Ms. Heming."

"Elsie's fine. You must be George. The roses are lovely, thank you."

"You're welcome."

"I'm told you rescued me," she smiled. She wished she'd put on a little lipstick. At least the scratches and bruises were fading.

"Glad I was there. But one of them would have found you. Your shoe prints going into the woods were pretty clear. You're looking a whole lot better since the last time I saw you.

Full name's George Watson," he said, drawing up a metal chair, the leg scraping lightly on the floor. His closeness gave off a hint of citrus and the outdoors, evidenced by his tan. After a brief shyness, they were chatting like old friends. He was a widower, with two grown boys, and almost grown grandchildren, he told her. Both families lived away, though visited quite often. Along with volunteering with the emergency team, where he'd spent most of his working life, he also taught an automotive class at the community college in the spring and fall

The nurse hadn't lied. He looked around her age, maybe a tad younger. Slate blue eyes, laugh lines fanning out from them. Two prominent lines bracketed his mouth, above a strong jaw line, if a little softer now. A face that had lived an interesting, if not an easy, life.

Over the next couple of weeks, George came to visit every day, always with a thoughtful treat. There was never a lack of something new to talk or laugh about. If someone else came to see her, or if he thought she looked tired, he would graciously take his leave.

"I'm going home tomorrow," she told him on the day her doctor signed the discharge form. "Nora is picking me up." She'd almost begun to regret going home. Almost. But the truth was she could wait to sleep in her own bed. And of course, see Molly.

He looked disappointed and she wondered if he might have wanted to drive her home.

"I'm glad for you. Please stay well, Elsie."

"Maybe I'll take your automotive class in the spring," she said impulsively, emboldened by the way he was looking at her. "Do you think you could teach me how to change a tire, George?" God, she was flirting like a teenager. It felt good.

"I'm quite sure of it," he said, grinning. "But I hope I don't have to wait until spring before I see you again, Elsie. "

Life can change on a dime, she thought. John had simply gone out to the kitchen and never returned to her. This could have been her last chapter. And death lasts a very long time.

"Call me," she said.

The End

I Hitched A Ride Into Hell

A time before we all had computers and cellphones

It was June, 28th, 1970, on a Saturday morning when my best friend Shirley and I started out to hitchhike across Canada. We live on the east coast in the small town of Belle-Arbre, population – 9,007 and were planning travel via our thumbs all the way to Vancouver, British Columbia.

The day was sunny and bright with a promise of adventure in the air. I could hardly believe we were on our way at last. As we walked along the shoulder of the road watching cars whiz past, waiting for someone to stop and give us a lift, I thought about all the things that had led up to our being here now.

Shirley Masson is my best friend and we had been kicking around this idea of hitchhiking across country all during our last year in Belding Senior High. When we decided for sure to do it, we could hardly wait for graduation.

"One day to pack our jeans and toothbrushes," Shirley had bubbled as we sauntered the two blocks from school, "and the next we're off to see how the rest of this corner of the world shapes up."

I caught the glow of excitement on her pretty face and I had to grin. I felt the same way. Beneath her blond hair, Shirley has wide blue eyes that can manage to look both innocent and worldly at the same time. And when she talks it's in this excited, breathless way with the kind of enthusiasm that rubs off. Somehow she makes you feel that around every corner there's a new adventure if only you'll risk taking a chance.

"You're like color TV and I'm like black and white," I told her once when we were analyzing one another during a sleepover at her house. Shirley thought it was a nutty comparison and laughed that tinkling laugh of hers when I said it. But I kind of think she agreed with me even though she'd never say. But that's how I see us. Even though we're both similar coloring, although she's a little fairer than I am, we could even be mistaken for sisters, we're different. Even to our looks despite the blond hair. Where Shirley is really built, I'm kind of tall and angular. I guess that's why we've stayed such good friends. Our personalities complement one another. Shirley brings me out of my quiet seriousness and I stop her from bubbling over completely, and somehow manage to keep her feet touching the ground, just a little.

Anyway, back to what made us decide to cross the country via our thumbs. Part of the idea came from an article we read called, "Crossing the Miles on a Shoestring'. Not that it recommended hitchhiking as the best way of transportation exactly, but it was the cheapest, and we figured the most fun way. But what really gave us the fever was knowing that lots of kids were planning to do the same thing. Many we'd already seen along the highway thumbing rides, knapsacks on their backs, just like Shirley and me. I also had my old suitcase I'd packed with stuff. We'd seen college kids, bearded, long-haired hippies and other travellers who looked no older than us finished their last year in high school, I figured   and not quite ready to settle down to the dull grind of a job or more classrooms.

Shirley had her guitar with her. She was a budding songwriter and never went anywhere without it. She was good too. Everyone said she sounded a lot like Joan Biaz, except her voice was a little deeper. I just knew she would make it big one of these days. I think it was my dream as much as hers. But I had my own dream too; I wanted to be a writer and wrote in my journal almost every day. The teacher said I showed a lot of promise, and I got an A+ on my last essay. I'd packed scribblers and pens to record our travels. Shirley was pretty good with the camera so we'd have pictures to show when we got back home. Maybe I'd write articles for the local paper, and Shirley could submit her photos.

Neither Shirley or I were brainy enough to take academic or go on to college (not to mention our families had no money) so we'd both enrolled in the commercial course the school offered. This meant we would be working in offices somewhere typing letters, taking dictation, filing stuff or whatever else office clerks did to earn their paycheques. I'd made decent marks in school, especially in Geography and English, so I thought I could be a good secretary. Or even enventually go to college. But I didn't want to think about that now. But whatever the future held in store, I still wanted to take a year off before starting all that. Right now, we just wanted a summer of freedom and fun, and a chance to see some of the country, outside our boring hometown before we had to become 'responsible adults', as my father termed what seemed really dreary to me.

Just as Shirley had promised, it was two days after school closing, our diplomas were framed and we were on the road. We had $487.00 between us that we'd saved from babysitting jobs. We figured when our money ran out, we'd get odd jobs waitressing, or whatever, and at the end of summer, we'd just head on back home.

Both our parents were dead set against what we were doing, but we presented so many good arguments, I guess in the end, we just wore them down. Even though dad said teens and young adults with their thumbs out, were becoming a familiar sight on Canadian highways, mom wasn't persuaded.

"Why don't you and Shirley work for a year, Karen," Mom coaxed. "Save enough money so you can go first class, like ladies."

"Who want to go first class?" I came back, ignoring the plea in her voice. "That would just take all the adventure out of it. And besides, money in your jeans doesn't make you a lady, mom."

"It can make you safer, Karen. It's dangerous getting into cars with streangers," she argued. "You don't know who you're getting in with."

"So, there's danger in crossing the street," I said. "Come on, Mom, we'll be okay, really. All the kids are doing it. Travel is broadening, educational."

She signed, looking anything but convinced.

I tried to ease her worries. "Mom, even our own Prime Minister thinks it's a great idea. He publicly promoting hitchhiking as a great way for kids to travel."

It was true. Pierre Elliot Trudeau had hitchhiked around Europe and the Middle East as a young man, long before he became prime minister. "His exact words were, "Hit the road. Drive or hitchhike and see what Canada's all about." I actually memorized that as a point of debate.

"Well, I like Mr. Trudeau, I think that was wrong of him to advise you kids to hitchhike," mom said. "But I can see that he's remembering his own experiences in a positive way. It's different for girls..."

My mother has dark hair and is petite. She has a cleft in her chin like Ava Gardner. She even won the Miss Belle-Arbre title when she was my age. Her looks passed me by. Everyone says I look like my father and I know I do. But my mother is more than just a pretty face. She's also smart and she's wise. Though sometimes I think she just frets too much and I think my dad would agree. But I still didn't feel good knowing I was responsible for putting those worry lines on her face.

"Look Mom. I'll send you a post-card from every point worth mentioning, okay? We'll keep change on hand and I'll phone you from a payphone now and then. Now please don't worry so much. Shirley and I are big girls now – big enough to earn our own living come fall," I reminded her. "We can look after ourselves just fine." I gave her a hug hoping to smooth out the frown between her brows. It didn't work. "Hey, and I thought there was no generation gap between you and me," I teased.

She smiled but it was a weak smile. "I hope I'm doing the right thing in letting you go, Karen. I could forbid you, you know? You're not of age yet and I'm still your mother."

"I hope you won't do that, Mom," I said solemnly. I knew my father would side with Mom whatever she decided, so I was arguing my case with her for all I was worth. If she had put her foot down and said absolutely no, then I would live with that. I would have been terribly disappointed, sure, but I wouldn't out and out disobey her. I was too big a wimp for that. Besides, I like my parents and I know they just want what's right for me. But I really, really wanted to go. And Shirley, too, would have been crushed if I couldn't.

Well, obviously in the end she didn't forbid me, but the worried lines were still there when I closed the door behind me. When we got far enough away from our small white clapboard house with its blue trim, that I couldn't see it anymore, I began to relax and look forward to our adventure. The very air smelled new and magical. And there was a lightness under my heart, as if a balloon were attached to it. We were about to begin a new chapter in our lives. But even with my anticipation, I could still see mom's worried face.

We'd been walking along the shoulder of the highway for about twenty minutes, trying to keep a space between ourselves and other kids we saw hitchhiking, when Shirley yelled, "Hey, Karen, they're slowing down," jolting me out of my guilty thoughts about my mother. "We've got a lift. Come on, slowpoke," she urged, tugging my arm, "before they take off again."

We both broke into a run toward the long, black convertible idling at the side of the road, signal light flashing invitingly. I was grateful and I knew Shirley was too.

"Hi, kids. Climb in," the blond, pleasant faced woman said, reaching around and opening the back door. She had mauve painted fingernails to match her lipstick. A small boy of about five sat quietly beside her. The car radio was on and the Supremes were singing You Can't Hurry Love, one of my favorites. She had it turned up loud. As we scrambled into the back seat, she lowered the volume a little to ask us where we were headed. We told her.

"Wow, you're brave girls," she smiled. "All the way to Vancouver."

* * *

We were in luck. She was going all the way out to Creighton Settlement, about 150 miles from where we were. Practically the whole time she chatted gaily from her front seat, telling all about how her husband was away in Vietnam, and that she was taking her son to their summer place for the holidays.

"Jack is coming home in September," she told us, smiling, showing her perfect teeth. "Then the three of us will be moving back to the city." She sounded like she'd had similar hopes before, but they'd fallen through. She was optimistic, but wary, not putting her whole self into the words.

"I didn't know Canada was in the Vietnam war," Shirley said.

"No, we're not, actually. Not in combat anyway. My husband joined the U.S. army. He was one of many young men who did. His father's American, also a military man. Jack wanted to help."

"My daddy's coming home when I go to school," her little boy said, with a big smile that revealed a space in front where his tooth had been. Nothing was held back in this excitement. He believed. His mother tousled his fair head. For the rest of the drive we were all silent.

We waved goodbye to Sandy Crandall, which we'd learned was her name, and to her son, Kevin, at an intersection in the middle of what appeared to be, nowhere.

"Good luck," she called out the open window. I could hear Monday, Monday by The Mama's and The Papa's thumping from the car radio, soon only an echo playing in my head.

We watched the car take a left turn, bump across some railway tracks then she was gone, taillights vanishing in a cloud of dust. I suddenly felt kind of lost and abandoned. Shirley and I both stared up at the wooden sign with arrows that pointed in three different directions – Brambles Fork, Deering and South Branch. The names meant nothing to either of us.

"Do you know where we are?" Shirley asked, feigning cheerfulness.

"Not a clue. And we didn't bring any maps." It was a statement of fact, and we should have thought of it before. I'd spent some time looking at our old globe before we left on our trip. "I didn't even notice where Mrs. Crandall turned off the highway. She would have told us how to get back on if we'd asked, but she must have figured we knew. Nobody in their right minds travels without maps."

"I didn't think of it," Shirley shrugged. "I can't read 'em anyway."

"Well, I can. Pretty well actually."

"Yeah, I know. You're the big geography whiz. So you're the one who should have thought of it. Oh, well, we'll get some at the next service station we come to and you can do your thing."   She turned her attention back to the signs. "I vote we go straight ahead. Follow the arrow that says 5 miles to Deering. We're bound to meet up with the highway eventually."

"You think?"

"Yeah, sure." She hitched the guitar up higher on her shoulder. We started walking. Along the way, I caught sight of a wide-brimmed old straw hat on the side of the road someone lost, and put it on, grateful for a little shade from the hot sun.

About ten minutes later luck caught up with us again. An old farmer with skin like burnt leather rattled to a sop beside us in a battered truck. "You girls lost?" he asked, spatting a wad of tobacco away from us, out of the side of his mouth.

"Sort of," Shirley said. "We're trying to get back onto the highway. And we need to find a service station too."

"Hop on," he said, motioning toward the back of the truck. "I'm heading right out to Mike's Body Shop. It's at the end of this road, and that's where you'll find your highway."

"Great!" we chorused, and clammered into the back of the truck. Another leg of our adventure.

At the combination body shop and service station we got some oil-speckled maps from a pleasantly plump man with thinning sandy hair and the fattest freckles I'd ever seen on anyone. He was wiping his chubby hands on greasy old rag. The place smelled of cars and grease, and a burning smell. Maybe a welding torch. He gave us the key to the washroom around back, and we were practically dancing as we fitted it into the lock. After doing our business, made more urgent from the jostling we'd gotten on the back of the farmer's truck, we washed up a little in the small, but surprisingly clean, sink.

"Boy," Shirley complained good-naturedly, pushing a comb through her tangled hair, I feel as if I've got half the countryside either in my mouth or on me."

"Yeah, me too." I sloshed cold water over my face, and patted it dry with a rough paper towel.

After we left the station, it seemed our good luck had come to an end. We'd been walking along the highway for what seemed hours and maybe ten cars went by us. It seemed this wasn't the main highway, but an old alternate route.

"Man, it's hot," Shirley complained, easing her knapsack and guitar off her shoulder and setting them down on the side of the road. "Let's just rest here for a few minutes."

"I'm with you. My feet are killing me. I sure wish someone would stop soon. If we get into Montreal soon we can ask around about where the youth hostel is. The guy at the service station said there was one somewhere in the area."

"Yeah, it said so in that article we read, for sure."

"We'll ask at their tourist bureau," Shirley said. "That's probably our best bet. But first I've got to get something to eat. My stomach is rumbling. I'm starved."

We'd packed a lunch but consumed it hours ago. Why didn't we think to get something at that service station? They had chips, bars and stuff. But we'd been just thinking about maps. And besides, I had an A & W or a Mcdonalds in mind. But there wasn't anything like that insight. Actually there wasn't anything, period.

All that stretched before us was miles and miles of shimmering pavement. On both sides loomed green hills and above us blue skies, with a blistering sun beating down. It looked like a place that hadn't yet been discovered, but because of the highway I knew it had. Not only was there no eating place in sight, but not a sign of a house or farm to show that people actually existed here. A long stretch of nothingness.

By our maps we figured we'd already covered close to 200 miles, which wasn't bad. But right then the only thing either of us was interested in was filling our empty stomachs and finding a bed for tonight. Even if it was in someone's barn. Actually, that didn't sound too bad.

"Tomorrow we'll just kick around wherever we happen to find ourselves and take in some of the sights," Shirley said. Then she got that familiar mischievious grin on her face. "Maybe we'll even get lucky and meet some cute guys."

I had to laugh. Nothing ever got Shirley down for long. I noticed that her skin, which was a little fairer than mine, beginning to pinken, and was glad I tanned easily. I gave her my straw hat to wear. Though I wasn't worried about sunburn, the back of my neck felt hot and sweaty. Sitting there on the side of the road, I pinned my long, heavy hair on top of my head. Shirley took the guitar out of the case, and sang a few songs, accompanying herself. I chimed in on a couple I knew the words to, but the truth is I'm not much of a singer.   She started making up a new song about two girls on the road, putting in the bit about the little boy who was waiting for his dad to come home from the war, and the farmer who picked us up in the truck, and one verse was about the little boy who was waiting for his daddy to come home from the war.   You just had to suggest a topic to Shirley and she could make up a song about it.

In a little while we got up and starting walking again. A few cars passed us, but none stopped.

The sun was beginning its slide behind a distant grey-green hill, and while I was glad for the cooler air, I was nervous about the oncoming darkness if we didn't get a ride soon. Shirley told me not to worry so much, (am I my mother's child?) at least it wasn't raining. Just as she was saying something about being grateful for small mercies, a small blue car passed us, then slowed. In one synchronized movement, we were alert and thumbing frantically. For one awful moment I was afraid it was going to keep going, but then with double sighs of relief, we watched it come to a screeching halt onto the shoulder of the road a couple of hundred yards from us, blinker flashing, as if to yell, 'Come on! Hurry!' before I change my mind. I had this crazy feeling that we'd get almost there and it would take off.

We were both out of breath by the time we reached the car.

"Sorry to make you run so far, girls," the man said. "At first I thought you were a couple of boys in those shirts and dungarees. Takes a little doing to tell the difference these days," he added, laughing. "And with all I read in the papers about beatings and robberies a guy can't be too careful about who he picks up on the road."

"We hadn't thought of that," Shirley said, looking both embarrassed and amused because he took us for boys. "Anyway, thanks a lot for changing your mind and stopping. Are you by any chance headed for Montreal?"

"Going right through," he said. I noticed when I got in the car that he was a nice looking man, probably in his early thirties. He had black, straight hair, kind of long so it curled up just a little above his shirt collar. From the back seat his shoulders were broad in the navy shirt. Someone's husband, I thought, noticing the gold band on his left hand. I pictured him living in a nice modern house, mowing his lawn on Saturday afternoons, a couple of cute kids with black hair playing nearby.

We were still a long way from our destination, so the conversation drifted back and forth among the three of us over the miles. I hadn't been far wrong in my thoughts about our driver. He told he was a traveler for a pharmaceutical firm and that indeed, he was married. But I did miss on one thing; he had three kids.

"Two boys and a girl," he said with a father's pride. "In fact, when they get as old as you girls, I'd like to see them doing the same thing you're doing. It's good for kids to see what the rest of their country has to offer. And those youth hostels you girls mentioned are a great idea. Should have had them long ago. Come to think of it, I know exactly where the one you is you've got in mind. Not too far off from where I'm seeing a client tonight. No problem to drop you both off at the door."

I felt a small twinge of discomfort when he said he thought what we were doing was a great idea, because he was the first grownup we'd told, to think so. Most thought hitchhiking was a bad idea, (but for Mr. Trudeau) and not just our parents, either. It was like hearing an off-note on the piano. Even the way Sandy Crandall, the woman with the little boy, had said we were brave, I got the feeling she really thought we were taking a big chance. I should have listened to my inner voice right then, but I didn't.

We thanked him, glad for the offer, and I'd already dismissed my uneasy feeling about the man. Instead, we were thinking about our stomachs. We still hadn't had anything to eat and I felt on the verge of starvation. It was getting dark out and I figured once we reached the hostel which was probably in some out-of-the-way place, there likely wouldn't be any fast-food restaurants. We couldn't know that for sure, of course, but I for one hated to take the chance. Morning was a long way off. Still, I couldn't bring myself to say anything because he was already being so generous. I guess Shirley felt the same way because she just sat there, grim-faced.

He must have read our minds, or else we were drooling. "I don't suppose you girls could eat a cheeseburger?" he said over his shoulder.

"Wow! Could we," Shirley beamed.

"We'd sure appreciate your stopping somewhere if it won't make your late for your appointment or anything," I added.

"No problem at all," he said. "In fact, I haven't had any supper myself. I could do with a little nourishment."

Ten minutes later we pulled onto the small gravel parking lot of a roadside dinner. It was white with dark red shutters and trim and looked almost like someone's house but for the big store front window showing booths, and the hanging sign that said, "Jenny's Lunch". Just the word lunch made my mouth water. The smell of food cooking wafted from the diner.

Charlie, as he'd introduced himself, passed a twenty dollar bill back to Shirley. "Get me a burger, coffee and get whatever you and your friend would like."

"Oh, no," I protested. "We have money; we can pay for our own, but thanks anyway."

"Nonsense," Charlie said firmly, pressing the money into Shirley's palm. "Call it in the interest of education," he

joked. "If my guess is right you girls probably aren't flush with money. You want to save every penny you can. Maybe some guy will do the same for my kids when they're old enough to strike out on their own.
"

"Well, thanks loads," Shirley said smiling and getting out of the back seat. "I'll just be a few minutes."

I started to follow her out when Charlie said, "Karin, your friend can handle it okay. I want to pick your brain. You're pretty good with maps and I need to help me out with one of the stops I have to make."

Everything in me said to get out with Shirley, but he was already unfolding a map that had been in his glove compartment and turning around in the seat. I couldn't just ignore him. Now when I think of it, that was twice I didn't listen to my gut, two chances I had to get to get out and I didn't take either. If I'd gone into the diner with Shirley I could have told her how I felt and she would have gone along with me, I'm pretty sure. But he'd given her a twenty, and he'd been nice to us.

The last thing I saw just before I saw him turn back around in the sea and felt the sickening lurch of the car was it sprinted forward was the screen door of the diner closing behind Shirley's head, still wearing my found straw hat. I heard the grinding of gravel, saw bits of it flying out from beneath the spinning tires. Smelled scorching rubber as we swerved back on the pavement, and went speeding down the highway. It all happened so fast, I couldn't even be afraid yet. I was too dazed, too bewildered. It had to be a dream, didn't it? Some terrible thing my mom worried could happen, now coming true.

I glanced numbly out of the back window. The restaurant – Shirley – were gone, disappeared as though they had never been there at all.

When I turned back around, I look straight into his cold eyes in the rear-view mirror. It was then that the fear, the horror of what was happening, curled in my stomach and mushroomed into panic. His eyes had a strange glaze, the pupils like slivers of dry ice. When he saw me looking, realizing what was happening, he grinned. And my blood ran cold. The grin did not reach his eyes. They were the eyes of something insane.

"Please," I managed to choke out past my constructed vocal chords, "take me back. Or just let me out here." I could hardly breathe my heard was pounding so furiously. "My friend – she'll remember your car. She'll be able to give them your description, and she knows your name. She'll – she'll call the police and they come after you. "

"Not where we're going, sweetheart," he said quietly. "And do you really believe my name is Charlie Drew?" He laughed and I heard the contempt in his laughter. He was smarter than the cops. Smarter than any of us. He'd rape and murder me and he'd get away with it. I could feel the tears flooding over and running down my cheeks. Does Shirley really know he took off with me? If she'd already called the police, shouldn't I hear their sirens by now?

Paralyzed with fear, I watched as the night darkened further, the sky a pale mauve, already scattered with stars. And then suddenly, he turned off the highway onto a narrow dirt road flanked with woods, and my heart sank even lower. The cops would never find me. A rush of panic swept through me like an icy wave.

Shirley wouldn't even be able to give them a license plate number. Who pays attention to such things, unless they're already suspicious, and we weren't. I was abducted in an ordinary dark blue car, and neither Shirley or I knew one car from another, unless it was a Lamborghini or something glamorous like that.

Behind me, the last light of the little village dimmed in the growing darkness, finally flickering and blendin into the night. This can't be happening, I told myself. You hear about these things happening on radio and television, and read about them in the newspapers, but they nevert happened to you or to anyone you know. Again, I felt my gaze drawn toward his eyes in the rear-view mirror, and I k new that this was happening. And it was happening to me – now. He was staring straight ahead, his knuckles white as his hands gripped the steering wheel. We were soon driving over pavement again but it didn't seem like the main highway. He was going so fast I couldn't make out the signs. It was dark out now.

A new sense of urgency had gripped him and the car picked up even more speed as it covered the long stretch of road, intent on its destination. Wherever that would be. I was terrified too let my thoughts go that far. I glanced out the window as the trees sped past, seeing everything like a blur through my tears. A small camp where an old lady was out chopping wood, flashed by. Then she was gone. I'll jump out, I told myself in desperation.

"Try it," he said, as if reading my mind. "We're going 90 miles an hour, so if you think you'll be lucky..." He grinned again. "You'll crack your skull wide open if you jump at this speed. And if you don't, then I'll just have to run over you and put you out of your misery. The cops will never find your body. Now why don't you just be a good girl and sit there quietly. You won't have much longer to wait."

I knew he was right about my jumping out of the car. It would be suicide to try. But what would it be if I didn't? As I said and waited, my fear mounted and a sense of my own helplessness made me feel sick to my stomach. I wondered if I was going to throw up. Instead, I began to cry softly.

"Please, please," I begged between sobs. "Let me out. I promise I won't tell anyone about you."

"Your friend would already have done that."

"She won't know your license number. And like you said, we don't know your real name. You can get away." But my only answer was in the monotonous hum of rolling wheels.

Without warning, the car turned off the highway onto another narrow dirt road, and for a short distance I felt myself being jostled about as the car suffered the deep ruts of the well-worn washboard road. Except for the headlights and the vague shreds of moonlight casting threatening shadows among the tall trees on either side of us, all was dark and silent. He cracked the driver's window open, and the scent of pine came wafted into the car.

Finally, the car came to rest, and as he turned out the headlights, the small span of trees that I'd been able to see a moment ago, blended into the darkness. I reached for the door handle but his own hand clasped around my wrist like a steel band. Then he was climbing into the back seat while I tried to scoot to the far end of the seat, but there was no way I could get away.

Without a word, he was on me, his strong hands groping, reaching, hurting, pinning me beneath him. I could feel the hard thrust of the door handle jammed against my back as I tried to fight him off. In the midst of terror, I heard the sound of cloth tears as he ripped my shirt wide apart down the front. His breath fell hot and scalding on my face, his wet, open mouth seeking mine was a vile, repulsive thing. I struggled frantically, my head turning crazily from side to side so he couldn't kiss me. His hand reached for my hair and slowly and deliberately his fingers wound themselves into it, twisting, pulling until the searing pan ripped through head.

We fought silently, but for the sound of his grunts. Perhaps minutes had passed, perhaps hours. I couldn't be sure. Time held no meaning. From time to time my strength threatened to give out, but my own terror seemed to create new burst of energy. In desperation, I continued to fight him.

And then, near exhaustion, I saw it. As though from nowhere – a knife. It was poised in his hand like the fangs of a snake, ready to strike. All time hung suspended, then the cold steel of the blade was touching my throat.

"I don't want to make you ugly, Karen," he crooned. "All I want is for you to be nice to me. You are the one I wanted, you know. I want you to know that. I could have had your friend. That's why I wasn't going to stop back there right away. It's not so easy with two girls, you know. But then I saw you and a plan formed in my mind to get you two apart." It was the boasting of a madman. I could feel my pounding like crazy in my chest, and my face was wet with tears. My head ached hurt where he had entwined his fingers in my hair and twisted it so hard I thought my scalp would come with it. "You were the one I wanted," he went on, "so soft and shy you are, like a little girl."

I could almost feel the sharp knife tearing through my flesh. Somehow I managed to force my body to lie limp, all the while praying for a miracle, a chance to escape.

"That's a good girl, Karen," he said softly as though praising a small child for a good deed. "I won't hurt you anymore, but you've got to promise me you won't scream. You won't scream again, will you, Karen?" As he said the words, he pressed the knife against my throat. I felt the surprise of a sharp sting, and the trickle of warm blood sliding slowly down my skin, beneath my torn shirt.

"No, no, I won't scream, honest. I promise I won't. Just please – please don't hurt me," I begged him.

I felt him hesitate a moment, then slowly the beginnings of a smile crept across his face. It was the smile of one who anticipated victory: he could taste it. He had stalked his prey and now he was going in for the kill. Because I had no doubt whatever that once he raped me, he would murder me and hide my body in the woods.

He raised himself off me long enough to place the knife on the floor, within reach.

And then he was on his knees before me fumbling with his pants. In that instant, I was no longer pinned beneath him and I knew it would be my only chance to get away. I had to try. With my full weight pushed solidly against the door, I brought the heel of my hand down on the door handle and with all the strength that remained in me, at the same time I slammed my feet against his chest. The door gave way and I felt an explosion inside my head, as it hit the ground. There was a dull moan from inside the car. With the door open, the lights came on and for a fleeting second I saw the look of surprise mixed with pain on his face, and then the insane rage that fast replaced them, and his hands curl into murderous claws.

I scrambled to my feet and ran into the woods. The muffled sound of his footsteps were following close behind me. His stream of obscenities defiled the night, naked and ugly. I ran blindly, tripping, getting up and falling again. Sharp branches stung my face, my legs, but I kept on running...running, hearing my sharp, labored breaths in my ears and my heart slamming against my ribcage. Finally, it pained me to breathe and I had a terrible stitch in my side and I knew I could run no further. I sat on the ground with my back against the massive trunk of a tree, trying to get my breath.

It was so dark I could barely see my hand in front of me. I crept deeper into the woods away from it and lay on the ground, and prayed he wouldn't find me. The stitch in my side was easing up, and my breathing had almost returned to normal. The brush was tall and thick where I lay. I flattened myself against the ground, and I prayed. Please let the night hide me.

"Karen ... Karen," he called through the trees. "Where are you, Karen?" came the eerie chanting through the darkness, freezing the blood in my veins. "Come out, come out, whever you are." I heard his mad laugh echo through the trees, seeming to echo. Then, a branch snapped beneath his feet and I stifled the urge to scream. I lay unmoving. Not daring to breathe as I heard him coming ever closer.

"Please, please God," I prayed silently, "Don't let him find me." The minutes passed. The chanting had stopped. All was quiet again, a deathly tomb-like quiet. I tried to focus my eyes in the darkness, but I could see nothing.

And then I heard him moving again, through the shadowy trees toward me. A passing cloud revealed a shaft of moonlight, and I could see him more clearly now, silhouetted against the night, his right arm raised above his head. There was no need to guess what he clutched in his hand. As he drew closer, his heavy, tortured breathing seemed amplified in the still night air. His features were more distinct now. His face had taken on the appearance of a crazed animal, eyes wild, mouth slack.

He began to flail at the tall brush in front of him exposing for an instant, the glint of shiny metal. My body tensed even more, flattening itself against the hard ground, hoping to disappear. The footsteps were loud in my ears now, each second becoming almost deafening in my imagination, until they had nearly drowned out the wild hammering of my own heart, which I was sure he could hear.

And then, beside me, they stopped.

My gaze drifted upward, up past the knife-blade that glittered in his hand, to his eyes. Eyes that were no more than evil slits in a grinning face. I felt the life's blood drain sickeningly from my body as he bent over me. A sharp, searing fire started in my chest and spread through me – and then merciful blackness moved in as he threw himself upon me.

Perhaps you read the headlines in your own newspaper:

Cross-Country trip Ends in Tragedy – 17 year old girl, raped, knifed, left for dead.

The paper said the police were still searching the surrounding area in Blackpoint Woods for clues leading to the capture of my abductor and would-be murderer. He was still out there.

Shirley had been able to provide police with a good description of the killer, though, and they'd put up a composite on TV, but though they got lots of calls none of them panned out.

There were other details in the paper, but I was in the hospital when I read all that, too weak from shock and loss of blood to be of much help to the police. I didn't remember the rape at all, which the doctor said was a blessing. The rest of it seemed like a horrible dream, but the bandages on my chest, the tubes and needles attached to my arms, told me differently.

"You're one lucky girl," old Doctor Bates had told me emphatically when I woke up in the hospital. He didn't waste words being tactful. "If you hadn't managed to crawl to the edge of the road that night, you might not have been found until it was too late. You surely would have died. Or if that knife had gone in one fraction of an inch closer..." He shook his head grimly. "But you're here, and we're all glad you are." He patted my hand, and told me to get some rest. As he was leaving the room, I heard him muttering something like 'Damned, stupid kids won't listen to anyone – think they know it all."

I was found the next morning by a woodsman and he took me to the hospital. I owe him my life. I don't remember crawling out of the woods to the edge of the road tha t night, like they say I did. I guess it must just have been survival instinct. But I think it was more than that. I believe my guardian angel was watching over me. Even after she'd warned me twice, and I didn't listen.

I still have the nightmares even though I've been in the hospital six weeks now. Part of that time, I've spent in the psychiatric ward with Doctor Waterman, trying to mend some of the emotional and psychological damage that predator caused. And I guess writing down what happened is supposed to be therapy. At least Doctor Waterman thinks it's a good idea, so that's what I'm doing.

"Get it all down on paper, Karen," she said. "Then try to put it to the back of your mind and move on with your life.

Doctor Bates knows about this special therapy, too, and he agrees, but for a second reason. "Maybe you can even get a few kids to have another look at this idea of seeing their country by hitching rides from strangers."

* * *

He's got a point, but the biggest lesson I learned from it all was to listen to that inner voice that tells you when you're in danger. I ignored that voice – twice. I won't again, and that's mainly what I want to tell other kids. Grownups, too. If I'd listen to my gut I would have gotten out of the car at the store, and confided in Shirley that I didn't feel comfortable getting back in the car with this guy, and she would have trusted my instincts. But I didn't trust my own.

Shirley suffered a lot of agony herself those first days when I lay in critical conditions in the hospital, and no one knew if I would make it or not. Just as my parents did.

"It's my fault," she had cried. "It never would have happened if I hadn't left you alone in that creep's car. I was near crazy when I came out and the car was gone, Karen. I didn't know what to do. The restaurant owner phoned the police, but there was just so much wooded area and back roads, they didn't have a chance of finding the car.

"Don't blame yourself, Shirley," I told her. "That guy was a real pro – a madman for sure – but a real pro." When the police searched the surrounding area that next day, looking for clues, they found the remains of a girl who had been missing for four years. It could have been me. We weren't the first hitchhikers he'd picked up. There may be more girls, in other provinces and maybe even states. No one could know for sure. "He definitely would have gotten one of us," I said.

I hated thinking of him still out there, preying on other girls who wouldn't suspect what he was until it was too late. And today there are many such predators cruising the highways.

"It's dangerous getting into cars with strangers," my mother had tried to warn me. You don't know who you're getting in with."

She was right. Maybe what happened to me was one chance in ten thousand, but it's a chance that neither Shirley or I would never take again. Sure, I admit there are plenty of kids who strike out across the country, have a blast, and get back home safe and sound. But the risk is always there. That's the obvious lesson. But the one I tried to impart to my own grown children is: always listen to that inner voice. It knows what it's talking about.

I'm proof of that.

Tragic Spawn

Chapter 1

The woman's voice reached down to her as if filtered up through deep bracken-green water, reminding her of when she was a little girl and had dived off the diving board at Shadow Lake and the voices above her would sound like that, all thick and gurgly in her ears. She felt herself rising to the surface, pins and needles of hurt prickling every inch of her body. Was she dreaming?

The words grew more distinct: "Melanie? Melanie Snow. Wake up, dear," said the irritating voice. "Open your eyes."

Someone was calling her. Trying to wrench her from this warm, dark womb of sleep. No, leave me alone, please. All she wanted was to sink back down into that soft place again, to just sleep and sleep, away from the hurt.

"Ms. Snow," the voice said again.

Every inch of her body throbbed with pain. She heard a moan and it took a moment to realize it came from her own parched lips. Why wouldn't the woman let her be? Let her sink back down into that merciful cradle of sleep. But it was not to be.

"Melanie, open your eyes now. Wake up. The doctor is on his way to see you." There was a note of excitement in the girl's voice when she asked, "Mr. Snow, are you sure you saw her eyes open?"

Daddy? Daddy was here?

"Yes, nurse. I'm positive. My little girl was born with those long smoky lashes and I saw them flutter and her eyes open. She looked right at me," he said, his voice breaking. "And then they closed again."

Why was her father crying? But like he was happy too. What happened? He had called the woman nurse. She must be in a hospital. Yes, that made sense. Her mouth tasted of chemicals and medicinal smells filled her nasal passages and coated her tongue. She tried to open her eyes, but they felt as if someone had glued them shut. She tried again. Her eyelids parted, mere slits, seeing nothing. Why doesn't Daddy put the nightlight on? He knows I don't like the dark.

"Daddy...?" The word came out in a croak, a rusted voice, unused, scraping the walls of her throat like sandpaper. "Is Mom here?"

She heard the intake of her father's sob and felt the comforting weight of his big warm hand on her shoulder. "Your mom's gone, baby. She died a long time ago. You were just twelve. Don't you remember?"

"Not to worry, Mr. Snow," the nurse said gently. "A little memory glitch is all. She's been in a coma for five days now, it's to be expected. Could you let me in there for just a minute, Mr. Snow? Thanks."

There was the faint whisper of fabric brushing against fabric. Then the nurse said, "Melanie, you've been in a car accident and you're at St. Bart's General Hospital. Do you know what year it is?"

She apparently replied correctly. "Very good," the woman said. "What city do you live in?

"Evansdale."

"Excellent. I'm Nurse Evans, Melanie. Lois Evans."

She got her to make a fist and then wiggle her toes. She ran a hand back and forth past her eyes but only Ted Snow witnessed it.

She took Melanie's pulse. Her fingers felt light and soothing on her wrist.

"Excellent," the nurse said. "I'm going to check your eyes now." Melanie heard a soft click close to her face, felt the slight warmth on her skin, and the milky grey at the outer corner of her right eye grew brighter. Another click and the brightness faded.

"Are you feeling any discomfort? Pain?"

Yes," she half-whispered. "Like I got beat up." She'd been in a coma, the nurse had said. A car accident. Melanie blinked her eyes and tried to focus them, but even on opening them wider, she saw nothing, only a blackish-grey, like peering through a wall of dense fog. Her father was in the room. Why couldn't she see him or the nurse?

"Would someone turn on a light, please," she begged.

* * *

"Ted, the doctor said the blindness is probably temporary," Doreen Snow said when they were out in the corridor, out of earshot of Melanie. She had been given something to calm her, but they could still hear her sobbing softly. Ted Snow had never felt so upset or helpless. For a moment back there, he had been elated that his daughter had wakened from the coma, but to have her be blind...

They were heading for the elevator when he broke down crying. He blew his nose and looked at his second wife through his tears. Not a platinum hair out of place, green silk scarf draped like a fashion model's about her neck, and he felt a jolt of resentment toward her. All those years when Melanie was growing up he was constantly pulled in two directions. His new wife and his daughter were forever at each other's throats. But it wasn't all Doreen's fault, he told himself, and it was unfair and cowardly of him to blame her when he was far more to blame. He had been weak. Knowing that didn't lessen the resentment against her, however; it sat in his gut like a smoldering fire. Doreen carried the stick and he wielded it against his daughter. Not literally, of course, he would never lay a hand on his child in anger, but still...

Ted had lost a wonderful wife, Ellen, his first love, and he had been devastated. But Melanie lost her mother, the real anchor in her life. They were close, best friends as well as mother and daughter. But he had thought only of himself. He met Doreen through a friend. He hadn't thought he would ever love again, but he fell hard. Ted had been lonely and she took away the loneliness, made his heart beat again. He hadn't even waited a year to remarry and now...

Oh, God, please let the blindness be temporary. The tears came again.

"Why are you crying, Ted? Is it for Melanie? Or for yourself because you married me?" Her own hazel eyes were swimming in tears, but he wasn't moved by them.

"Jesus Christ, Doreen," he lashed out, drawing a quick look from a nurse walking past them in the corridor. "That was twenty years ago. Does everything have to be about you?"

She looked like he had slapped her and he felt like the worse kind of creep. The truth was that she'd nailed it dead on as she usually did.

Chapter 2

Detective Matt O'Leary gazed down at the dead woman at his feet with a blend of sadness and anger. Dora Nabers had been a fixture at the corner of Logan and Horsefield Streets, next to Jake's Hav-a-Snack, for as long as he could remember. Even on the coldest days in winter she would sit in her wheelchair like a big, overgrown baby with that perpetual smile on her round face, playing her accordion with great zest and joy, all the old toe-tapping tunes like Turkey in the Straw and Orange Blossom Special, that made you smile right along with her. Passersby would sometimes drop coins, and occasionally a bill, onto the red felt lining of the accordion case that sat on the sidewalk beside her. Matt himself had dropped in a few bucks from time to time, often stopping to chat. Everyone knew Dora or knew of her. She was even written up in the local rag once. She was local color.

No matter the season, Dora always wore a white knit stocking cap with a Canadian maple leaf on the side, pulled down over her ears. She wore it now as she lay in her metal three-quarter bed in this rented room. Her body was discovered by her landlord who became concerned when she was late with the rent. "She was always very prompt about that," the short, jowly man told him. "Poor soul," he muttered, pulling a large white handkerchief from the back pocket of his pants and wiping his eyes. Matt thought the hanky was probably more to smother the putrid odor of human decay than out of any actual grief, since he quickly lowered it to his mouth and nose, and he showed no sign of removing it. Matt didn't blame him. The body was pretty ripe and he had to swallow back his own gorge. He smeared Vicks under his nostrils to stifle the smell. "You can go back up to your apartment," he told him. "Stay put. Someone will be up later to take your statement." The landlord, who had been hovering in the doorway nodded and fled, clearly grateful to be out of the room.

Dora had been here awhile, he thought. He ran a hand through his dark hair with its smattering of grey. Although he was only thirty-eight, he felt older. Sometimes he wondered if he'd chosen the wrong profession. Times like now. It had been expected of him; both his father and grandfather were cops. The thought was fleeting as he went about his work of investigating a murder.

The stocking cap hadn't even shifted on her head. Was it her habit to wear it to bed? he wondered. Or did her killer put it on her as a kind of parting gesture, for whatever reason? It was clear from the bruising on her neck, the petechiae (blood spots) in the whites of her eyes when forensic expert Harry Deagan lifted her lids, that she had been manually strangled. Harry worked quietly beside him, peering over the tops of his round glasses. Harry was a small man who did the comb-over and wore shiny polyester brown suits, but he was ace at his job, had been at it for a good twenty years. Matt liked him.

The coarse grey blanket was drawn up to her shoulders, as if by tender hands. Beneath it, she wore a faded blue cotton nightgown. Her eyes were closed. She might have been merely sleeping but for the smell. That and the green discoloration of her skin, the grossly bloated flesh.

"Matt, take a look at this," Harry said softly, holding up one of Dora's hands for him to examine. They had been folded over one another as if she was already laid out in her coffin. Like Jodie's had been. Dora had rather chubby hands, in keeping with the cherubic smile she always wore.

Her killer had cut her fingernails. "She managed to claw him then," Matt said, as much to himself as to Harry. "He was getting rid of the DNA." A quick search turned up no fingernail clippings. And no scissors. He apparently took them with him. Did he go out the same way he entered? Matt wondered.

Leaving Deagan to his business, Matt wandered to the window. It was at street level and Matt could see lots of shuffling feet out there; a crowd had gathered and excited chatter reached him. Murder draws curious onlookers like flies to dog crap, he thought.

The window screen was slit three ways, providing easy access into the room. Her killer would have waited until dark to enter, he surmised, otherwise, he stood a good chance of being spotted by neighbors. Matt turned away from the window and took in the sparsely furnished room, early Goodwill ambiance. Dora's accordion sat in its case on the worn brown linoleum in the corner, next to a round table marred with scars and burn marks. Since Dora didn't smoke, according to the landlord, they had to have been there when she moved in three years ago. Before that, she lived with her mother, who had passed on. She was alone in the world.

The room spoke of a sad life, belying how Dora had spent her days. Making music and bringing sunshine into the lives of everyone she met. She didn't deserve to die like this.

Neither had Jodie Ballard, he reminded himself, the young girl with Down syndrome, murdered two weeks earlier. When Jodie didn't arrive home at her usual time, her father called 911. After he hung up, something drew him outside. He walked around the back of the building where he found her. A neighbor said she had heard his howl from three floors up. The young woman he'd always called his special child lay next to trash bins, hands folded one over the other, in death. Like Dora, she'd been strangled to death. "Just had a bad feeling," Mr. Ballard told Matt. He was a sickly grey color, Matt remembered and looked as if all the muscles in his face had collapsed. Later that night Joe Ballard was rushed to the hospital with a heart attack and died on the table while the medical team worked on him, but failed to bring him back. So Jodie's mom was understandably in pretty rough shape. This bastard was inflicting a mountain of pain on a lot of people. The kind you don't easily spring back from, if ever.

For a time, a town would grieve for Dora as it had for Jodie. It seemed the whole town had turned out for Jodie Ballard's funeral. Many there to support Rita Ballard whose primal cries had torn at his heart. She looked pale and fragile, and as if she might crumble to the ground at any minute, and which she might have if friends hadn't been holding her up. She had lost everything. Matt had attended the funeral, along with half a dozen officers, though out of uniform. Often killers like to show up at the funerals of their victims, it gives them a rush. They scanned the faces in the crowd looking for the one that didn't belong, the one that triggered suspicions but came up empty. How could they know with so many people in attendance? Killers tended to look like anyone else.

The forensics team had come and gone. They had dusted for prints and taken photos from every conceivable angle. Dora's body was zipped into a body bag and transported to the morgue. No sirens. No need.

Alone now, Matt tried to get a psychic beam on the killer, gain some sense of him. But nothing came to him. Just a conjured image of a dark figure slithering in through the window like a deadly cobra. Did Dora hear the noise and wake up? Or was she asleep when her killer attacked? The room provided no answers. No special insights.

Out on the street, the crowd was thinning. Nothing more to see. The yellow crime tape was in place and a couple of uniforms were guarding the perimeter of the crime scene. He turned the key in the ignition and the car purred to life. As he buckled himself in, a small voice whispered: serial killer. He reminded himself that two killings did not a serial make. A coincidence? Somehow he didn`t think so. Before pulling away from the curb, he glanced out the side window to see a couple of teenage girls with iPhones snapping pictures of the rundown, green wooden building, aiming their shots around the tall blond kid who Matt recognized as Terry Maroon from the local TV station. He was shooting video for the evening news, presently focusing on the torn screen in the window.

A female reporter he didn't recognize, with slick blond hair, eyes made up to put Tammy Faye to shame, rushed over to Matt's car and shoved a microphone in the open window at him, asking him if they knew who killed her. How would they? Eager, ambitious eyes and glossy coral lips posed more questions. The new face had bigger plans for herself than the local TV station in Evansdale. He gave a few short answers before closing the window, nearly on the mic, and pulling away from the curb. He didn't enjoy being rude, but some of them gave you no choice.

Dora would be missed. That spot alongside Joe`s Hav-a-Snack would be pretty empty and quiet now.

On the drive back to the station, Matt made mental notes, comparing the two victims and their circumstances. Jodie Ballard had worked at Newton`s Groceries over on the west side. Although born with Down syndrome, she was highly functional, according to her co-workers and family. She smiled easily and was eager to please. Customers loved her, Mr. Newton told Matt. Like Dora, she had made a worthwhile life for herself, despite her challenges. Yet someone had decided these women didn't deserve to live.

In his office, with the door closed, Matt transferred his thoughts and observations onto sheets of legal paper and slipped the sheets into the file folder, a pathetically thin folder at the moment, similar to that of Jodie Ballard's.

They were making no better headway with the hit and run that had blinded

Melanie than they were on these killings. Matt heaved a sigh and rose from behind his desk, reaching for his brown suede jacket on the wooden clothes tree. His shift finished, he looked forward to home and a long, hot shower. He'd feed his goldfish, Rosencrantz and Guildenstern, then head on up to the hospital. He would like to have had some good news to report to Mel, she sure could use some and that was an understatement. But he didn't have a clue as to who the bastard was that struck her Honda and kept on going. One witness said the vehicle was a dark van, possibly navy or black, and that the driver was wearing sunglasses and a peaked cap. That was it. No one got a license number or a good look at the driver. Could be male or female, but Matt would put his money on 'male' ¬¬-- just a hunch.

Up until now, Melanie had little recollection of the accident, but maybe with a little more prodding something would click in. It was worth another try. Besides, he liked spending time with her. He just wished the circumstances were different.

* * *

The Eraser was riding his bike past the house on the other side of the street when they carried the woman's corpse on a gurney out of the house and down the steps to the waiting ambulance. He was wearing his blue helmet and looked like any other ordinary

151

young man on a bike, craning his neck, interested in seeing what was going on. No one paid him any attention. A flesh-colored Bandaid concealed the scratch on his cheek.

A small crowd was milling about, silent, watching. He had to go around the white van from the local TV station which was parked helter-skelter at the curb. He noted the length of yellow crime scene tape stretched across the outer front door, the end flapping in the breeze.

Where will you go next? he silently asked, hearing the ambulance doors shut behind him.

He had been on foot when he passed Dora sitting on that same corner where she'd always sat with her accordion. And there she was, staring at him through Dora's eyes, mocking him. He'd felt the other's presence even before he looked into Dora Nabers' eyes, but then he knew for sure. Was it only a week ago?

"It doesn't matter," he said aloud, his sneakered feet pumping harder on the pedals now as he turned up Queen Street on his way to work. "I'll find all your hiding places, and I'll destroy every last one."

Chapter 3

It was mid-afternoon, overcast, and The East End Mall in Kingsdale was crowded with shoppers. The Eraser, as he liked to think of himself, sat at one of the molded plastic tables by himself, nursing a Pepsi and eating fries from a small cardboard plate, and people-watching. It was one of his favorite things to do, especially in nice weather when the girls wore shorts or tight jeans, some with their tanned midriffs bare, skimpy tops that showed off their boobs, and skinny jeans that accentuated their tight little butts. Why not? He was a normal guy, he told himself. He avoided looking at the ones with flab hanging over their waistbands. He had a girlfriend once or twice, but it didn't last. The last one said he was weird and just stopped returning his calls. Well, to hell with her.

His eye strayed momentarily to the big screen monitor advertising Nike sneakers. Then it changed to a rent-a-car commercial and on to something else, but he'd already looked away. Idly dipping a French fry in the small pool of ketchup on his plate, he popped it in his mouth and went back to girl-watching. They did little for him today. His hand moved to cover the scratch that the retard left on his cheek, though it was fading now. That Polysporin ointment was good stuff.

Music played over the sound system, competing with the jabbering of shoppers, nothing he recognized. Probably supposed to keep people shopping, buying junk they didn't need. His gaze narrowed ever so slightly as a young girl with a silver ring in her lower lip and wearing black eyeliner got up from a table not far from him and limped heavily to the waste bin and dumped in the remainder of her meal, a half-eaten hamburger, fries. She sat the tray on top of the stack. Behind her, someone called out, "Hey, Lana," and the girl turned in his direction and took a step forward so he could see her full-length; she looked past his shoulder and waved. He felt his heartbeat rev up, his throat go dry.

She had short dark hair and was wearing a khaki skirt and cream-colored blouse. Her dimpled smile, the gleam of white, even teeth barely registered on him. He didn't even glance behind him at the woman who had called out to her. He had no interest. As he had no genuine interest in the woman who returned the wave.

No. It was her foot in its big brown shoe that drew and held his attention. Not brown exactly, but like tea when you put milk in it. Taupe. Yes, that was what his mother called that color. It was all he could see when he looked at her: that big clunking shoe. So ugly it offended him, as deformities of any kind offended him. Even horrified him. A chill had crept down his back. He had to work extra hard to keep the disgust and pity from his face. She was a mistake. A blight, a tragic spawn. She must be erased. Like when you're a kid and you draw a picture of something and it doesn't come out right. You just erase it. Or rip out the page, and start again.

He was the eraser of mistakes. The good Lord had chosen him to do this work. Not that he was blaming God. No, there was no blame to be handed out here. Some small voice told him his reasoning was flawed, that that wasn't why they had to die. But he wasn't listening. As people were born of sin, women carried the faulty limbs, twisted features, and minds within them. Carriers. As his mother had been a carrier, her womb spewing forth a defective, barely human—thing. Not the defective's fault either. But since the flaw couldn't be repaired, the whole issue had to be erased. The burden lifted. The Eraser held that kind of power; he could end suffering, and change lives for the better. He remembered well the very moment he had changed his own life. But no time for that now. She was heading for the exit doors. He rose casually from his chair, tossing the remainder of his own fries and drink into the trash, dropped his tray on top of hers, and followed. He was following the 'shoe'. His eyes were riveted on the shoe. It filled his vision, his consciousness. That big, ugly shoe that rose and fell, rose and fell, her left hip dipping in sync, the shoe dragging it downward, seeming an entity in itself. When she stepped through the automatic doors into the grey, drizzly day, he was right behind her. Close enough to touch her. He buried his hands deep in his pockets to stifle the urge.

The bus pulled up with a hiss of air brakes and a belch of exhaust, and she hitched herself up onto the step. He followed, paid his fare. His bike was chained and locked in the parking lot; it would be fine. She took a side seat near the driver, and he sat two seats behind her and pretended to look out the window.

In the grayness of the day, his reflection in the glass was faint, but almost at once he could see his reflection begin to morph into that of another, as she had once been. A raindrop ran down the window and caught one corner of her mouth like the drool he remembered, couldn't forget, and could not tear his eyes away. The small voice in his head spoke to him, sending the familiar chill through his body as if his heart had just received an infusion of ice water. The voice could form words now, whereas once it was capable only of mindless gibberish. "You know it's me in there, don't you? I'm watching you. I've come back. I'll always come back. I'll never leave you."

"No! No!"

Fearing he had cried out, he jerked his head around in sudden panic, but no one on the bus was looking at him. One man was reading a newspaper. A woman was talking and smiling at her little boy. Relief swept through him, but he was trembling just the same. A Chinese man seated across from him turned the page in his paperback, paying him no mind.

The girl had put earphones in her ears and her lips were moving to a song only she could hear. Her legs were crossed, the shoe swinging in time, mocking him.

Chapter 4

Melanie was sitting up in bed when Matt walked into her hospital room around seven that evening. She recognized his footsteps, purposeful, yet respectful of where he was. She was wearing the blue brushed satin nightgown Francie had brought from the house along with some other things she'd needed. One of the volunteers had washed her hair and she had to admit, it perked her up a bit. She had even put on a little lipstick.

"You look beautiful," he said. "Practically all the bruising is gone," Matt said. Telling her she looked beautiful made her smile. But for the fact that she was still blind, they said she was doing well physically. She had suffered a cracked rib and a broken ankle in the accident, but they were both healing nicely, as was the two-inch gash she'd sustained on her chin. She traced the C-shaped wound with her fingertip. The doctor said it wouldn't even leave a scar.

"Wow, you've got a flood of get-well cards here," Matt said. "They cover just about every surface in the room."

"People are thoughtful. The nurse read every message to me. They're from patients, old friends. Schoolmates I haven't seen or heard from in years. People are kind, Matt. Most of them, anyway." Her smile dropped away. "I don't suppose you have any news on my hit and run."

"Sorry," Matt said, drawing the chair up to the side of her bed. The leg scraped on the floor.

"No, I am sorry. That sounded like an accusation, didn't it? I didn't mean it to. It's hardly your fault."

"It's okay. And we will find out who hit your car. It's just taking a while. How are you feeling?"

"Not so bad. Doctor Howell says the blindness could be temporary. They've done more tests. If you pray, and I know you do, say one for me, okay?"

He promised he would.

St. Bart's hospital was always a place of hustle and bustle, and tonight was no exception. Gurneys rattled past the door on squeaky wheels, a nasal voice on the intercom summoned various doctors to different parts of the hospital. One was a 'code blue' on the geriatric unit which was close enough that you could hear running feet.

Melanie was near enough to the elevators to hear the bell ding every few minutes. People coming and going. A hospital was a world onto itself, a microcosm of the outside world complete with all the drama, heightened by the constant battle against illness and death.

She heard the whisper of pen on paper and wondered what Matt was writing. Maybe something about the Dora Nabers' case. She knew he'd been at the scene. Cops saw gruesome sights in their line of work, some becoming desensitized, and hardened over time. But she knew from experience that certain things got to Matt. He was a tough enough cop but he had a tender, sensitive streak a mile wide. She'd had him as a patient a few years back after he'd sunk into a depression following a particularly tragic case. But he got through it, and was fine now, as far as she could tell.

He was also tenacious and right now he was prodding her to remember something more about the accident, but it was no use. She knew that victims of a physical trauma that rendered them unconscious seldom recalled the details. And she'd been in a coma for five days. It seemed strange to lose a piece of your life, along with your sight and you couldn't even recall how it happened. Amazing that we take our sight for granted, even though it's a huge part of how we function in the world. We depend on our eyes to tell us so many things. She'd always known this, but now she knew it in a very personal way. She was fighting to hold the terror of permanent blindness at bay, to cling to hope.

"As I said, Matt, all I remember is driving to work and singing along with the radio. It was a nice day. I was expecting a patient at 10:00 a.m. but I only know that from my calendar, and because you read it to me." Her finger found a looped thread on the blanket and she plucked at it. Then she removed her finger and smoothed it down. "Anyway, I do recall catching something dark out of the corner of my eye and then nothing. But that's it. It's like a dream, in a way. A bad dream. But I guess it was real enough."Oddly enough, she remembered all that went before the impact. She'd relived it many times since she woke from the coma. The doctor had been surprised that she'd remembered with such clarity and told her it was unusual considering her serious head injuries. But remember she did.

It had been a cool Tuesday, and she was driving down Main Street in her maroon Honda, on the way to work, singing along with the radio just as she'd told Matt. Not unlike any other weekday morning.

Her office was located on Bayard Lane, in a strip Mall wedged between Shoppers Drug Mart and the Dollar Store. She shared a waiting room and receptionist with an Ophthalmologist, Dr. Jeff Davis. The song she was singing along with was Aretha Franklin's Respect. She was finger-tapping the steering wheel to the beat, feeling good. Traffic was light. The sun shone through the window reflecting the diamond on her finger, its stone large enough to be slightly embarrassing. Alan didn't do things in a small way. She'd met him in the produce aisle of Sobeys. He had asked her if there were ways of telling if a butter squash was dry. Not exactly an original line, but cute, she'd thought at the time, like something out of a romance novel. He was cute too, right down to the cleft in his chin, and with no shortage of charm. They'd chatted about one thing and another; she found out he was in pharmaceutical sales and she told him she was a therapist. The following week he called her at the office and asked her out to dinner and that was the start of their relationship.

She was smiling to herself, thinking about all that, when the van, (if it was a van) struck her car full force, catching her corner bumper and sending the Honda spinning out of control and into a deep ditch, where it burst into flames. These details she knew nothing about until she woke from the coma and learned about it. She'd even read the write-ups in the paper. She'd glimpsed that dark mass from the corner of her eye just before the lights went out. Literally. She related all this to Matt, leaving out the part that included Alan, which was hardly relevant. He might think (though he'd never say) that she was daydreaming and not paying enough attention to her driving. Was there an element of truth there? Maybe. But she didn't think so.

"You're lucky to be alive," he said, not for the first time.

"Yeah, everyone says that." But she knew it was true. She was lucky. The man who pulled her from the burning car just seconds before it exploded, had been in to visit her last week and she was glad of the chance to thank him. He was a nice man, a shy man, a family man, and a reluctant hero. She would have burned to death in her car if not for his quick action. Whatever the future held for her, she was not sorry she had escaped a fiery death. Not sorry to be alive.

Although she knew Matt was assigned to investigate the hit and run which put her here, she was glad of his company. They had become good friends over the years.

`"There was another murder," she said sadly. A statement, not a question. "Dora Nabers."

He didn't respond right away and she sensed he was surprised she knew about it. "I'm not all that cut off from the world," she said. "The nurses were talking about it. And I heard it on the news. The television reporter was questioning you. I could hear the stress in your voice. Subtle, but there, just beneath the surface. How are you doing?"

"Of course, you would have heard. Okay. Yeah, I'm okay, Mel."

"I remember Dora. She was a sweet, good person. I used to stop and talk to her sometimes if I was passing by. Who would do something so horrible? Do you have any leads?"

It was a relief not to be talking about herself. Besides, she had a feeling they weren't going to find her hit-and-run any time soon. If they did track him down, they'd probably find out it was some kid driving his father's car, maybe talking on a cell phone, distracted. After he hit her car he'd just panicked and took off. Finding him would be like finding the proverbial needle in a haystack. And even if they did find him, it wouldn't change anything.

"No. Nothing yet. Dora's mom is gone and she had no other family. No brothers or sisters. At least that's what her landlord said. We're questioning neighbors."

"That's two mentally challenged women now, isn't it?"

"As far as we know. There could be others that we don't know about. In other towns, other... Oh, hello," Matt said, letting her know they were no longer alone. She hadn't heard the footsteps enter the room. "Deverson, isn't it? I'm just on my way out, help yourself to the chair." The chair leg scraped again as he got up to leave.

"How are things, Detective? You any closer to finding out..."

"Following up on a couple of things," Matt interrupted with strained pleasantness. "See you later, Mel. I'll drop by tomorrow."

Melanie hiked herself further up in the bed, smiling. "Thanks for coming, Matt. Alan, hi, Honey. I'm so glad you're here." She knew when he leaned down to kiss her, for the sliver of white in her right eye grew darker, and then his lips were on hers, soft and gentle. She felt his weight settle on the edge of her bed, smelled his faintly spicy cologne. Cartier.

"Me too. How are you doing? When did the doctor say you can go home?"

"I haven't seen him yet today. Still awaiting the results of the latest tests. How's work?"

"Good. I'm going to have to be out of town for a few days. I don't want to go away with you in here, but I need to close a deal. It's important. But don't change the subject. I want to hear from you. Is there anything you need? Can I get you something from the cafeteria? Be a nice change from the hospital food, I'll bet."

She smiled. "It's not so bad. Francie took me down to the cafeteria for coffee and a sandwich earlier today. We've been down a couple of times; a nice change of scenery from this room."

When he said nothing, she elaborated, "I know I can't see what's around me, but I can smell and hear and touch and taste. Yes, it's a change of scenery for me."

"I didn't mean to imply it wasn't. I just..."

"I know. Actually, I don't mind hospital food that much. They're good to me in here. If I want a piece of toast at night, for example, or a cup of tea, all I have to do is ask. I think hospitals get a bad rap."

"And I think you're an exceptionally good patient. I'll just be glad when you're out of here. When you can see again. When we can set our wedding date."

She hesitated, not wanting to infect him with her doubts, nor offer false hope, no matter how much she wished for that good news that would give her back her life. She didn't miss the order in which he'd placed those things he'd be glad for. "There are no guarantees, Alan."

"You've got to think positive, Sweetheart. Of course, you'll see again. They can do so much today."

She could only smile and pray he was right.

"You look so pretty in that blue nightgown," he said. "It brings out..." His voice trailed off.

He'd been about to say it brought out the blue in her eyes but stopped short. Why? True, she couldn't see out of them, but they were still blue, weren't they? Was Alan embarrassed by her blindness?

Anxiety knotted in her stomach and she let it escape on an exhalation of silent breath as she visualized him in her mind's eye - handsome, with that movie-star cleft in his chin, longish dark blond hair. Absently, she reached up and let her fingers trail the open collar of his shirt. Crisp. Probably white. He'd be wearing a blazer and slacks. Alan always looked like he just stepped out of GQ magazine. Even when he deigned to wear jeans and a tee-shirt, which wasn't often, he looked photo-shoot ready. He gave no hint that he was aware of it, which only added to his appeal. A sadness swept over her and she wasn't even sure why.

Late that evening Doctor Howell dropped in to see her. Visitors had gone mostly and the hospital's heartbeat had slowed to a soft murmur. She had known by the heaviness of his step, the way he hesitated in the doorway before coming into the room that he hadn't come bearing good news. Still, she could be wrong.

He took the chair that Matt, then Alan, had occupied earlier. Not wasting words, Doctor Howell told her in a sympathetic voice that she had Traumatic Optic Atrophy, which also put her in a coma. "To be technical," he'd said, "the optic nerve axons have been damaged from blunt head trauma. Your head, evidently, slammed against the window at the moment of impact."

He went on talking, explaining her condition in layman's terms, but offering words of encouragement, of hope. He talked about stem cell research, breakthroughs in laser surgery, and so on, but she'd been beyond hearing by then and could only sit there, feeling cold to the marrow, knowing that her life was changed, not temporarily as she'd tried to convince herself, but forever. She was a blind person. This was her new reality. She had tried to prepare herself for this possibility. But she hadn't succeeded, not really. Because she had not believed it possible. She had rejected it just like when someone you care for, dies. Even though they've been sick for a long time, it's always a shock. It always stuns you that you will never see them again. At her deepest core, she had been in denial. Blindness was unacceptable. Blurred vision perhaps, where glasses would be necessary, possibly with coke bottle lenses to peer through. If only. The thread of hope she'd clutched onto, broke. There was nothing they could do. "Maybe in time..."

Before the doctor left, he laid a hand on her shoulder and told her he was sorry. And then he said it again with more emphasis. And a few seconds later, he left her alone to deal with the news.

* * *

One week later Melanie was in her room by the window, her overnight case at her feet, her hand on the sill which was warmed from the sun, waiting for the orderly to come with the wheelchair and take her down to the main entrance. Down on the street, someone was operating a jackhammer.

"Thanks so much for all you've done," she said to the nurse she'd come to think of as a friend.

"Just my job, dear," the older nurse replied with her usual cheerfulness. She was stripping the bed in preparation for the next patient. "Besides, you're a pleasure to do for. You look lovely, by the way. I don't think I

168

could have done near as well putting myself together if I didn't have my sight."

"Not too much makeup then?"

"Not at all."

She'd been careful to apply it sparingly. Better than ending up looking like Bozo the clown. "As a kid, I learned to put my lipstick on without a mirror," she said, "away from the disapproving eye of my father."

"Ah, he's one of those, is he? I had one myself. But he seems like a very nice man."

"Oh, he is."

The nurse chuckled. "He's here just about every day, isn't he? I know the feeling though. Not like today. Today little girls are dressing to look like hookers at ten, most of them. Not their fault, though, what with all the focus on sex in the media. But then I'm probably just an old prude."

"I don't think you're a prude at all."

Nurse Evelyn Raynes was one of Melanie's favorites, compassionate while being no-nonsense, every inch a professional. And she had a point in what she said. Looking back, Melanie understood why her father had been so strict with her, although not then. No, not then. After her mother died, he had changed, and became obsessive in his parental duties, as he saw them. He was relentless. Who was she with? Where was she going? How long would she be? Was she really going to wear that? She understood now, of course. He was trying to be both mother and father to her, trying to protect her from the world, from herself. He'd lightened up after he met Doreen. She was fourteen then and hadn't counted on hardly being able to talk to him at all once the new wife was in the picture. She and Doreen were constantly at loggerheads. He took sides, seldom Melanie's. It seemed she was always in the wrong. So many crazy emotions inside her battling for dominance. She hated her stepmother with a vengeance and resented her for trying to take her mother's place. She was angry at her mother for leaving her. At her father for bringing that woman into their lives. For his disloyalty to her mother. The perfect storm for creating a rebellious teenager. She had dropped out of school, went a little wild, and married the town bad boy. She found out later that he'd slept with one of the bridesmaids the night before the wedding. They divorced after two years and she had the good sense to go back to school, and then on to university on a scholarship. She'd majored in psychology probably because she wanted to understand human behavior better, wanted to understand herself better, like a lot of people who went in that direction. Someone had been looking out for her...a guardian angel? Maybe her mom, she thought. She could have ended up on the streets, or worse. So why this? Why now when she had her life on track had this happened to her? She had a successful career, she was getting married to a man she loved and who loved her.

"Your fiancé coming to fetch you?" Nurse Raynes asked, as if picking up on her patient's thoughts.

"No, he's away on business. Otherwise, he'd be here." Her words sounded defensive even to herself. "My uncle's picking me up at the entrance; he drives a cab." She opened her watch and felt the position of the hands. "He'll be here in twenty minutes." She could have pressed a button and been told the time but chose not to. "An orderly's coming to take me down." The nurse already knew this, of course. It was as if she were trying to convince herself that she was going home.

She had thought of calling Francie, who'd already offered to come and get her, or even her father, but decided instead to call her Uncle Carl from her new talking cellphone, a special one for the blind and visually impaired. One of the nurses' aides had entered her contacts, including emergency numbers. She told Carl what she'd be wearing, not that he wouldn't recognize her, though it had been a while since he'd seen last her. Of course, there was the white cane; he couldn't miss that.

Food smells wafted from the corridor. Dinner carts rattled past the door. She wouldn't be here for lunch today. She felt anxious. Nurse Raynes was plumping up the pillows now: pat...pat...pat...

Across the hall, The View was on television. She recognized Whoopi Goldberg's rich deep voice. She liked Whoopi. She was real, easy inside her skin.

"That's a beautiful diamond," the nurse said. "I love a solitaire."

"Yes, it is pretty." She became acutely aware of it on her finger, wound it around once, and felt the sharpness of a prong with the pad of her thumb. She wished Alan was here to take her home but he couldn't very well neglect his work to be with her. He would be back soon, she told herself. She must be careful not to be too clingy, too needy. Alan loved her. Didn't he? Yet there'd only been a couple of guilty phone calls in the past two weeks.

"Now there's an understatement if I ever heard one. It's a rock. Fire and ice. He's a nice-looking man, isn't he? Looks like a young Robert Wagner. When's the big day?"

Before she could answer, the orderly came into the room preceded by a wheelchair, his big voice cheerily saying, "Well, are we all set?" A voice she hadn't heard before.

As she was being wheeled down the corridor toward the elevators, she felt almost like she was floating through the darkness, but for the whisper of wheels on the polished floor, and the muffled footsteps behind her. "I'll bet you're glad to be getting out of here," he said. "Everyone always is."

"Yes. In a way." She sensed a heavy man gripping the handles of her wheelchair. Round, cheerful face. Was she wrong in her perception? Her own hands clutching the overnight case on her lap felt cold.

"Yeah, I get it. A little scary out there. You live alone?"

She hesitated. "I do. Why do you ask?" They stopped. Seconds later the elevator doors slid open and they got on. The elevator hummed and she felt the sensation in the pit of her stomach of dropping through space.

"Oh, no reason. Sorry, Hon, didn't mean to pry. Terrible about those murders, isn't it? Those poor women. I saw an old black-and-white movie once where the killer preyed on women with any sort of affliction and murdered them. I don't remember much about it, but I think it rained all through the movie. Weird, eh?" She felt the wheelchair take a sharp turn, before proceeding down another corridor. They stopped. "Well, here we are. That looks like your guy by the information desk. He's looking in this direction. Big guy, grey curly hair, sunglasses?"

"Yes. That's him." Her relief was out of all proportion.

Her Uncle Carl used to come to the house when her mother was alive. They would sit in the kitchen drinking tea and talking. After her mother died of a brain aneurysm when Melanie was twelve, he stopped coming around. Now and then she used to see him driving his taxi around town, and he would wave out the window to her.

"Hey, Melanie, sweetie," the familiar male voice said. "Papers all signed and ready to roll. So glad you called your old uncle."

He led her outside on his arm. The sun's rays were warm on her face. She breathed in the fresh, clean air, devoid of hospital smells. A lovely day. She thought about Uncle Carl in his sunglasses. She would get sunglasses, too, a fashionable pair, nothing too dark. Francie could help her pick them out.

The car smelled of leather, and faintly of cigarettes. He probably smokes with the window open when he's by himself and thinks no one else can smell them when they get in. She smiled to herself while at the same time trying to ignore the fist of fear in her stomach, her racing pulse. She thought of the times when she sneaked cigarettes from Doreen's pack when she was a kid, blowing smoke out her bedroom window, but her father always knew. She was too angry back then to give a damn. Another memory of her father and herself came to mind: she was sitting on the kitchen table, and he was teaching her to tie her new black patent-leather shoes. Another of him turning the hands of a big round alarm clock, teaching her how to tell time. Always so patient. Every small achievement brought her a sense of pride, more so because she knew her father was proud of her too.

She ran a hand over the plush velvety seat, found the seatbelt, and buckled herself in, feeling a small satisfaction at the click.

She understood why she'd called her uncle to come and get her. Aside from wanting to take control of her life, it was because he'd been there in happier, safer times. And he'd always been nice to her.

* * *

The man watched the brake lights go on and then the taxi disappeared around the next bend in the curving exit road leading into town. Before that, his eye had been riveted on the woman's white cane like a fox sighting a rabbit.

"Did you know her?"

His heart banged against his ribs like an anvil and he turned slowly. The nurse's aide was smiling at him. He'd almost forgotten she was walking beside him. "She looks like a girl I went to school with," he said, keeping his voice matter-of-fact. "Can't think of her name or I would have said hi."

"Melanie," the girl said. "She's a therapist. Probably will need some therapy of her own now. Car accident, poor woman. Left her blind. The jerk who hit her car just kept on going. But she's lucky to be alive. How are things with you?"

He answered easily and the momentary alarm fell silent. They entered the building and went their separate ways.

* * *

Melanie gave her uncle a bill folded in that special way they'd taught her in 'personal adjustment class', and told him to keep the change. He tried to give it back, but she insisted. "This is your living, Uncle Carl, and if you don't take it, I won't feel comfortable calling you when I need a cab."

He sighed and took the money. "Your mother wouldn't thank me. Melanie, I'm so sorry about what happened to you. I hope they get the son-of-a-bitch soon, pardon my French."

"No pardon necessary. I hope so too." She unsnapped the seatbelt and took the key ring out of her purse. Now that her car keys were no longer on it, it was easy to locate the house key.

Carl opened the passenger door and she maneuvered her cane out ahead of her body. His hand was at her elbow. "Watch your head." He made a protective cap of his big hand as he had when she got in. Such a decent man, she thought, and wondered why he'd stopped coming to the house after her mother died. Did her father not like him? Or maybe it was the other way around?

"We're right in front of your house, honey. And a nice house it is, too. Suits you. Take my arm if that's better for you. I'll walk you up to your door. Stay with you for a bit if you like."

"No, no, Uncle Carl. That's okay. I'll be fine. I want to try to do it on my own."

"You sure?"

"I am. Thanks. If I invite you for lunch sometime will you come?"

"Sure I will. I'd like that."

His hand dropped from her elbow but he didn't move away.

Forest Street was one-way, ending in woods that would eventually be cleared for further housing development. But for now, the scent of pine was in the air. She was home. She saw her house in memory, white with blue trim, and lacy curtains in the windows. Walk tall, she told herself. Chin up, as the therapist had advised her. Take sure, straight steps.

Feeling for the edge of the curb with her cane, she stepped up onto the sidewalk and then focused on walking in a straight line, trying not to hesitate, and to seem confident. She navigated the short walkway with no problem and after tapping either side of the first step to place herself just a little to the right of center, she went up the concrete steps, holding onto the wrought-iron railing. There were four steps. Yes, four. Her key on its ring was clutched in her hand, digging into her palm. Don't drop it!

Behind her on the sidewalk, someone laughed. A young girl's laugh. A person with all senses intact and no thought that that could change in an instant. The footsteps went on past, on down the street, conversation fading. Grasping the doorknob, she ran the pad of her thumb over the keyhole, inserted the key, and let herself into her house.

She'd purchased this house long before she met and fell in love with Alan, and was proud of having her own place, paid for with her own money. It was good though that Alan had no aversion to living here with her.

Just before shutting the door behind her, she heard the chunk of the car door closing and the car pulling away from the curb. Uncle Carl had stood on the sidewalk watching her until she was safely inside the house. So kind of him. People were kind. But she'd be damned if she'd be a variation of Blanche Dubois, dependent on the kindness of others, whether strangers or friends, to get through her days. She would learn to be self-sufficient. And yet even now, her heart pounded as if it too was afraid. As if she was kidding herself. She did need people. And now more than ever.

At that moment, she felt as if she were standing inside a dark room with no way out. You'll adapt, she told herself, repeating the words of the therapist for the newly blinded. This is the hand you've been dealt and you must make the best of it. They were words she might have offered to one of her patients in similar circumstances, couched in more gentle terms, of course. It's not what happens to you that matters, but how you cope with it. God, would she really have given anyone such pat, Oprahesque advice? And yet it was true. People lived with far worse things than blindness.

She visualized the room she stood in. Creating the calming, cozy ambiance in her home, especially this living room, from the pearl grey walls to the sofa and chairs with their chintz covering imprinted with big coral and green leaves, had been a labor of love. The furniture consisted of pieces she'd picked up in antique shops and restored to their original beauty. A lovely old pine bookcase with glass doors was the last treasure she'd restored; it stood against the far wall, by the hallway. The hallway went straight through the house, front to back, rooms branching off it, her bedroom last on the right, past the washroom. The Den and kitchen were on the left.

Melanie took a cautious step forward, reminding herself not to trip on the braided rug in the center of the hardwood floor, and moved in the direction of the fireplace. Photos were displayed on the mantle, one of herself receiving her master's degree in psychology, another of her mother and father on their wedding day, and next to that a glamour portrait of her mother alone, taken in a studio. She had always been able to see something of herself in her mother's face, the wide-set blue eyes, the defined cheekbones, the slightly too-narrow mouth, and in the chestnut brown hair that wouldn't curl.

She stood her cane in a corner by the fireplace and made her way down the narrow hallway, her hands reaching to either side of her, fingers groping smooth egg-shell painted walls and wood door frames.

She had expected the house to smell stale and musty considering how long she'd been away, but instead, it gave off a fresh lemony fragrance. Francie. What would she do without her? They'd been friends since grammar school, always there for one another, sharing secrets, venting personal angst. She'd probably got the better end of that deal, with all her complaints about her stepmother. But she didn't want to be a burden to Francie now, or to anyone else. She'd done well in the hospital. Those last couple of weeks she'd been able to walk up and down the hallway and find her room again, just by counting doors. She saw so much through touch now, as well as through sound and smell. She would practice getting about in her own house. By the time Alan got back, it would be second nature. He'd be proud of her.

Orienting herself in the bedroom doorway, she moved to the bed and ran her hand over the pretty quilt she'd bought at a quilt fair last summer. Turning right, she walked toward the vanity. There, she placed her hands against the mirror; the glass was cool against her palms. Of course, she saw no reflection, as if she were some creature of the night. But then she couldn't see the mirror either She was being melodramatic. She was real enough. She didn't have to see herself in a mirror to know she was wearing her off-white linen pantsuit. The nurse had even commented on it. She knew that her eyes were light blue. That her hair came to just below her ears, (easier to care for, the girl who cut it said) and she wore small gold hoop earrings. Now those ears were forever cocked, listening, trying to pick up clues as to what was going on.

Because it was true -- they were -- you were. The sunglasses would help camouflage the blindness. She remembered there was a pair on the vanity, not what she had in mind but they would do until she got the new ones.

Feeling for them, the side of her hand bumped the top of a bottle which immediately fell over with a clunk and the fragrance of L'Air du Temps filled the air. Damn! Tears of frustration stung her eyes. She managed to upright the bottle of lotion and mop up the mess with a wad of tissues. After groping around on the floor for the wastebasket, she dropped them in. She hadn't put the top on the lotion tightly the last time she'd used it. Well, she'd just have to be more careful in the future. To paraphrase Clint Eastwood, a woman's gotta know her limitations.

Hearing the soft closing of the front door, her thoughts scattered and she turned around. The faint fall of footsteps was headed in her direction. A smile broke from Melanie. Francie. Her heart lifted.

"Francie, I'm in the bedroom," she called out. "Oh, I'm so glad you're here. I know said I'd call you when I was being released, but I wanted..." She stopped.

The footsteps halted in her bedroom doorway, came no farther. Frowning, she thought: No, not Francie standing there. Not her father, either, she would know if it was him. But someone was there. Someone who had followed her into the house. A burst of adrenaline shot through her veins. How could she have been so stupid as to forget to lock the door behind her? What was the matter with her? And then she saw movement in that milky whiteness at the corner of her eye. Felt a shifting of air in front of her. Don't show fear, came the warning voice inside her mind. Stay calm.

"Who is it?"

No answer. The fine hairs prickled on the back of her neck and it was hard to breathe, let alone speak. "Can I help you? Have you come to the wrong house?" She heard the tremor in her voice. Receiving no answer alarm quickly turned to panic, a reaction that both angered and frightened her. "Who are you?"

Instantly the bit of whiteness in her eye went dark and a hand touched her cheek it was as if spider webs were draped over her face, and she was suddenly screaming,

screaming, her hands flailing about, beating at him like a mad woman.

He had backed away from her reach, backed from the room. And then she heard him walking away. Even when she heard the front door close, the terror did not release its grip on her. She stood frozen. But at last, her legs obeyed the urgent command from her brain: Hurry, lock the door before he decides to come back!

Hands outstretched, Melanie navigated her way back through the darkness of the hallway and living room with all the grace and agility of a broken robot, bumping into furniture and striking her hip against the corner of the bookcase, tripping over the living room rug, while somehow managing to stay on her feet. Finally, with trembling, clumsy fingers she managed to lock the door. Then she sank to the floor, sobbing and rocking like a child trying to console itself, which was exactly how she felt. She had not cried so hard or so loud since she was a little girl. Nor had she felt such rage at her helplessness. She was still huddled there on the floor a half hour later, or maybe it was longer when the doorbell rang. By then, all her tears had been cried out. She was drained of emotion and feeling like a bundle of soggy rags as she rose shakily to her feet and asked who it was, her voice sounding thin and reedy in her ears, barely recognizable as her own.

"I've got a couple of coffees from Timmy's here if you're interested," Matt called through the door. She unlocked and opened the door. "Hi, just what I need. Coffee from Tim Horton's. Smells great. Thanks, Matt." She tried to smile. "Come on in."

"I dropped by the hospital earlier and they told me you'd been discharged. I had a favor to ask..." He paused, and she felt him scrutinizing her. She tried to keep a normal expression on her face. "I was surprised you'd been released, you never mentioned it last night. I thought...Mel, what's wrong? You look like you saw a ghost. And you're shaking."

He wasn't buying her act. She saw in her mind's eye his craggy face, the slight bump on his nose, just a little crooked, from what exactly she could only guess. She saw the warm amber-colored eyes beneath dark brows, the fine lines fanning out from the corners. There would be concern in those eyes right now and it was all she could do not to lean into his wide, comforting shoulders so near to her. She resisted the urge. The last thing she wanted or needed from Matt was his pity. The concern she could handle. Besides, he was holding those hot coffees.

"Has something happened?" he prodded.

"C'mon into the kitchen. I'll tell you about it."

When she finished telling her story, he said, "And you're sure someone was here? After all, this is your first day home. It would be natural to..."

"Matt, I'm blind, not crazy. And I didn't imagine it. Someone was here. I heard him breathing. And I saw movement. I can, you know. Not much, but like when you see something out of the corner of your eye. Maybe a little more than that. And then I heard him leaving, heard the door close. When he ...touched my face,..." She gave an involuntary shiver. "I freaked. Like I never have in my life before. I was terrified. I thought..."

"I know what you thought. But it was probably just some joker who saw you get out of the cab with your white cane and decided to have a little sport. It's a nasty world out there, and getting nastier every day. A lot of ugliness around, Mel. I see evidence of it every day in my job."

"I'm believing you. I don't want to but I do." She took a sip of her coffee. It was still hot, black, just the way she liked it. She felt the spread of warmth through her body. She wasn't shaking anymore.

"Good. So you should."

"So you don't think it was any joke at all? I'm pretty sure I knew that. Anyway, it's my own damn fault. I'm madder at me than you could ever be. I stupidly forgot to lock the door behind me."

"Well, you won't get an argument from me there." His tone softened. "You shouldn't be alone right now. What about staying with your dad? A week or so. At least until..."

"No, Matt, that`s not going to happen. I'm fine, really. My stepmother's a nice enough woman, but it's not a place for me. Anyway, I love my house. This place isn't fancy but it's home. Aside from that, how can I expect to learn to get around within my own walls if I`m somewhere else?"

"Point taken. It's a great house, too. Cozy if not fancy, elegant if not grand, but I've never been big on fancy. You did a great job decorating."

"Thanks. Appreciate the kind words. You mentioned you needed a favor."

Melanie felt a warmth to her face, but it wasn't Matt's compliment on her decorating that did it, nice though it was. No, the sun had come round to this side of the house, pouring its rays through the kitchen window. A pleasant sensation. Like having Detective Matt O'Leary sitting across from her at her kitchen table, sharing coffee with him was pleasant. She was grateful for his friendship.

"More than a favor. I need your help. I wanted to ask you if you would consider putting together a profile of our killer."

"A profile? Oh, Matt, I don't think I..."

"Why not? You did it when we had that arsonist running around setting fires and we got him."

She remembered. He turned out to be a firefighter by day, a pyromaniac by night. She would have wished for a different outcome but was relieved to have had a part in ending his nefarious activities before he killed someone. "But that was a long time ago and I..."

"I transferred the file to tape. Everything I've got to this point. Mel, I need your help here."

She heaved a sigh. "I'll listen to the tape, Matt. But I can't promise anything."

"I'm not asking for promises. Just give it your best shot. Oh, and I have one more bit of news to share with you. We got a note in today's mail from the person we think may be the perp.

"Oh, Matt."

"It could be a hoax, of course, but it rings authentic. Only a few sentences. The message he wants to get it out there is that he's not the monster everyone is making him out to be and that he's doing the Lord's work -- ridding the streets of 'defectives' as he called them. It's on the tape, verbatim. The page he used came out of a five by seven-inch writing tablet, lined. Black ink, print small. A couple of spelling mistakes. They could be deliberate, but I doubt it. It was mailed here in town, and sent to the station. Addressed to me personally."

"Too bad he didn't email it. You could have put a trace on it."

"Yeah. Guess he's not that stupid. Or maybe he's not into computers."

"Or he wants you to think that." Still thinking out loud, she said, "He tells himself that he's doing the Lord's work. Good work. Because it's the only way he can deal with the fact that he's a vicious murderer, preying on vulnerable women. He wants people to think well of him. To like him. He cares about that. He also wants you to be impressed at this holy service he's taken on. That's why he sent the note."

"He signed himself 'The Eraser'," Matt said. "So he's taunting the police. He wants us to think he's smarter than we are. He's daring us to stop him."

"Maybe. It's a characteristic of many serial killers, we know that. But I'm not so sure in this case. I'll know more after I listen to the tape."She was warming to the subject. It was good to have purpose again, to be useful. She was sure this wasn't lost on Matt and was thankful to him. The name echoed in her mind: The Eraser. Though the room was warm, it brought a chill.

* * *

It was a day for company. After Matt left, her dad showed up to check up on her and bring more gifts - a pretty pink robe, and a basket of fresh fruit. She wished he would stop with the presents; he couldn't afford them and she didn't need them. But it was

188

sweet just the same. Later Francie dropped by with pizza, Pepsis, and a rant because Melanie hadn't let her know she was being released. They were sitting at the kitchen table, and through the chewing, Francie said, "You know I would have driven you home."

"I know. I wanted to see if I could get myself home. I wasn't on my own. My Uncle Carl drove me. But I did call the cab," she joked. She said nothing about her visitor today. No point in upsetting Francie over something that had happened and was now over. She'd probably tell her eventually.

The plan to curl up under the blankets and let the world drift away wasn't in the cards. Not that it was a great option anyway, now that she thought about it. "Thanks for cleaning the house while I was in the hospital, Francie. I appreciate it. Everything smelled so nice and fresh."

"Wasn't me. Thank Doreen, your stepmother. Not that it wasn't clean already. But she ran a vacuum and dusted."

"Oh." She was more than surprised, and not as pleased as she should have been. She didn't need to see Francie to know she was grinning. Melanie found no humor in it. She'd given her father a key, but he wasn't supposed to share it. Not even with his wife. Especially not his wife. Doreen always had an agenda. But maybe she was being unfair. It hadn't even occurred to her it was her stepmother who readied the house for her homecoming.

"I thought it was sweet," Francie said.

"Yeah, I guess." Melanie was still a little taken aback and mildly irritated at the idea of being obliged to her...or to the idea of her going through her things. But she could tell this was one time Francie wasn't going to commiserate with her on the subject of her stepmother. That was the downside of having a best friend; they told you the truth, whether you wanted to hear it or not.

"So," Francie said. "What are your plans?"

"A shower later. Lay out my clothes for tomorrow."

"Don't be a wise-ass. I meant long term and you know it."

It was Melanie's turn to grin. "I haven't had time to think about it yet. I still have to work so it's a matter of finding something I can still do."

"You can do anything you want. What's stopping you from doing what you've been doing? Being a therapist. You're a great therapist. You should get yourself one of those seeing-eye dogs, though."

"You're not the first one to mention it, Francie, but I'm not so sure I can take care of myself, let alone an animal." That sounded so self-pitying she wished she could take it back the instant it was out of her mouth. Francie let the comment lay unchallenged, but Melanie could almost read her thoughts. And she'd be right in her assessment.

She was still herself, after all, still Melanie Snow. A reasonably attractive woman, a good friend, intelligent, educated, (hadn't Matt asked her to work up a profile on this killer?) And she liked to think she could be fun to be with. At least she used to be. She needed to take her life back. To fight the part of her that wanted only to curl up in a ball and hide away from the world. What happened to her vow to be independent? She was pretty sure her unknown caller had sent that bit of bravado into hiding. But only temporarily, she promised herself. She'd simply have to let that unpleasant experience go and move on.

"You're right, Francie."

"About what? I didn't say anything."

"I know. But you're right." Francie didn't answer, but Melanie knew the grin was back. They had always been able to tune into each other's thoughts and moods, from the time they were kids.

Sometime after Francie left for home, Melanie heard the faint rumble of thunder not that far off and something flashed in her right eye, like a small starburst. Lightning. A small shudder of foreboding rippled through her. The drapes had been left partially open, considering her eye had caught the flash of lightning. She closed the drapes.

Alone now, the silence of the house seemed to drop down into an even deeper silence. A certain eeriness in it. As if it were waiting. But that was silly; just her imagination. She shook off the sensation and sat down on the living room sofa to listen to the tape Matt had made for her. She slipped the tape into the recorder, clicked the on button, and hit play. The shape of each button record, play, fast forward, backward and pause was diffcrent, and her fingertips had memorized them all. Immersing herself in interesting work would be very good for her.

When she'd listened to the entire tape, she turned it off and slipped in a blank tape. She pressed record and spoke into the built-in mic. She planned eventually to get a new laptop and figure out the text-to-speech function, but until then, this would do fine.

"June 30th. Dr. Melanie Snow. Unknown subject."

Based on the information Matt had transferred to tape, (including the note from the killer) her training as a psychologist and therapist fortified with a ton of material she'd read over the years, took over. Melanie painstakingly began to draw up a basic profile of their killer, even while knowing that profiling was not an exact science and that she could be wrong on any number of points.

Though there are similarities in the backgrounds of serials, each with his reason (over 90% of serial killers are men) for killing, his method of operation, or modus operandi. M.O. Sometimes those methods changed. For example, someone who strangles his victims might conceivably stab his next one. Child abuse was usually found somewhere in the background of most of them, whether real or perceived. And sometimes there was just evil. Even though she was a psychologist, she believed in evil. Some acts were so heinous psychology couldn't explain them.

She remembered reading somewhere that there was something like three dozen serial killers active in the U.S. at any given time, and though Canada's population is far less, we have our share. Names like Paul Bernardo, Robert Pickton, and Clifford Olsen came to mind. There were more. And now this unnamed one. Well, not exactly unnamed since he called himself 'The Eraser'. She knew a few things about him after talking with Matt and listening to the file. She could almost feel him drawing closer. Not a good feeling.

She remember Matt telling her that a couple of weeks before Jodie Ballard was murdered she'd confided to a co-worker that she thought someone had followed her home from work, though when she turned around she saw no one who looked suspicious. Did Jodie describe any of the faces she had seen? Faces she had dismissed as unthreatening? It might be worthwhile for Matt to talk to the co-worker again. She could suggest it. Though it was unlikely they hadn't covered that angle thoroughly. Still, she would mention it.

Whoever he was, he probably gave off no danger signals and appeared normal to the untrained eye, or even to the trained eye if it came to that. Psychopaths learned how to mimic appropriate behavior which is why they can go undetected for so long. They're often charming, even with sunny personalities. At the very least, they're adept at blending in.

Matt said Jodie's co-worker was devastated because she hadn't reported the conversation to her boss, or to the police at the time. She had believed Jodie was imagining things, but unfortunately, she was wrong. Melanie doubted that it would have made any difference in the outcome unless she'd decided to accompany Jodie to and from work every day. He would have gotten to her sooner or later.

A gust of wind rattled the window and made Melanie jump, the recorder near slipping from her hand. It had begun to rain in earnest, drumming on the glass like some clawed thing that wanted in. An involuntary shiver went through her. She needed to leave this task for a while. She was creeping herself out.

Chapter 5

Angie Gray lived only four blocks from Melanie, although they didn't know one another. She was a widowed librarian who lived with her cat, Misty, in a dark green and cream A-frame house set well back from the street, as did Melanie's house. At a flash of lightning in her picture window, Angie glanced away from the book she was reading, ironically enough a new Stephen King novel. Her son kept trying to persuade her to get a Kindle, but she liked the feel of a book in her hand, the smell of it, even though she was very computer literate. She liked turning real pages. She supposed it was the librarian in her.

Another flash. The blue-white light spotlighted the expanse of lawn, producing a negative of the old crabapple tree standing at the edge of the now rain-battered, deserted sidewalk, its leaves bowing low in the wind as if conceding power to the night. Thunder crashed and rolled across the sky, vibrating in the very marrow of her bones. The wind-driven rain drummed on the roof and chattered against the glass. She had always loved a storm as long as she didn't have to go out in it. And she didn't, not since cancer took her left leg two years ago and forced her to give up her job at the library. Now and then she went to lunch with one of her old co-workers, and she enjoyed the camaraderie and catching up on everyone's lives. Her next-door neighbor, Nancy Wedge, had invited her for lunch tomorrow. So Angie's life was full. She had friends and she had work to do. being alone.

She shifted position in the big chair by the fire and continued to read, never suspecting that she would ever know the ending of the story. In the particular scene she was reading, the day was bright and sunny. Have a nice day. Though not here in Evansdale. It would be easy enough to spook yourself, let your imagination run away with you on a night like this. For instance, she might make something of the fact that when she was downtown last week she'd sensed someone following her, sensed eyes like hot lasers on the back of her neck. Felt the tightening of her skin. So strong was the feeling she'd actually stopped and turned around on the sidewalk and scanned the faces of strangers, but no one was looking at her. And even if they had been, people often did look at her. Or tried not to. It was human nature, she supposed. You didn't see a one-legged woman every day. She could have worn the prosthetic leg, but it chafed the stump and she found it uncomfortable and preferred getting about on her crutches. Crutches that at the moment leaned against the gray stone fireplace until they were needed again. Angie had no thought that they would not be needed by her.

She had shut down the computer earlier, pampered herself with a bubble bath, and donned her nightgown and cream-colored velour robe in anticipation of a pleasant evening, reading. Angie worked at home for a publishing company, editing books, a job her background as a librarian had qualified her for and which suited her circumstances perfectly.

She took a sip from the glass of red wine on the end table beside her. The fire crackled and snapped cozily in the fireplace, sending shadow flames dancing on the wall. It was mid-May, but the air felt cool tonight and Angie was perfectly content to curl up here in her attractive little cave with its modern furniture polished by lamplight. The midnight blue carpeting added a certain lushness to the room. She turned the page, a soft sigh contrasting with the storm outside her window.

Books had always been a friend to Angie, even in the worst of life's storms. Yet after Mike died of a sudden heart attack three years ago, she could find no pleasure in them. Couldn't focus on the words which ran together in a meaningless jumble. Could barely draw a full breath for that matter or put one foot ahead of the other. (That was when she still had two feet of course.) But gradually life reasserted itself and she rejoined the living. The books were there to reach for like old and faithful friends. Not that she didn't miss Mike, but now she found she could remember the good times and smile to herself and let the memories comfort her. Their son Michael was doing well in university; he wanted to be a teacher like his dad. Mike would be proud of him. Correction. He was proud of him. Angie believed Mike was up there smiling down at them.

As much as she had been enjoying the book, for some reason, her thoughts kept veering away from the character's dilemma to mulling over her own life. Or maybe the storm was just making her edgy. It had turned up its volume, making such a racket with the wind keening under the eaves and wailing down the chimney like some tormented banshee, she couldn't concentrate. The rain that had chattered against the window earlier now sounded like someone was hurling handfuls of stones at it. There was the briefest moment when Angie thought she heard a different sound from the kitchen. A soft thump... tinkling of glass... and she looked up. Seconds later, Misty, her grey Persian cat came slinking into the room. Jumping up on Angie's lap, she looked straight at her out of those moss-green, knowing eyes. Angie smiled and stroked the small silky, knobby head. "Did you knock that poor old African Violet plant over again, you bad girl? I guess the storm's got you antsy too? Well, we'll clean it up later. Settle down then if you're going to sit here with me."

Misty circled a couple of times and then curled up in her lap, but her eyes remained open, ears flicking. Oddly, she wasn't purring. Angie gave her another pat and went back to her book. Not until moments later when a dark shadow fell across her page, did she look up again. When she did her heart shot into her throat at the sight of what looked like the grim reaper standing there in the archway, dressed in a black hooded coat shiny with rain dripping from it, down to the black-gloved hands. Before she could scream or even process what was happening, he came at her, sending Misty to the floor with a howl. Then he was on her, his hands around her throat, cutting off her air, taking her to the floor. She was only vaguely aware of the book hitting the carpet beside her with a soft thud, her glass of wine toppling off the table, as she tried to fight him off, tried to pry his fingers away, to breathe. But his hands were like steel and held firm, his thumbs pressing ever harder into the soft flesh of her throat. Her nails tried to find his face, but then his hands left her throat just long enough to grasp her wrists, forcing her hands to her sides and kneeling on them. She gasped in precious air, but then his hands were around her throat again, squeezing, squeezing until blood pounded in her ears as some great falls and colored lights flashed behind her lids. Her lungs strained for air and her body convulsed, her one sad heel thumping the floor as if in protest.

"Shh," he whispered. "Stop fighting. Go to sleep now."

Chapter 6

Melanie sat bolt upright in the bed, her cotton pajamas plastered to her body like a second skin, her heart racing. She listened intently, every nerve on alert like an animal sensing danger. Someone had been pounding on her bedroom door trying to get in at her. She heard nothing now, only the storm outside. It must have been a dream.

Yes, only a bad dream, she told herself. A nightmare. One that had followed her into waking, still echoing inside her head. But it was only the thunderstorm outside her window she heard, the noise morphed into a nightmare, her subconscious creating one sound from another, one far more threatening than any thunderstorm.

Working on the profile must have triggered the nightmare. She pushed back the blanket and slid her legs over the edge of the bed. She'd spent too much time peering into the mind of a madman tonight. She'd heard it said that when you look into the abyss, sometimes the abyss looks back at you. Made sense. She sat for a minute until her heartbeat returned to normal, then, donning robe and slippers, she took her cup into the kitchen and plugged in the kettle for fresh tea. She dumped the bit still in her cup into the sink and rinsed the cup. As she waited for the water to boil, she hugged herself, unable to shake off the sense of something deadly and menacing creeping ever closer. The pounding on the door from the dream echoed even now, even though the claps of thunder had long faded.

She thought of the title of a Ray Bradbury book 'Something Wicked This Way Comes', and shivered again. Goosebumps rose on her arms, beneath the sleeves of her robe. She jumped at the kettle's whistle.

Knowing she wouldn't get any more sleep tonight, Melanie took her cup of tea back into the bedroom with her. She stacked the pillows behind and around her and went back to work. The rain was coming down harder.

It had taken Matt time to read the murder file aloud to her, then put it on tape. It would have been a lot easier for him just to hand a copy of the file to a more experienced profiler. She hadn't lost the sneaky suspicion that this was his way of keeping her mind occupied and off her problems while also allowing him to keep an eye on her. She had to admit, she didn't mind at all. She just hoped her efforts would help bring down this killer and end the terror for so many women.

After another half hour of talking into the recorder, alternately listening to the tape Matt had given her, Melanie set the recorder on the nightstand and huddled under the blankets. In the living room, the clock on the mantle bonged three times. The house was locked up solid, both doors and windows, and Melanie finally went to sleep and slept soundly, waking early the next morning anxious to give Matt her insights on the man who had murdered two innocent women and was probably already targeting the next victim.

Chapter 7

"I knew something terrible had happened to her," Angie Gray's neighbor sniffed into a wad of tissues, her other arm cuddling the cat against her shoulder. She was standing inside the back door in the spotless aqua and white kitchen where she'd told Matt she'd shared many a cup of tea with her friend and neighbor. She'd invited Angie to lunch today, and it was just not like her not to show up, she said. "I phoned and when she didn't answer, I threw on this raincoat and came on over. I saw her car in the drive so I thought she just forgot and I knocked on the door. I figured Angie might have gotten immersed in her work – she's a book editor you know... well, was –" She was on the verge of breaking down again. Matt put a steadying hand on her shoulder and it seemed to calm her. She stopped and sighed, and went on. "When she didn't answer the door, I went around back and saw the broken window. I called you right away."

"You did exactly right, Ma'am."

If she'd thought to look through the part in the living room drapes she would have seen her friend sprawled on the floor. It was good she didn't. She'd have a hard enough time closing her eyes tonight, as it was. She hadn't moved from the doorway. Her eyes were swollen from tears and her hair was mussed, bits of it standing up like tiny copper wires.

"I could feel it in my bones that something terrible had happened to her," she repeated. "My God, it's that killer, isn't it? That one who murders handicapped people."

"We don't know that, Mrs. Wedge, but of course it's possible." It was more than possible, he thought. This was the third victim, this one with a physical handicap. There could be others, he thought again. In other towns and cities. Departments didn't always share information. Sometimes it was territorial and sometimes just a matter of a small force spread too thin. But this was his territory, his responsibility to get this cowardly creep off the streets. It was clear now he wasn't just going after women with intellectual challenges, but physical challenges too. He couldn't help thinking of Melanie all alone in that house. So vulnerable. They had to stop this psycho before he killed anyone else. Before he got to her.

Matt had already noted Mrs. Wedge's small shoeprints in the mucky trough outside the kitchen window, and confirmed that they were hers. But there was also another set of shoeprints, larger, deeper.

Boots, he concluded, that luck more than anything had kept her or anyone else from trampling on.

Officer Dave Malacky was standing guard to secure the area until forensics did their work. They'd get a cast of the boot print. He'd also observed mud on the window sill both inside and out, with a smattering left on the kitchen floor, a few more prints heading toward the livingroom. None returning. There could be other evidence   a cigarette stub, a pop can... a button...you never knew what small thing could help I.D. a killer.

The quivering mewling cat had been under the sofa when they got here, and it took a lot of coaxing to persuade it to come out. Misty, as Mrs. Wedge called her, would now be cared for in her house. As much as Matt liked cats, he thought Angie Gray would have been better served with a Rottweiler. He'd already been trying to persuade Melanie to get a dog.

"You have to stop him," Mrs. Wedge burst out, and the dissolved into sobs again. "Oh, poor little Angie. She's had so much trouble in her life, but you couldn't find a sweeter person."

"We will, Ma'am. We will."

But would they? Hadn't he made the same promise to Jodie Ballard's mom? And to Dora Nabers' spirit as he'd stood over her in that depressing room where she met her horrible end. Melanie's in danger, he thought again, and ice crystals crawled down his back on insect legs.

He had an officer escort Mrs. Wedge home. He would interview her again in the event there was some small detail she might have overlooked and would recall after the shock wore off, something that would help them in their investigation. Perhaps some comment the victim made to her in passing. Before they left, Matt asked her if Angie had mentioned anyone suspicious to her. If she'd felt like she was being watched.

She shrugged and looked sadly at him. "Angie always felt like she was being watched. People can be so insensitive. She never let it get to her though. But no one in particular, no. Not that she mentioned to me anyway."

When they were gone, Detective Matt O'Leary walked back into the living room where the victim lay, and gazed down at her still form on the carpet. She'd been dead maybe eight, ten hours. He'd know more precisely when forensics got here. Her eyes were closed. Her hands folded one over the other, in the same funereal pose as he'd left his other two victims. What breed of animal would do this? According to her friend, her husband checked out with a heart attack three years ago and then she'd lost her leg to cancer. Their one son, Michael, named for his dad, was in first year university. Matt would need to inform him of his mother's death before the news hit the media. Not something he looked forward to. He flipped open his cell and put in a call to the university. Then he knelt down beside the body. The carpet was damp beneath him, a blend of rain and wine, he surmised. He'd already bagged the fallen wineglass. Her crutches were propped against the wall near the fireplace. He had a brief image of her sitting in her chair, reading by the fire, death stalking ever nearer. Bastard!

She'd been a nice looking women in life; her shoulder-length hair was still shiny in the light coming through the narrow part in the drapes. A couple of uniforms guarded the perimeter, keeping rubberneckers hanging wanting to see more, away from the house. He drew the drapes fully closed to discourage morbidly curious eyes.

Serial, Matt thought, then reminded himself to keep an open mind, not jump to conclusions. There was always the possibility someone else had killed her, even a copycat. They'd check out the son, along with anyone she might have been seeing romantically, though the neighbor said there was no one special in her life. But maybe she didn't share her every secret with Mrs. Wedge. Everyone loved Angie, the distraught woman had assured him. Apparently not everyone.

There was faint bruising on her neck. He predicted forensics would find high levels of carbon dioxide in her blood, although he'd been told that measuring post-mortem blood could be so unreliable as to provide no worthwhile information.

He could detect no trace evidence of hair or fibers, but that would need to be confirmed by other than the naked eye, and by experts, which he definitely was not. Her fingernails hadn't been recently cut, but he had bagged her hands anyway. As far as he could tell, there'd been no sexual assault. His gaze travelled down to her lone bare foot peeking out from beneath the robe. Her neatly manicured toenails were painted a soft shade of coral. That somehow got to him. A certain defiance and courage in the face of incredible loss. Qualities that made him think of Melanie.

The blat of a police siren outside, followed by the squeal of brakes, brought him to his feet, his knee protesting with a soft crack, and he walked to the window. He let them in to tramp through the victim's house, albeit wearing the required paper booties. Sometime later, photos taken, prints lifted, shoeprint cast in plaster, they all traipsed out again. Like Jodie and Dora, Angela's body was zipped into a body bag and removed to the morgue in an unhurried ambulance.

Who would be next? He couldn't dismiss Melanie's face from the screen of his mind.

With everyone else gone, the house felt eerily quiet. Matt's heart jumped when his phone rang. It was the son, Michael Grey. He had a good voice, strong, manly, yet with something of the boy still evident in it. Matt closed his eyes and let his breath out. "Michael, this is Detective Matt O'Leary of the Evansdale Police Department. I'm afraid I have some bad news for you."

After Matt hung up the phone from talking to Michael Grey, he felt sick. The kid was in shock, naturally, on his way home now to plan for his mother's funeral. Small mercy that exams were over, at least he hoped they were. He'd do a routine check on him, but he knew in his gut Michael Gray had nothing to do with his mother's murder. He was a victim too. This would be a dark time in the boy's life, a time that would change him forever. Matt sometimes wondered how people retained their sanity in the face of so much loss.

He'd come very close to going over the edge at one time himself, and the deaths did not even involve members of his own family, which consisted of his mom, one sister, married with two kids, living in China where she taught English as a second language. His father, who'd been a cop was dead fifteen years now, shot in a domestic dispute. His mother lived with her older sister in Sarasota, Florida. No, it wasn't a loved one he'd lost, or even anyone he knew personally, but it hit him hard just the same. Melanie had helped him over that very bad patch in his career. The incident that had pushed him toward the brink involved a custody battle in which a father shot his two little boys to death, then turned the gun on himself. After finding those kids dead in their beds, he'd lost his way for a time. He couldn't close his eyes at night because the visions would be there, waiting for him. Even in the daylight hours, their bloodied little bodies appeared to him, those half open blue eyes looked into his. Why didn't you save us? they seemed to say. They haunted him. He escaped inside a bottle to forget, and that's what outed him. He hadn't expected the therapist to help, but the chief had ordered him to see her or take a long vacation. So he went and she had helped him. Not that he was over the experience, but he did learn how to put it in a compartment by itself so it didn't bleed, so to speak, into every moment of his day. Melanie was an excellent psychologist. The fish were her idea, a way to calm the mind, a sort of meditation as he watched them swim leisurely about in their ten gallon tank. It worked. Rosencrantz, who was electric blue, and Guildenstern, a sunny orange, had become his buddies. He hoped she would be able to help him again, in a different way and wondered how she was progressing with the profile. What manner of beast had she come up with? Whoever The Eraser was in real life as opposed to his twisted fantasy life, he was wrong about one thing; he was a monster.

He was on his way to Melanie's when Officer Jack Eldridge called him from the station informing him that a couple had come in to report a 'peeping tom' and was waiting for him in his office. "The husband thinks it might be our killer."

The news of the latest murder had already broken and the phones were ringing off the hooks. Matt turned the car around in a Wendy's parking lot, already on the phone requesting a car to stake out Melanie's house. "Our perp may already have paid her a visit," he said, to ensure that his request was not taken lightly. He knew it wasn't the only request for protection they'd get. Fear would be rampant, it already was, albeit some of it born of paranoia. The quirks of ex-husbands, neighbors, in-laws would suddenly take on new possibilities. Darker possibilities.

Officer Jack Eldridge was one of the old-timers, long a widower. He'd been manning the phones up to now. Jack was well over six feet, balding and softening a little around the middle as retirement drew near. The job was his life. Matt wondered what the hell he would do the day after retirement. You get used to the life, crave the adrenalin rush, and many cops liked the feeling of control. He wondered how much of that described himself. Except that he felt anything but in control of this situation. Maybe they'd get a break.

"One call came in from a woman who's wheelchair bound," Jack said, "and is convinced her son-in-law plans to kill her. She thinks he's just murdering those other women first so the police won't suspect him when he finally gets around to doing her in. There's a flood of calls with the same theme, Matt. My own mom is a nervous wreck lately. She wears a hearing aid and tries to hide it with her hair when she goes out to do her errands to avoid looking like prey."

"I'm sorry, Jack. I met your mother at a Christmas party a few years back. Nice woman. She doesn't seem the hysterical type."

"No, she's not. Not usually anyway. But she's getting on, near eighty now, a little more fragile than she used to be and she knows it.

"Someone's already been around to check out the wheelchair-bound woman," he went on, glancing down at his notes, "and her daughter says her mother is having some mental problems, but not so bad she's ready to place her in a nursing home just yet."

They would keep an eye on the situation, he said, but were satisfied for the moment that the woman was in no immediate danger. Jack turned the page in his blue spiral notebook. "Another caller believes her son wants her dead so he can take all her money, which apparently amounts to a few hundred dollars. There's no life insurance on her, not even enough to bury her should she die of natural causes." He sat the notebook down on his desk. "As it is, the guy works two jobs to pay a caregiver to come in daily. But we won't ignore the possibility that her fears might be valid."

"Great Jack. You never know." Matt knew elders were abused by their kids all the time, as inconceivable as that might seem. Elder abuse was on the rise. Or maybe it was always there and we just never heard about it in the old days. This killer could be anyone: the mailman; the bagger at the grocery store; the meter man. Who knew? Chances were the guy looked ordinary; serial killers generally did. A parade of faces floated past his mental vision: Wayne Gacy, Ted Bundy, Gary Ridgeway, Dennis Rader, (BTK) Jeffrey Dahmer...

They'd follow up on every lead, no matter how unlikely. Most of the tips would prove fruitless, others given more weight. The couple presently waiting in Matt's office would belong to the latter group. They were sitting patiently, holding coffees someone had bought them, both turning to look at him when he came through the door. Almost in unison, they sat their coffees on his desk.

Good-looking kids, both dark-haired and dark-eyed. They might have been siblings. The woman's name was Lana Drew, the husband Will Drew, an electrician who worked for the city. Matt sat down behind his cluttered desk and grabbed a report form out of the basket. Pen poised, he said, "Thanks for coming in. I've already been given a rundown of the incident, so maybe you can fill me in on the details. And what makes you think your peeping tom was our killer."

"We didn't think so, not at first," the woman said. "But now..."

After a slight pause, she stood up and walked around to the side of his desk, which, for a moment, took Matt by surprise. She walked with a heavy limp, and he saw at once why, and it made the fine hairs on the back of his neck stand up. He saw her fully now. Lana Drew had a leg-length deficiency. Her left leg. She wore a custom-made shoe to help compensate for the difference. No doubt it helped, but not a hell of a lot as far as he could tell. It was a pretty shoe, more a full-foot sandal with a red and yellow stripe across the top, just the toe peeking out, the nail polish the same soft red as the stripe on the sandal. It made him think of Angie Gray.

Easy to understand why the couple was so concerned; they had good reason to be. Their 'peeping tom' could very well have been targeting her. He must have spotted her somewhere and followed her home. Luckily her husband was home at the time, otherwise, they might be having a different conversation. Lana returned to sit beside her husband, clutching her matching leather bag nervously in her lap. She picked up her coffee again, and sipped it, not taking her eyes from him.

Matt nodded. Point taken. "So tell me what happened? Don't leave out anything."

"There's not a lot to tell. I was about to get ready for bed, and when I turned to the window to pull the blind, this man was peering in at me. For a second we just stared at each other. Then I screamed."

Her scream woke their little boy who'd been sleeping in the next room, and alerted her husband who took off after the guy. "Unfortunately he vaulted a fence and managed to get away," Will Drew said. "He was fast."

"It happened a couple of weeks ago. We thought he was just your run-of-the-mill perv, your know? Until we heard the news a couple of hours ago about the latest murder. They said the woman had lost a leg to cancer." He covered his wife's hand with his and looked at her with pride and love. And worry, Matt thought. Lana could give no definite description of the man. "Just this long, pale face staring in at me," she said, fear lingering in her pretty dark eyes. The tiny silver ring in her lower lip winked under the fluorescent light. "Creeped me out. Those eyes -- Jesus."

"What do you mean?"

"They were light. Not blue though. Gray, maybe." She shivered perceptively. "Like rotting ice."

"He was at least five, ten," Will Drew put in. "Around my size. He had to be in pretty good shape too from the way he flew over that fence. I couldn't catch him, and I'm no slouch."

He wasn't. Will looked like he hit the gym regularly. No bragging there, just a stated fact. So the peeper could be something of an athlete. Or else just a guy who was fast on his feet naturally. He'd known kids who were, growing up.

"Wish we could have been more help," Lana said.

"You've been more help than you know."

Will Drew told him he was driving his wife and baby out of town to visit an aunt for a couple of weeks. Matt thought it was a very good idea. He wished he could talk Melanie into going someplace safer until they got this guy off the streets. But he knew that wasn't going to happen.

* * *

Matt pulled together a task force. A hot line was set up to field the increased incoming calls, too many now for Jack to handle on his own. There were so many questions without answers. How did he find his victims? Did he just spot his prey on the street and start stalking them, as he speculated had happened with Lana Drew? As for Dora, she'd been pretty much a sitting target. Literally. Or was there some other connection he was missing? What would cause someone to have such hatred against women with a disability? Those victims may have faced challenges the average person didn't, but they had carved out lives for themselves, lives that were working. But for their killer, that didn't matter. He was like someone working in a warehouse, given the job of tagging for destruction anything he deemed faulty or defective. He was eager to see Melanie, see what she'd come up with.

Matt gathered his team together in the squad room. When he first joined the force, the place smelled of vomit, coffee, and sweat, and the walls had a film of nicotine accumulated over many years. Now, in the new building, where smoking wasn't allowed, it was as sterile as city hall, or most offices. You wouldn't know it was a police station but for the 'Most Wanted' posters on the wall. And the uniforms, of course. He waited till the shuffling and muttering simmered down and everyone was seated before he spoke. He opened by sharing his thoughts on the case. Laid out what they already knew.

"There might be some connection between this guy and the victims we haven't zeroed in on yet. For example, did they patronize the same doctor? Dentist? Church? Maybe had some legitimate reason to be in their neighborhoods."

"He's a freakin' sadist like Dennis Rader," Officer Andy Perkins piped up from the back of the room. Andy was a stocky guy with a shock of red hair and freckles. "BTK."

"Possible," Matt said. BTK, as the killer had tagged himself, was short for bind, torture, and kill. Rader was a vicious killer who simply got off on his victim's pain and terror.

"Although our unsub did give himself the name The Eraser, he doesn't quite fit into the usual pattern. As you all know, Jodie Ballard was born with Downs Syndrome. Dora Nabers also had some mental challenges. And Angela Gray lost a leg to cancer. For some reason known only to him, they had to die because of those challenges. We know Jodie worked at a grocery store over on the west side, so maybe that's where he saw her."

He was reaching, but you had to start somewhere. When an offender has some connection to the victim, you have a chance of ferreting him out. You start with the victim and work backward. You dig into backgrounds and look for a motive. The victims themselves can tell you a lot sometimes. In most cases, murder is a crime of passion, ignited by rage over some issue, real or imagined. Love triangles were right up there. Lust. Greed too. But murderers who kill for their own twisted reasons, often for the simple thrill of it, can be the toughest to nail. They can go on killing for years before they're caught, if ever. Yet these murders weren't entirely random, were they? As he'd pointed out, the victims were required to have some visible flaw that set them apart. Like Melanie, persisted the disturbing thought. He banished it, couldn't let his concern for her become a distraction. It wouldn't help anyone.

The media had a grip on this thing and were riding it for all it was worth. Murder was big news, scary news, especially in a small town like Evansdale which was for the most part a quiet town, a good place to raise your kids. And with this third victim, the pressure to stop this psycho was mounting, not least of which was Matt's stake in his capture. He told his team about Lana Drew's peeping tom. "Might or might not have been our perp. But I've got a strong hunch he was." He believed in his hunches, they were based on long experience.

"We need to take this guy down," someone else said unnecessarily.

Chapter 8

While Matt was wrapping things up at the station, Melanie had just slipped the tape she'd made for him into a padded envelope. She was about to go into the kitchen and make herself a sandwich when the phone rang. By her watch it was 2:05 p.m. She'd been too caught up in her work to eat lunch. She hit the speaker button on the phone. She was getting good at this. "Hello."

"Melanie, it's me," came the familiar voice, "just driving in from the airport. I was on my way to see you if that's okay."

Alan. She smiled to herself, tears springing to her eyes. He was home. Everything was fine again. "Of course it's okay. It's more than okay. I can't wait to see you." After hanging up, she quickly dabbed on lipstick and ran a brush through her hair. She was wearing jeans and a light blue Tommy Hilfiger shirt. Francie had sewn tactile tags on the inside of all her clothes. B for the blue shirt, with the braille symbol beside it. She knew a little Braille, but being fluent wouldn't happen overnight. It would take time like so many other things she needed to learn.

The doorbell rang ten minutes later and for some reason she just stood there in the middle of the floor, feeling anxious. You're over-emoting, Melanie. Relax.

After making sure it was Alan on the other side of the door, she unlocked and opened it.

"Roses," she smiled. "They're beautiful. Thank you."

"How do you...?"

"I can smell them, silly. I still have my other four senses. No other flower smells like a rose. Are they red?"

"Yes," he said, surprised yet again.

"I'm just guessing," she laughed. "Red roses have the strongest perfume, almost spicy." She imagined his handsome face, his Tom Cruise haircut.

"I asked the woman to put them in a vase," he said.

She thought he sounded as nervous as she felt. Why was that? "Come in, please." She took the vase of flowers and sat it on the coffee table, then went into his arms. He held her gingerly as if she were made of glass. She withdrew from his embrace. "That was thoughtful of you, though I do still know where my vases are and I can find the kitchen faucet." She laughed softly, and at the same time, she wanted to cry. Why? What was wrong? "I'm so happy you're here, Alan," she said, meaning it. "I've missed you."

"Me, too. I'm sorry I've not been in touch; I've been so busy with work. How are you? You look great."

There was a small sick flutter in the hollow of her stomach. He hadn't kissed her. Did he think she had become too fragile for loving? Or had he just lost interest? She moved to the sofa. "It's okay. You're here now. Sit down, please. Tell me about your trip."

She felt the cushion sink a little as he sat down beside her, leaving a space between them. "It went well. Great, actually. Closed an important deal."

She nodded. "I'm glad. Then your time was well spent."

"What about you? How are you?" he asked again.

Alan wasn't his usual self either. Conversation always came easy to him. His stock in trade. Smooth, fluid. Together. Now he was repeating himself, struggling with small talk, trying to find words when they should come like the flow of a river. He had said he loved her and asked her to marry him.

"I'm okay. Better now that you're here." The flowers smelled strongly, almost too-sweetly in the room. Anxiety pushed her to her feet. "You must be hungry. What can I get you? I was just about to make myself a tuna salad sandwich. I'm still a bit limited in what I can cook right now but I'll get better. If you don't fancy a sandwich how about scrambled eggs and toast? I've got that down pat."

"Melanie, you don't need to..."

"I know I don't need to. I want to. Alan, please don't treat me like an invalid. I'm perfectly capable of scrambling a couple of eggs. To prove it, I want to show off my new skills. I've been practicing, learning every inch of this house and everything in it. I still mess up, a few stumbles here and there ..." she gave a laugh that had a hollow ring... "but pretty darned good if I do say so myself." She started for the kitchen, a tactic to halt her rambling as much as to serve any other purpose.

"Wait, Melanie. Please."

She stopped and turned around and he finally took her into his arms the way she'd needed him to. But it was too late, like having to ask, and the tears stung hot behind her lids. Something was wrong. So wrong. What was it?

"It's going to be okay, isn't it?" he asked into her new short hairdo, his warm breath like a sigh against her ear. He's scared, she thought. She understood. Of course, she did. She was scared too.

"Given time," she said. "I   think so."

She had heard the fear in his voice, a need for reassurance which immediately transferred to her, and some of her new-found confidence slipped away. Alan was having second thoughts about their relationship. Even knowing that, what he said next didn't fully register for several beats. Tears making him choke out the words, he murmured, "When I saw you standing there before the mirror, looking so lost, unable to see, knowing that you would never..." He stopped in mid-sentence, but not in time. "...In the hospital," he said, grasping at the false words. Faltering.

For a moment, she felt only confusion, sure she must have heard wrong. But the pieces clicked into place, almost with sound, and the truth swept through her veins like a transfusion of ice water. Her hands fell away from the smooth fabric of his jacket. She disengaged herself from him and took a step back. "The only mirror in my hospital room, Alan, was in the washroom and anytime I was in there, the door was closed. Oh, my God. It was you, wasn't it? You're talking about the vanity mirror in my room. You're talking about this house."

"What? No, you don't understand..."

"But I do. I understand perfectly." Her voice was quiet, calm. Belying what she felt inside. Disbelief, mostly. And yet she knew it was true. That she was devastated was an understatement. She was repulsed. Sickened. Betrayed. "It was you who followed me into this house the day I got home from the hospital. You must have called the hospital and they told you I had been released. So you drove over here. You waited out on the sidewalk. You watched me get out of that taxi, go up the steps, tapping my way along with my white cane..." The tears came silently now, flowing down her cheeks and there was nothing she could do about it. "How could you?"

He tried to touch her shoulder, but she jerked away. "Don't."

"Please, I know what you must think. You have to understand..."

"Oh, but I do," she cut in. "I understand better than you know." Despite the tears, her voice remained calm and steady, when what she wanted to do was to scream, to beat him with her fists like she tried to do that day he had been only a malicious entity in her house, a dark shadow seen from the corner of her eye. The day he had touched her face, then walked away. Turned his back on her in the very worst way. She wanted to tear into him, but she didn't. Instead, she said, "I understand that you walked into my bedroom and when I asked who was there, you refused to answer. And kept refusing. I understand that you left me there, hysterical, because I couldn't see who it was. I was terrified. There's a killer out there murdering people like me. Yet you never spoke a word. You just...left."

"Melanie, I'm so sorry, I..."

She could feel her heart splintering into a thousand pieces and knew what it was to have a broken heart. How could he? Why? And yet something inside her had recognized his presence that day, maybe the way his body had shifted the air in front of him. She hadn't smelled his Cartier cologne, she supposed, because the lotion she'd spilled on the vanity had overridden its fragrance. Or if she had smelled it, however faintly, she'd blocked it out, denied it in some deep part of herself. Alan loved her. He couldn't do something so cruel. But he could. He had.

"I just didn't know if..."

"I get that too, Alan. No need to explain yourself. You had doubts and I never would have blamed you for that. I had doubts too. But what you did ... leaving me like that. No, I could never trust you now. Not ever. Who would do that, Alan? Who would be so cowardly?"

"I'm sorry. I still love y..."

"Love me despite my blindness? How noble of you. Just go. Please, just go now."

"Melanie, you can't mean that. You..."

The numbness was leaving her now, replaced with indignance, and fury. Her fists clenched and fire rose to her cheeks. "I never meant anything more in my life. I want you out of here. Now! We're done. And you're off the hook." She wrenched the ring off her finger and thrust it at him. After the briefest pause, he took it. She almost sensed his relief.

"Melanie..."

This time she did scream. "Get out. Go! Now!"

As before, but when his identity was unknown to her, he turned from her and walked to the front door. The door opened and closed. Not a slam, but a soft closing, making it even more final. She locked the door behind him. Her pounding heart slowed, the rage subsiding. The anger seeped away, there was just the pain now. She sagged down on the sofa and let the tears flow. After a moment or two if this, she rose and took the vase of flowers into the kitchen (in what was the best march she could muster), and dumped them, vase and all, into the garbage can. When the lid wouldn't close, she jammed the flowers as far down into the can as they would go, then yanked her hand back suddenly as it drew fire from one of the thorns. "Prick," she said aloud to the silent house as she sucked the offended finger.

And surprised herself by laughing.

Chapter 9

When Matt dropped by later that night, Melanie both surprised and dismayed him by telling him she was planning to reopen her practice in her basement in a couple of weeks. When the hell had she come up with this idea? He didn't want to throw cold water on her plans; he felt like someone had just thrown cold water on him. It just wasn't a good move right now. It was a terrible idea. She was making herself vulnerable to anyone coming in off the street. "I think it's great that you're getting on with your life, Mel," he said carefully. "But don't you think you're pushing it a little? Especially, with this..."

"No, no, I don't," she cut in. "I have to earn my living. I'm a therapist. It's what I do. It's perfect, actually. My lease is just about up on the office downtown, so why not? They're putting a sign in the window for me with the change of location and the new phone number. It just makes sense, Matt. I have a finished basement, and it won't take much work to get it ready. I just need some electrical work done, and my office sound-proofed and that's about it. The rest is cosmetic." She was high on her plans, even animated. He had to admit, he loved seeing her like this. "A coat of paint, carpeting," she went on. "I've made some phone calls and the zoning bylaws allow me to have my practise in my basement. There's even a good-sized parking space in the back. And I won't have to worry about catching buses to get to my place of business. Come on out to the kitchen. I just put the kettle on. Tea? Coffee? I made tea earlier but I let it get cold." This comment seemed more directed at herself than at him. "I've done more work on the profile, and made changes, hope it will be helpful."

No point in arguing further; her mind was made up and he wasn't going to change it. "I know it will, and I'm grateful," Matt said. And he was. Leads called into the station were going nowhere. Not to mention the barrage of complaints about the damn lazy cops who are doing nothing to protect its citizens. The mayor was down the chief's neck and the chief was down his. The city was on terror alert. Anyone with even the slightest infirmity was barricading themselves inside their home. Baseball bats were retrieved from garages and closets and kept within easy reach. Locksmiths were making a killing, so to speak, and dog adoption at the shelter was at an all-time high. He wished he could think of that as a benefit, and for some, it would be, but once this was over, what then? What happened to the poor dogs?

He'd love to know how that name 'The Eraser' got leaked to the press. It made its way into the morning paper. Could be anyone from a cop to one of the secretaries. Regardless, titillating bits had a way of getting out there, inflaming an already inflamed public, and not much you could do about it.

Earlier, he got a call from a cop buddy reporting that a well-dressed man carrying flowers rang her doorbell and was let in. He stayed about twenty minutes. As soon as he heard the description, Matt knew it was Deversen. He didn't know much about Alan Deversen, but he knew he didn't like him. There was something weak-kneed about the guy. He was good-looking; even being a straight guy he could see that, and apparently Deverson had loads of charm, since according to Malanie he was successful in his work which was in sales. That, and the fact that she'd fallen for him. Matt had been less than enchanted the couple of times he'd met him. Other than that, he didn't know Deverson and didn't particularly want to. You're jealous, O'Leary, he told himself. Admit it. Maybe. Probably. But it was more than that.

"Tea would be great," he said as Melanie preceded him into the kitchen, hands held out slightly to her sides as if to put a space between herself and any object she might encounter. An instinctively defensive walk. His eye ran the length of her slender, tapered back, down to the gentle swell of her hips in the jeans, as if with a mind of its own. He reproached himself for his male shallowness. Not in a big way. "You opened the door before you knew it was me," he said, his protective side coming to the fore. "Just an observation."

"You phoned and said you were on your way. Anyway, I recognize the sound of your car. The engine has a lovely purr."

"I'm sure it's not the only one that does. As much as I'd like to believe it." The 1963 Rambler was Matt's only indulgence. He'd bought it a couple of years ago for a great price, drove to Montreal, and brought it back. Since then, he'd put some money and a lot of work into it, happy work, without regret. He'd always had a fondness for the make, which was once the chosen car for cops back in the day.

The sun poured through the kitchen curtains and caught the curve of Melanie's cheek, her lovely neck, which was smooth and pale as alabaster but for the small brown mole there. A vision of phantom hands around her throat covering it sent a chill to his heart and drummed up a rush of anger. "You do need to be more careful, Mel."

As if privy to the awful image in his mind, she said, "Afraid the bogeyman will get me?"

"Don't joke, Mel. That's three murders now."

"I know." She sat a cup of steaming tea before him. "And I fit right into his preferred quarry." The mockery was gone from her voice. "My bad jokes are just me whistling in the dark, Matt." She sighed and shook her head. "That poor woman. Lost her husband, a part of her body. And now her life."

"Yeah." Matt caught a whiff of flowers and noticed the rose sticking out from behind the garbage can. She'd missed it. Well, he had a pretty good idea of what went down here. The way his heart leaped for joy made him feel like a fool. Melanie wasn't interested in him as anything more than a friend; she'd made that clear a long time ago and numerous times since.

She was rummaging in the cupboards. "I'll take the trash out," he said. "Where are the bags?"

"Thanks. Left, bottom drawer." She laughed and there was sadness in the laugh. "Okay, so you know. The engagement's off. Take the vase too if you like, I don't want it in the house. You probably should know; it was Alan who came and left like a ghost in the night. He followed me into the house the day I got home from the hospital."

"You're kidding."

"Nope. But I get it, you know. He didn't bargain for a life with a blind woman and just didn't have the guts to tell me to my face. Anyway, he tripped himself up and I knew it was him. And this conversation is done with."

"Okay." Matt was so stunned that anyone could do something so cruel, let alone the guy who was supposed to love her, he could find no words. And then he got busy thinking of ingenious ways to kill the son-of-a-bitch. Matt had him figured for a jerk but even he hadn't expected him to pull a stunt like that. He knew he probably shouldn't be happy that the engagement was off, but he was. So what kind of a jerk did that make him? She was hurt and upset. "I'm sorry," he said, finally.

"Don't be. As for the real bogeyman, I've not been outside my doors, so it's not likely he's even laid eyes on me, so he has no reason to come calling."

Matt didn't miss the fear beneath the feigned bravado. Nor when she said, "You've got to stop him, Matt."

"That's the intention."

Shaking her head, shoulders sagging, she said, "I know. I'm sorry. Any leads?"

"Maybe a small one. We'll talk about it. First, I want to hear more about you opening your business in the basement in a couple of weeks."

"Not much more to hear. I've hired a receptionist, just out of university. I used to share one with an Ophthalmologist."

"I remember. Didn't take you long."

"Just a phone call, actually. She'd registered for work with unemployment. I interviewed her on the phone and she seems perfect. Kind of an old-fashioned girl, very sweet, and responsible. She was raised by a grandmother who went blind in her later years, so I won't be an oddity."

"Seems like it was meant to be. I'm glad you won't be alone. So what kind of precautions have you taken to protect yourself?" The question had to be asked.

"Double locks on the windows and doors. I'm also considering taking everyone's advice and getting a dog."

"Now you're talking. That's great, Mel. A guide dog?"

"Just a dog. From the shelter. A friend. It will be company for me, and also let me know if anyone's lurking about. Lots of people are adopting dogs lately. I need to get the right one for me. It will also put my father's mind at ease. I know he's worried."

"He's got reason to be. And if I'm scaring you, so be it. You need to be very careful until we nail this guy. In the meantime, we've got a car assigned to your house and I don't want any argument on that."

"You won't get one from me. Matt, I refuse to live my life cowering in fear. It will swallow me whole. But neither am I a fool. Thanks."

She was back to moving about the kitchen like someone who had lost her sight years ago, instead of the few weeks it had been. He watched fascinated as she made the tea, and arranged Oreo cookies on a plate. Matt observed all the little tricks she'd learned in such a short time to compensate for her loss of sight; he was proud of her. He thought about offering to help, but also knew she was showing off for him, and he was content to let her. She'd been practicing.

Melanie sat down across from him, turned those blue eyes on him, and smiled warmly, openly. He felt a sudden fury at whoever did this to her, followed by frustration in knowing they were no closer to finding out who it was. Uncanny, though, how it seemed to him she could see him. But maybe that was just wishful thinking on his part.   Matt told her about Lana Drew's experience with the peeping tom.

"Did she get a good look at him?"

"Not really. A long pale face, and light eyes, but probably not blue. Like rotting ice was how she described them." He also told her about the husband's effort to run him down. "He got away, leaped a fence, he said, so we know he's got to be fairly young. In good shape."

"That follows the profile. Although he may be younger than the average serial, mid to late twenties. Perhaps Lana saw more detail in his face than she knows. If she did then you could consider an artist's sketch. What about hypnosis?"

"There'd need to be more evidence that he wasn't just your regular low-life peeping tom before the station would spend the time or money. Lana's affliction suggests only a possibility that he's the killer, and that's not enough. But good thoughts, Mel."

The clock in the living room began to bong and they waited for it to finish. Eight o'clock. "A present from dad. I always know what time it is." She laughed lightly. "I'm awash in buzzers and bells."

Throughout the bonging, his thoughts shifted back to Deverson. He was thinking how satisfying it would be to show him what it felt like to be afraid. He was some piece of work. It broke his heart to see her like this and struggling so hard to be brave, to move forward. He had a feeling that given time, she was going to be okay.

Given time.

She was holding her cup halfway to her lips, when she said, "So much violence in so little time." A frown furrowed across her smooth forehead. "I wonder if something significant happened in his life recently to trigger this explosion of rage."

"Do we know that it's sudden?" Matt said. "And why against disabled women?" The question was directed as much at himself as Melanie. No matter how many times he asked it, there seemed no clear answer.

"Many people have an aversion to or are even repulsed by people like me, Matt."

"Melanie, I don't..."

"No, it's true. The blind, amputees, and others with disfigurements are often subject to hatred. It's human nature to distrust what's different. To fear it. It's always been so. There was a time when someone like me might have been hidden away, made to feel shame. They were even thought to be possessed by the devil. Or had somehow brought the wrath of God down on themselves. You know better than most that hate crimes are committed against the disabled. I don't know if you ever noticed when you were at the hospital, but there was one nurse who was very uncomfortable around me. Oh, she wasn't obvious about it and always outwardly kind, but I could feel it. I think I was even more relieved than she was when she left the room."

"I didn't know. I'm sorry you had to endure that."

She shrugged. "No big deal. Most of the nurses were great. I'm just giving you an example. And I know I'm not telling you anything you don't know. We live in a society where violence against the disabled, gays, women, the homeless, elderly people, other races, you name it, is common. When we objectify, devalue, and dehumanize people, we all become vulnerable to all manner of abuse."

He nodded. "You're more than just a psychologist, Melanie. You have a special insight into the human psyche. You're extraordinarily sensitive to people. I know that from experience."

"Thanks. That's kind of you to say, Matt."

"I wasn't trying to be kind. It's only the truth."

"Well, I'm flattered. Thank you. It's second nature to me to wonder about human behavior. And I am sure these murders relate in some way to the killer's past. That's always a safe guess, I suppose. More tea?"

"Yes, please." She grasped the handle with thumb and forefinger, touched the rim with the side of her hand, and poured carefully. Eager for anything she could give him, Matt said, "None of the victims were sexually assaulted. We have shared this with the media. What does that tell you?"

She set the teapot down on its thick knit holder, feeling for it first. "That the murders weren't sex crimes would be the obvious answer, I suppose, but that's not necessarily true. Just because there was no intercourse, no penetration doesn't mean there still isn't a sexual component."

"How so?"

"He could be impotent. Or just into disabled women; some men are, as sick as that sounds. So he feels shame for his perversion and takes it out on them. Like killers of hookers. Just a couple of possibles, Matt, but I'm speculating."

"No, please go on."

"Well, we know he doesn't kill them right away. He stalks them first. Makes him feel like some kind of God, with power over life and death. 'I can get to you whenever I want,' he's telling his victims." Matt saw a quiver go through her as if she had somehow tapped into their psycho's consciousness. Not a good place to be, he thought.

"That's all pretty elementary, Matt, I know. I want to think on it more." There was a memory of a past patient that had been nagging her lately. But she wasn't ready to share it yet. She could be way off base.

"Okay. Listen, Mel, you said you haven't been out of the house in a while, so I'm wondering...since I'm off duty tonight, if you might like to take a little drive."

"Oh, Matt, that's sweet of you, but..."

"You got other plans?"

"No, but..."

"Business. Strictly business. I've got a hunch you're going to be the key to solving this case. I brought the murder book. It's gotten thicker since the last murder. I'll read what's been added. Tomorrow I'll record everything you don't already have."

After a hesitation, she said, "Okay. But only if you promise me we'll drive with the windows down for awhile."

"You got it."

"I'll just get my jacket."

* * *

They'd been driving around for half an hour or so, neither of them saying much, both deep into their private thoughts, when she felt the car veer left off the main road. Gravel crunched briefly beneath the wheels and they stopped. "Care for a drink? Listen to some good piano?" Matt asked.

She grinned. "Since we're already here, wherever here is, why not?"

"It's called Bailey's, only been open a few months. One of the guys retired last month and we came here to celebrate. Thought you might like it."

Matt thought right. She did like it. Almost as soon as they were inside, she felt herself relaxing. Someone was playing some very good jazz on the piano, the kind that stirred deep emotions and made you feel mellow. "There's a vacant table at the back," he said. He maneuvered her between the tables, his hand at her waist, the other lightly on her arm.

The place smelled faintly of cedar and malt, a pleasant scent. She felt the cool air from the fan, hearing its soft whirring above her head.

He held out the chair for her and guided her into it. She slid her fingers along the small table's roundness as she sat down. "Only a few people here tonight. A weeknight. What would you like?" Matt asked. Above the music, a faint murmuring of conversation.

"A glass of white wine would be great."

He ordered for them both, deciding on a beer for himself. For the first little while they chatted about this and that. He told her he was thinking about getting a bigger tank and two more fish to keep Rosencrantz and

Guildenstern company. She talked about how much she was looking forward to getting back to work, about how lucky she'd been to get Emma May Wilkins for her receptionist, but soon steered the conversation back to the case. There'd been no further murders since Angela Gray, but they both knew it was just a matter of time until he struck again. The murder book was still locked in the car; he hadn't gotten around to reading the additions to her. She had a feeling he hadn't intended to. He'd bring a new tape tomorrow, he said.

The lack of added information didn't stop her theorizing, however. Matt was a good listener. She had been told she was too, a definite asset in her profession. She was genuinely interested in people and loved nothing more than to help where she could. It was her calling. The calling was never louder. In this instance, Melanie wanted to believe they'd get this predator off the streets and that she would play a small part in that, hopefully before the next woman was chosen to die. Or did he already have her in his sights? If she could nail down the motivation for the murders, she thought it could make all the difference in stopping him. But she wasn't sure she had. Lately, she'd been remembering a young girl, a patient who came to her when she first opened her practice, and her thoughts on motive had taken a different direction. Her patient had a sister who was paraplegic and serious troubles had evolved from that. Both at home and school.

Her thoughts were interrupted as the waiter came with their drinks. Melanie waited until he was gone before she picked up her glass of wine, and said, "I was probably too technical on the tape, Matt, though I tried to keep the psychological jargon to a minimum." She decided to put off telling him about her patient. It might just muddy already muddy waters. Too, she wanted to mull it over a bit more. "Anyway, to summarize, I'm thinking the person you're looking for is someone on the quiet side but manages to blend in. He's easy to be around, pleasant, and eager to please. Intelligent, though he probably did poorly in school. He has a menial job, and little power there or in his personal life. I believe it's why he stalks his victims first. It gives him the illusion of power. This is the basic profile for serial killers, I know, but it's not always the case. Some have very big jobs and are highly thought of. Consider rapist, serial killer Russell Williams."

"Yeah, he was a piece of work. The guy was a Colonel in the armed forces, base commander at CFB Trenton. Also, a decorated military pilot who flew Canadian Forces VIP aircraft for dignitaries like Queen Elizabeth and the Prime Minister of Canada."

"Even Wayne Gacy, though nowhere near the level of Russell, was into politics and had his photo taken with celebrities," Melanie said, "including Rosalynn Carter. I think in this case, though, the profile will come close. He likes his prey to be aware of him, even if only at a sensory level. Enough to disturb their sleep. Maybe even their waking hours."

"You're making him real, Mel. He's not a ghost anymore."

"Well, it's pretty general stuff I've given you. But thanks. I could be way off on this like I said. I've speculated and made some assumptions. Aside from that, you said you know from the shoeprint outside Angela Gray's kitchen window that he wears a size 11 shoe. And according to the woman who caught him staring in her window, he's narrow of face, pale, and her husband attested to the fact that he's fairly young, agile, seeing how he vaulted that fence. Like I said, probably mid to late twenties, even early thirties. If he is the killer, and I think we both believe he is."

"You know, Mel, coming in here was intended to take your mind off this case for a little while. I figured you could use the break. I know I could. But maybe that's not possible right now. For either of us." When he spoke again there was a new note of optimism in his voice. "We found that dark blond hair at the scene of Angela Gray's murder. Longish. It was on the shoulder of her robe. I probably told you. Now all we need is someone to match that hair and shoeprint to."

"True." She smiled. "But I'd say you've already put bone and flesh on this ghost, without me."

They left a half hour later. Matt had an early appointment in the morning. "I'm meeting with a woman who thinks her brother might be our guy. Says he hates all women. Amazing how many do. Fortunately not enough to make them killers."

"I think your job has skewed your vision of people, Matt. There are lots of good guys out there. Look at you."

She was teasing him and he knew it. Maybe flirting with him? Matt was one of the good ones. Be careful, Melanie. He's a good friend. Just a friend. And that's all he can ever be. She was just feeling vulnerable right now that was all.

Chapter 10

The Eraser was riding by her house earlier just as the door opened and the blind woman appeared on the arm of the man he recognized as Detective Matt O'Leary. He kept on pedaling, not daring more than a glance in their direction.

The detective had been in the news a lot lately, in the newspaper and on TV. In one segment, a reporter shoved a mike in the open window and was hammering him with questions. Sonny was sitting in the living room with his mother, watching it on TV. His mother remarked that she hoped they'd get the monster who murdered those poor women. He felt her looking at him when she said it, but he didn't meet her eyes, just mumbled his agreement.

The couple descended the steps and got into the dark car parked at the curb, the cop hovering over the therapist like a mother hen. He dared not slow down, but he could see them in his rearview mirror. He drove around the block, stopping at the back of her building. There was little traffic. He straddled the bike, feet on the pavement, and surveyed the entryway. Dr. Melanie Snow, Therapist, the sign above the door said.

She'd been easy to find. There'd been only one Melanie in the phone book under therapists. He went to her office downtown that first week but it had been closed. A few days ago there was a flyer in the window that gave this address. Melanie Snow. Snow. There was purity in the name. Snow hid the dirty slush in early spring. Old tires, and other filth that accumulated over seasons. Snow covered a myriad of sins; would it cover his? Was this a sign that Emmie forgave him? Would she stay dead this time?

Sometimes he got confused about the purpose of his mission. Because if it was Emilene returned in one more of her various disguises, how did that add up to his being chosen by the almighty to erase them? It was hard for him to reconcile the two. It didn't make sense in a way. And in another way, it made perfect sense. She couldn't enter the bodies of her hosts without their willingness, could she? So they were co-conspirators in her mischief and must die. Yes, they had invited her in. He couldn't think too much about it because it just made his head hurt when he did and then he couldn't think at all. He knew though that he could change lives for the better. To lift burdens. Hadn't he changed his own life? His mother's? When he thought of his mother, a heavy sadness settled on his shoulders like a grey shroud. He shook it off as he took in the house and its surroundings. Noted the fenced-in back yard, the big doghouse. He'd have to find a way to deal with the dog problem. And he would. His gaze traveled to the far window on the main level; he wondered if it was her bedroom window.

From the corner of his eye, he caught cruiser lights in the rearview mirror. The police car had just rounded the corner and fear shot through him like a hot arrow. He pretended to check his tire, then hopped on his bike and cleared out of there.

He wasn't a bad person, not the monster the papers and the talking heads on TV were saying he was, he thought. The police would have read his note by now. Would they understand his mission? Of course, they wouldn't. He had been foolish to send it. They wouldn't see those women as he did, sucking energy from those around them, ruining lives. Melanie Snow needed people just to exist. She needed them to prop her up. Now there was an interesting phrase: prop her up. Like Emiline had needed to be propped up, literally.

The heart of the matter was, Melanie Snow was a mistake, whether by birth or accident. A blunder. And she must be erased. It should have been done by now. What was he waiting for?

Soon, he thought. Soon.

Chapter 11

Sometimes when Melanie woke in the morning, she'd forget for a moment that she was blind and fully expect to see her room in all its glory; her blond oak dresser that she'd sanded and finished, and above it the watercolor of the orange tabby cat she'd bought from a local artist in the park last summer. Then reality would wash over her like a wave of sickness, sucking her down into a mire of depression and she would just lie there and cry, or wail her despair at the world, and God. But she tried to do this as little as possible. It didn't help anything and served only to keep her from going forward. This morning, though, she felt optimistic. Being with Matt last night, even with the conversation dealing mainly with the business of a killer being on the loose, had been pleasant. If she were being honest with herself, it was more than pleasant. He was great company. She had liked sitting across from him, sipping wine, talking. Hearing the murmur of conversation around her, the bluesy tunes issuing from the piano both stirred her blood and relaxed her at the same time. Or maybe she'd just had too much wine.

He was coming over again tomorrow night and she realized she was looking forward to his visit more than she probably should. She had to be careful about that. The last thing she needed was more complication in her life.

There was a time when Matt was attracted to her, she knew that. During the custody case in which a father had shot his two children to death and then turned the gun on himself, Matt had come to her as a patient. Finding those little boys dead in their beds, amidst blood and brain tissue, had done a number on him. Melanie was occasionally called upon to work with policemen and firefighters who were having difficulties psychologically and emotionally, and Matt had been one of them. He became infatuated with her, but she recognized it for what it was   'transference of affection', (known in the profession as feelings of love for one's therapist) and was careful not to take it seriously and made a point of discouraging any overtures. Anything else would have been unethical. Being the sensitive guy he was, he didn't need to be hit over the head with a hammer to get the message. But she treasured his friendship. The small niggling voice inside reminded her that the attraction hadn't been totally on Matt's side. Yes, she'd have to be careful of that.

Besides, he was seeing someone at the time. Maybe still was. Gretchen, was it? Not blond, as the name would suggest, but a stunning redhead with a body meant for catwalks. Once, toward the end of the sessions, she came to an appointment with him and sat in the waiting room, which surprised her. Matt was such a private person. Melanie remembered feeling a twinge of jealousy at the time and wondered if it had betrayed her. She didn't think so; she was a pretty good cover-upper. But enough of that, she thought, throwing off the blankets and getting out of bed.

She dressed in the pantsuit she'd worn home from the hospital. She and Francie were going to spend a couple of hours shopping, maybe lunch downtown, then head over to the dog pound to pick up Sadie. She'd decided that with Francie beside her, she wouldn't need the cane. Though she didn't exactly feel like a kid on Christmas morning, she felt good. Better than she had for awhile. Hopeful. Excited about reopening her practice. Also excited about getting Sadie. The name Sadie rang in her mind. A nice sound.

When she'd phoned the shelter last week and described what sort of dog she was looking for, the woman told her about Sadie, a terrier/lab mix that had just come in. They'd had others but adoption was up since those terrible murders. Melanie said she'd take her. Sight unseen seemed redundant. She gave her her credit card number to hold her. And also made a small donation, wishing she could afford more.

* * *

"An elderly woman owned her," Melanie told Francie at lunch. "The woman at the shelter said Sadie was very gentle and smart."

"She sounds perfect," Francie said. "When you phoned me about getting Sadie, I think I was excited about her as you were. Funny, though, I figured you'd want a guide dog."

"I thought about it. A lot, actually. But aside from the fact that it would take a year or two at least before I could get one, they have to first train the dog, then you with it. Seems complicated, not to mention expensive. Anyway, I don't think I'm a good candidate. Knowing me, I'd be feeding it when I shouldn't be, playing with it, and making a pet out of what is supposed to be a working dog. I just want a mutt. A companion."

"Did Sadie's owner die?"

"No. She had a stroke. She's in a nursing home now." They both fell quiet. Then Francie said, "That's so sad. But she couldn't have a better new owner for her friend than you, kiddo."

They were sitting in a small cafe downtown, still chatting about the dog. They'd be picking her up from the shelter

252

this afternoon. Melanie was wearing the new glasses she'd bought at the Pharmacy earlier. Francie said they suited her face and didn't look like a blind person's glasses. "No way anyone would know you're blind," she said. They talked about one thing and another, including Francie's two boys going off to hockey camp for the summer. Francie sang Norm's praises and Melanie tried not to feel jealous. In truth, she couldn't have been more pleased for her. Francie deserved all the happiness life could give her.

Norm worked as an x-ray technician at the hospital and was a teddybear of a guy. He adored Francie, bringing them around to the subject of Alan, Melanie's almost second husband. No way to avoid it. But she was grateful to have a good friend she could talk to about what happened, and Francie being Francie, wasn't shy about pumping her for details. Just like when they were kids. And Melanie didn't hold back.

"No, I haven't seen or heard from him since I gave him back his ring and sent him packing," she said, in answer to her question.

"You did right. He's a jerk."

"Yeah. I couldn't agree more." Nothing better than having a good pal who will trash your old boyfriend. Even Nick Slater, Melanie's ex managed to find his way into the conversation. The last she heard, he was still single and making his living in real estate. She'd seen his ad in the paper from time to time. As for her, her relationship history had been pretty well mapped out at twelve, she reasoned. She'd felt betrayed by her father and so picked men that were sure to betray her. Psyche 101.

They were munching tossed salads and sipping iced-tea amidst the pleasant sounds of soft chatter, mostly female, the clatter of cutlery, and laughter. Melanie speared a piece of what she expected to be a tomato and which turned out to be zucchini. She managed not to grimace, though she had nothing against zucchini if it didn't sneak up on you.

"Do you miss him?" Francie asked.

"Alan? At first. I guess I missed who I thought he was. But I think at some level I'd been preparing myself for a breakup so it didn't come as a total shock. Only the way he handled it. Getting over him won't be a problem."

All she had to do was remember how she felt that day: like a two-year-old abandoned by her mom in a dark place, where demons with red glowing eyes and clawed hands, crept ever closer. And even that didn't come close to the terror she'd felt. One thing she did know: she never wanted to feel that way again. Better to be dead than to cower helplessly in fear for the rest of her life. She didn't tell Francie about being curled up on that floor in a fetal position, sobbing like a child, though maybe she guessed it. Melanie couldn't dwell on the memory too long without writhing in her very soul. Francie didn't push.

"How are you doing?" was all she said. Her voice had dropped discreetly and Melanie knew she was leaning toward her. "Fine."

"No, I mean really. How are you emotionally?"

"Well, depends on when you catch me. Sometimes I'm so angry I want to beat someone with a stick. I still get frustrated, and scared… but mostly I'm okay. Or getting there. Good friends help."

"I'm glad. Like the title of that old TV show advised: 'One day at a time'. I think it's great you're re-opening your practice. Having your office set up in the basement is the perfect solution."

"Yeah, I thought so too. Opening in a week, actually. Uncle Carl and his partner are doing some work down there today, sound-proofing my office. The electricians are coming tomorrow to modify a few things. I'm also having classical music piped in. Some final touches."

"You're getting to know your Uncle Carl again. That's so cool."

"Yeah. He's been to lunch a couple of times. I never knew he was gay. Why would I? I was a kid when Carl used to come around. That's probably why dad doesn't feel comfortable around him, being the homophobe he is."

"A lot of his generation are like that. But despite that, I always liked your dad. Except when he sided with what's-her-name."

Melanie laughed. She was throwing her a few crumbs after the house-cleaning issue. "Carl and mom used to play together as kids. He tells me little stories about her and it's so great imagining her as a little girl. It brings her closer to me."

"Yeah. You two were close. But life goes on. It's terrific that you're moving ahead with your life, Mel."

"Well, I've always believed that taking any action is better than wallowing in self-pity. They say on the other side of fear is liberty. So I'm practicing what I preach." She managed a grin.

"You're doing what you should. You're a great therapist, Mel."

"Thanks. Matt was nice enough to say that too, and I guess I'm needy enough to want to hear it. At first, I was gung-ho about opening my practice downstairs. Then I started doubting myself and wondering if anyone would even want to come to a blind therapist, but I think I'll be as busy as ever if the phone calls are any indication. I do wonder how difficult it's going to be though. I'm used to looking at people when I talk to them when they talk to me. Watching their eyes, their body language to get at a truth even they might not aware of. I can't do that now."

"I never thought of it that way before. That's right, you won't be able to see them." She was quiet for a moment, then, "I guess you'll just have to listen harder. Sadie can be your co-therapist."

Melanie laughed. It was good to laugh again. To be here with Francie, having lunch, just like before the accident. She felt almost normal."

"A dog will be good protection along with being a buddy," Francie said. "I remember you had a dog when we were kids. You called her Candy. She was black and white and sweet as her name."

"Yeah, I've been thinking of her too. A Heinz-57. She ran out in the street that day straight into the path of a truck."

"You blamed yourself."

"Well, it was my fault. We were playing fetch and the ball went out in the road and she ran after it."

"God, how you cried -- like for days. There was no consoling you."

It was true. She had loved that dog, they were the best of pals. She told Candy all her secrets, cried into her furry body, and vented her frustrations. Melanie could almost resurrect the pain she'd felt that day seeing her dog lying on the road, bleeding. "I tried to comfort her and she licked my hand. As if she were trying to comfort me. And then she was gone." A lump formed in her throat.

"It was at the beginning of summer vacation," Francie said. "I remember your mom died that fall."

The lump in her throat got bigger and it was hard to swallow the piece of cucumber she'd just put into her mouth. "Yeah. A long time ago. Let's talk about something else, okay? Like the fact that I've got a great fenced-in yard with a nice big doghouse awaiting its new occupant. Carl painted Sadie's name on it. Although much of the time, she'll be either in the office or upstairs with me."

"This is going to be one lucky dog," Francie said. "What time did you say you're supposed to pick her up? It's just past one."

"One-thirty." They paid their checks and left.

Chapter 12

The cacophony of barking in the animal shelter was almost a roar and seemed to come from everywhere, echoing off walls and ceilings. The place smelled musky, reeking of animal stress, born of fear and confusion. Some of these animals would be euthanized, but maybe not so many now that adoptions were up. She wished she could have taken them all home, but she could at least save one. She could give one dog a good home. The woman had gone to get Sadie, who she had said would be a fine companion for Melanie. Hearing the heavy panting as the dog panted nearer to her, she felt an immediate anxiousness.

"Sadie's four years old this fall. Let her sniff your hand. She's very gentle like I told you on the phone, although she's a bit nervous right now."

Melanie held out her hand, palm down, and felt the warm rough tongue lick the back of her hand. She crouched down and patted her, feeling the animal's body trembling beneath her hand. Poor girl. She has no idea what's going on, Melanie thought, her own anxieties fading with her concern for Sadie.

"She does seem sweet-natured," Francie said beside her. "She's caramel-colored with white patches, Mel. The perfect size. Liquid brown eyes. She could use a bath though. Whew."

"Just didn't get around to it yet," the woman said defensively. "We've been so busy. As I mentioned on the phone, Sadie belonged to an elderly woman who is no longer able to care for her. Even before the stroke she was quite ill and wasn't able to give Sadie the same quality of care as before. The daughter couldn't take her in. Sadie, I mean. Or the mother, come to that," she half mumbled to herself. She sounded stressed out to Melanie. "I haven't even had time to put out an ad for her yet. If you decide you want her, I'll have someone bathe..."

"Oh, no, I've already decided I want her," Melanie interrupted. "Of course I do." She already felt a connection to Sadie and almost panicked at the thought of losing her before they even got a chance to know one another. "I'll bathe her myself. It will be fun and give us a chance to bond. She needs to get used to me first, though. I'm sure she's missing her owner terribly."

She felt sad for the woman who had owned her and was now in a nursing home, just a different kind of prison from this one as far as Melanie was concerned. At least she could spring Sadie. I'll take good care of her for you, she promised the woman she had never met and probably never would. On the other hand...

"Go ahead and walk her down the corridor and back," the woman said, putting the leash in Melanie's hand. "There's nothing in your way."

They walked a few steps up and down the narrow floor. Holding onto the leather leash, she could feel Sadie's anxiety and was sure Sadie could sense hers. She was eager to get home, where they could get to know one another without anyone else around. Francie filled out the papers and Melanie signed them and paid the required fee, then they left. It was good to get out in the fresh air and sunshine again. To be under the wide open sky. She was positive Sadie shared her sentiments.

*   *   *

Despite it being her first day home Sadie allowed Melanie to bathe her. She was edgy at first. Melanie could feel her body shaking beneath her hands, but after a few minutes of getting a deep soapy massage from her new mistress, and listening to baby talk, the shaking stopped and she actually seemed to enjoy it.

Sadie was by nature calm and intuitive. The woman at the shelter said she was part lab, so maybe, with patience and work, she could be trained to be a sort of guidedog. By bedtime that first night home they had bonded and instead of sleeping in the new bed she had bought for her, she lay down on the scatter rug at the side of Melanie's bed and heaved a long sigh, as if she had come a long way to find contentment. Soon she was snoring softly. It was a comforting sound and made Melanie smile. And for now that was enough. She was a presence. A warm and soothing spirit. I'm not alone, she thought, as she drifted off to sleep.

Sometime in the night Melanie was awakened by Sadie's growls rumbling deep in her belly. Melanie reached down and stroked her and murmured to her and was rewarded with a warm, moist lick to her inner wrist. The growling stopped but after a couple of minutes, resumed. Suddenly, Sadie leapt to her feet and gave a couple of barks.

Melanie sat up in bed. "What's wrong, girl? What did you hear?"

She listened, but could hear nothing except for the occasional hiss of traffic out on the back street. Probably raccoons rummaging in the garbage can for scraps, she told herself, but a ripple of fear washed through her just the same. She reached for the phone on her dresser and held her thumb over 911 button. But she heard nothing else and after a while closed the phone and put it back on the dresser. She patted Sadie who had already settled down on the mat again. "Maybe you just had a bad dream, eh girl. Everything's different now, isn't it. Yeah, I know what that feels like."

Sadie thumped a tail on the floor. A soft thump, unconvinced that it was just a dream.

While Sadie went back to snoring, Melanie lay fully awake in the bed, ears atuned to every sound in the night. The whisper of passing cars outside her window, the creaks and groans of the house settling. Normal sounds you often hear in the small hours somehow took on an ominous feel. She thought how wonderful it would be to be able to turn on a lamp and see what was around her. To see Sadie. A normal everyday thing she took for granted in the years she had her sight. It was near dawn when she finally fell back to sleep and woke a couple of hours later with Sadie's nose nudging her arm.

Chapter 13

Detective Matthew O'Leary felt like they were all sitting on a time-bomb waiting for the killer to strike again. With many citizens demanding police protection, and Melanie opening up her practice, he could no longer justify to the powers that be the special considerations for Mel and he was feeling more than a little uneasy about her situation. He was driving home from a meeting and decided to give her dad a call. He wasn't sure why he wanted to see Mr. Snow, only that he needed to talk to someone who cared about her as much as he did. They had met a few times at the hospital and he seemed like a good guy. He knew Melanie would have his head on a platter if she knew what he was up to, but he'd just have to risk it. Especially now that she was opening her practice in her home. Though she'd had new bolts installed on the door leading upstairs and into the kitchen, a determined killer could always find a way inside. As a special favor a couple of the guys were still driving by her house at night, keeping an eye out, but it would not be enough to ensure her safety. He was glad she'd decided to get a dog. A barking, growling dog could make a potential intruder hesitate and maybe move on.

Ted Snow sounded pleased to hear from him. Matt asked on the phone if he had a few minutes to talk, and he replied that he had whatever time Matt needed. Twenty minutes later Matt was sitting across from the man in the living room of his small bungalow on the outskirts of Evansdale.

"Thanks," Matt said, taking the earthenware mug of coffee he offered, and thought he smelled something a little stronger than coffee rising out of the dark brew. Ted Snow limped slightly as he sat down in the chair, gestured Matt to the other one. He knew from Melanie that her father was a retired bus driver and that the job had left him chronic back problems.

"Doreen's visiting her sister," he said, letting him know they wouldn't be disturbed and that Matt could talk freely. "Laced that coffee with a little brandy," he grinned.

He rarely drank on the job, not for years now, but he couldn't see himself refusing the coffee, spiked though it was. "Thanks, I can use it."

They were sitting on big stuffed burnt orange chairs angled toward one another, a glass-topped coffee table between them.

"I'm not going to hedge here, Mr. Snow. As you know there's a killer out there and I think Melanie could be in danger." It occurred to him to tell him about the stunt the old boyfriend had pulled, but decided it wasn't his place. Anyway, it was better left in the past.

"I'm well aware of that, Matt." Ted snow's hair was almost as white as his name. His face was lined and the worry was evident in his blue eyes. Matt didn't like being the one to add to those worries, but it was important that everyone close to her realize how vulnerable she was right now and do whatever was possible to protect her until they had this animal locked up.

"I'm not sure what more I can do, Matt. I'm glad you're there for her, though. I didn't see too much of the boyfriend in the hospital. There's something about that guy I don't cotton to."

"That's over, I think." Despite himself, he ended up telling him what happened.

"Bastard," Ted spat, his face reddening. "I dropped in later that day, not long after you left, I believe, and she seemed fine. But maybe I wasn't paying close enough attention. I just figured the anxiousness had all to do with   with the blindness. She didn't mention any intruder of course. She wouldn't. Not to me. I ... I've let her down too many times when she was growing up, I'm afraid." He swallowed hard then took a swig of his coffee as if to wash down some bitter truth. Matt guessed he really needed the fortification. He knew the feeling. He set the mug on the glass coffee table, sliding a coaster under it, and looked at him squarely. "If you have any suggestions, Matt, I'm listening. Melanie won't come here. Not that I blame her. My daughter and my wife get along reasonably well these days, but I don't see them living together, though to Doreen's credit she's offered to turn the study into a guest room for Melanie. But it would just sit empty. And I doubt my daughter will let some stranger come live with her either, though I'd be more than happy to pay for it."

Matt doubted retired city bus drivers were all that flush with money.

"Melanie has always been a girl who likes her space," Ted Snow said.

"I've gathered that," Matt replied. "We're keeping an eye on her place but the department's short-handed, especially now with the recent cutbacks. Not to mention all the deserving citizens demanding protection. And of course there's an avalanche of tips to follow up on, so it's doubly busy. I just think if everyone..."

"I get it, Matt. Of course I'll do what I can short of tying her up and bringing her here. Now that she's opened her practice in her basement, there'll be all sorts of people coming and going. How can you monitor that situation?"

"I guess you can't," Matt said, and realized the truth of it.

"You care for her, don't you? That's why you're here."

"I do, Sir. Very much."

"I'm glad. You seem like a nice young fella. So do I. I love my daughter and I obviously want her to be safe. At first I hadn't even thought about that madman out there killing women in connection with Melanie. As naive as it sounds, I hadn't thought that she would be in any danger from him. I guess I just have a hard time thinking of her as disabled. She's always been such an independent girl."

"That hasn't changed."

"No. But she is disabled, isn't she?" His Adam's apple rose and fell. His blue eyes swam with tears. Anger laced his words. "I don't suppose you're any closer to finding the bastard who blinded her?"

An accusation. He knew Matt didn't. What he really meant was why don't you assholes get off your donut-fat duffs and find him.

"I wish I could say yes, Ted. I wish it more than you know. One of the witnesses got a glimpse of him, but not enough details there even for a composite drawing. I guess you know all that from the media. We don't have a license number, not even a partial. This town is filled with dark vans. And it's highly possible the perp isn't even from here, just passing through. But we haven't given up looking, I promise you that. Melanie's car burned up in the fire but some of that maroon paint had to have been scraped off in the impact. Honda Civic maroon. It would be great if..."

"If someone saw a dark van with transfers of maroon paint on the right front bumper and wheelwell," Ted finished with sad humor. "Yeah, that would be great, Matt. It surely would." He sounded about as optimistic of that happening as Matt felt. A long shot to say the least. Even if paint had ended up on the van, it's a good bet it was sprayed over the same day.

"Hang in there," Melanie's father said. "And don't worry. I won't tell her you were here. As far as Deverson's concerned I'm just relieved he's out of the picture. No need to let her know I know."

"Thanks. Appreciated."

"Not a problem. I know my little girl. She'd be sorely ticked at you for upsetting the old man. She may not trust me wholly, but she's my kid. She loves her old dad even if she doesn't always like him. Hell, I don't always like him." He managed a grin despite the worry still etched in his face and Matt didn't miss the way his mouth crooked slightly at one corner, the way Melanie's did when she smiled.

At the front door, Ted Snow said, "Thanks, Matt. Thanks for caring."

"It's not a chore, Mr. Snow, I promise you."

He nodded. "Somehow I think I knew that. It's Ted. Okay? You and I are friends."

He grasped Matt's extended hand as if it were a lifeline, and Matt felt the heat of the man's emotions through his grip.

Chapter 14

Allison Greer was Melanie's third and last appointment of her first day back to work. After years of physical and mental abuse from her husband, Allison had finally gotten up the courage to leave and take her little boy Kevin with her. She took out a restraining order against him but told Melanie she was still getting hangup calls, but from a blocked number. "And sometimes he sits across the street in his car and looks up at the window," she said anxiously.

Melanie told her to be careful. An unnecessary warning, but she'd felt an urgency about giving it. "The most dangerous time for a woman is when she's leaving the relationship," she said. "I know you know that." She could sense her fearful nod.

"I know it's Ed," she said. "Sometimes when I look out the window I see his car parked across the street. He just sits there long enough to make sure I see him, then takes off before the cops can get there. It's his word against mine."

Melanie suggested she be ready next time with a video camera.

"Yeah, that's a good idea. I was hoping he'd stop on his own, just tire of all the drama and move on but it's not happening."

Melanie hoped he would too, but she wasn't overly confident it would happen. She knew his type. He was a man who needed control over the woman in his life and Allison had taken that control back from him, leaving him reeling.

The first time she saw Allison, she had a shiner and a split lip. But you could still see that she was a pretty woman with lustrous dark hair, a nice figure, and little idea of her attractiveness. Her husband had done a good job at whittling away at her self-esteem, making her believe no one else would want her. He also promised her that if she ever left him, he'd kill her. Would he? Melanie wondered. Or was it just talk? You could never be sure until the unthinkable thing happened.

"How are you doing, Dr. Snow?" Allison asked. "I'm so sorry about what happened to you. I couldn't believe it when I read it in the paper."

"I got your lovely card, Allison. Thank you. And I'm okay. Working on it, anyway. Making my peace, as best I can. But you're not paying out good money to listen to my problems."

"No. I want to hear. You're more to me than just my therapist, you know. You're my friend. I couldn't have gotten through all this without you, Dr. Snow. I'm a different person because of you."

"It's you who deserves the credit; you did the work to bring the change about. But I'm glad I could help. And it's Melanie, okay?"

"Melanie," she repeated almost shyly. "You know it sounds crazy and I hope you don't mind my saying so, but being blind gives you a sort of -- mystique. You have an all-knowing aura about you now. Like you can see out of those blue eyes into a person's soul as well as her mind. Even more than you normally do."

"Really?" Melanie sat back in her new swivel chair to contemplate Allison's words. She grinned. "You mean like a fortune teller or clairvoyant?"

"Yeah, like that. Does that sound crazy?"

"No, not too. I rather like the idea of appearing all-knowing." She waggled her fingers at Allison, chanted an eerie 'woo oo woo oo,' and they both laughed. "Didn't see how there could be a positive spin to being blind," Melanie said. "So - tell me about the new guy."

A pause. "How did you know?"

"I'm all-knowing, remember. No, just kidding. I hear it in your voice. Despite being hassled by your ex, you sound happy. There's a new brightness in your voice. I could even hear it in your step when you came in the door."

"He's nice. Not as good-looking as Ed, but he's gentle and funny. I feel safe with him. We're like - friends, you know."

Melanie warned her to be careful and also to get that video of him stalking her so she'd have proof to show the police. "Make sure it's dated," she said, as she followed her to the door.

"What about you? I-- uh -- noticed you're not wearing your diamond."

"Ah. Observant."

"Well, it was a pretty big diamond," she giggled. "Hard not to."

"Yeah, it was nice, wasn't it. Well, as you've surmised, that's over. Just didn't work out."

She'd had time to take it in and understood now why Alan did what he did that day. He hadn't planned it that way, she was sure; he wasn't a cruel man generally. But when he saw her standing in front of the mirror, seeing her reflection and knowing she couldn't see it, it creeped him out. He panicked. He probably wanted to say something to her and then he'd just missed too many beats of silence, and he couldn't bring himself to speak. Yes, she understood. She almost wished she didn't have a penchant for seeing things from more than one point of view. Didn't mean she liked him any better.

She felt Sadie shift position on the floor and let out a half-yawn. "Okay if I pat her?" Allison asked.

"Sure. I know you're an animal lover so I kept her in here with me for your session. Some people are nervous around dogs, or allergic. Emma, my new receptionist, always asks first. That door behind me leads right out into the yard."

"She's really nice, your new receptionist. I like her better than the old one. Pretty, too."

Melanie envisioned Emma. Pretty, as Allison said, but probably not aware of it. Light brown hair, green eyes, Emma had told her when she asked. Almost as tall as Melanie, went maybe 130 pounds. Dressed conservatively. Skirts, white blouses. She kept a cardigan draped over the back of her chair. Melanie's hand had fallen upon it once when she was reaching for her coffee. Bet she keeps hand lotion in the drawer. Probably Jergens. Something old soul about her.

"Cool. Sort of like a real doggie door. Sadie must be wonderful company for you."

"Oh, she is that for sure." Melanie gave the dog a scratch behind her silky ears to let her in on the conversation. She felt the warmth of her body gently press against her leg.

"It -- it must be so hard, being blind."

"It's a challenge, but you play the cards you're dealt. I'm pretty organized and that helps. And I have a friend who helped me rearrange my closet for funtionality. She stuck little labels on the inside of my clothes with raised letters for color -- 'W' for white, 'B' for blue and so on. And you can tell the texture of fabric by feel. I'm still learning lots of little techniques to help me."

"I think you're so brave, Doc...Melanie. I think I'd go mad if I went blind."

"Well, you only think so. But you wouldn't."

"I always wanted to ask a blind person: when you dream..."

"I dream in color the same as I did when I could see," she said before Allison could finish. It was the first time she'd been asked the question, probably not the last. Funny, she herself had never given it any thought before the accident. "And that's because I had my sight for most of my life. If I had been born blind, I expect my dreams would be made up of other senses rather than visual - smells, sounds and that sort of thing."

"Yeah, I guess. Makes sense."

The bell dinged lightly. Time was up. "I'm not going to charge you for this session, Allison. We mostly talked about me. We'll call it a neighborly visit." She expected one or two of her patients came just out of curiosity and that she might not see them again. Allison wasn't one of them. She smiled as she walked her patient to the door. "You be careful now. Keep your cellphone close to you, and remember to get that video."

"I will. Thanks, Melanie."

After Allison left, Melanie took Sadie outside and led her to the far corner of the yard by the fence to do her business. Melanie was exhausted and had a slight headache.

Surprising how draining it could be when you were intensely aware of every step you took, every move you made, hour after hour. Even listening to inflections in a voice took intense concentration, always while trying to appear as you were before the blindness, when in reality nothing was the same. On the upside, she was managing pretty well, even with Sadie. She was keeping all her ducks in a row, so to speak, even if she couldn't see them. She could even tell when Sadie had to go number two by laying a hand on her rump, which made it relatively easy to scoop it up and drop the bag in the garbage bin. The mundane chores sometimes took the longest to conquer. But Sadie was her responsibility and she didn't mind the less pleasant tasks in the least.

This done, they played a little fetch with her blue and white ball which provided the exercise Sadie needed. She'd been thinking lately of getting her a special harness and venturing outside, but she knew that would be premature. She needed to get in lots of practice at home first; she had already ordered a couple of audiobooks on the subject. Sadie would do fine. She was special.

Chapter 15

Emma loved working for Doctor Snow. It was sad what happened to her but you could tell she was determined not to let it stop her from living her life. She was always here early. Right now it was just past eight o'clock in the morning and Emma watched at the window as her employer, dressed in jeans and a yellow tee-shirt, tossed the ball to Sadie, who raced after it. What a lovely looking woman she was, even without a drop of makeup.

Emma frowned, noticing that the doctor had gone very still, just standing there holding the ball in her hand. She seemed to be staring at something on the other side of the fence out on the sidewalk, her head slightly cocked. Emma tried to see what she was looking at but the window was at the wrong angle to let her see out onto the street. Sadie was watching too. She let out a short bark, her tail straight up, not wagging.

Behind Emma, the coffee perked with little popping noises, filling the office with its rich aroma. She'd come in and have a cup of coffee then go upstairs to change into appropriate clothes for the office.

Whoever it was out on the street was gone now and they were back to their game of fetch. Dr. Snow threw the ball and Sadie brought it back and dropped it at her mistress' feet. When the ball rolled away, Sadie went after it and pretty much put it in her Dr. Snow's hand. She was looking up at the doctor with those soulful eyes, tail wagging happily. Emma was sure Sadie knew she'd been rescued and was saying thank you in the only way she knew how. You could see it in the way she looked at the doctor with such devotion. Emma believed dogs had great understanding, even if they didn't have the human words to convey it. Sadie and Dr. Snow had formed a real friendship.

There was something regal about her boss, a certain dignity in her blindness. An air of independence that her grandmother never had in those last years of her life. She wouldn't venture outside at all unless she was on Emma's arm. Of course her grandmother had been much older when she went blind. She was also of a different generation. Emma wished more than anything for one more walk with her.

Doctor Snow had asked on their first close-up interview if she could touch her face, and Emma had no problem with it. Her grandmother often cupped Emma's face in her hands, just to see her again, she'd say. The doctor told her she had a nice face, not only lovely, but honest, trustworthy. Emma knew she was putting her on her honor. Everything in a doctor's office was confidential. She didn't have to spell it out. But it was okay that she had. She needed to be careful, especially with strangers. She touched her hair too, and Emma had been glad it came to her shoulders and that she'd just washed it.

Most days Doctor Snow (she had told her to call her Melanie but somehow she hadn't been able to do that. Not yet, anyway. It would seem disrespectful). She usually brought Sadie inside with her and let her sit under her desk, but it was beautiful out today so she'd probably leave her out there for awhile. She'd lie in a sunny, grassy spot and watch life in the next yard, on the other side of the fence. An elderly couple who owned a black scotty dog lived there and Sadie seemed to find the little dog fascinating. If it got too warm Sadie would find shade under the lone apple tree in the yard or go into her doghouse, which was white with blue trim. Her name was painted on the side in big, curvy blue letters.

Her thoughts fled at a light rap on the door. She glanced at her watch as she went to see who it was. It was only 8:20 a.m. Doctor Snow's first appointment wasn't until ten o'clock. She closed the venetian blind and left the window.

She opened the door to see a young man standing there, a tentative smile on his face. He had red hair and that pale complexion some redheads have. No freckles though. He wore dark-rimmed glasses and his shoulders in the beige bomber jacket were slightly drawn in, as if he'd been heavily rained on. Not possible on this bright, sunny day though.

"Good morning. May I help you?"

"I - I'm Randall Walls and I was wondering if I could see Dr. Snow this morning."

"I'm sorry, but you'd have to make an appointment. Are you a patient of Dr. Snow's?"

"No. But I've heard she's very good and I... my little girl died a few weeks ago and I've just been so depressed I ... I can't eat or sleep." He made to run a hand through his hair, then changed his mind and shoved the hand in his pocket. "Or even think straight. I won't take much of her time. I just need... wanted to talk to her for a few minutes. I've heard she's very good," he repeated.

He looked so wretched, so distraught, Emma could not bring herself to say an out and out no, not without first talking to Dr. Snow. It couldn't hurt to ask though she generally didn't see patients without an appointment, not unless it was urgent and she knew them. "Please, sit down. Would you like coffee? It's all made."

"No. I'm fine, thank you. I'm sorry for bothering you." That's her out in the yard, isn't? I saw her when I was walking past. I recognized her from her picture in the paper.

Terrible what happened. Will she bring the dog inside? I'm afraid of dogs. I got bit as a kid. I - I'm sorry."

"There's nothing to be sorry about, Mr. Walls. It's not a problem. I'm sure she'll leave Sadie outside in your case. She understands about phobias." Of course she did. "Though you have nothing to fear from Sadie. She's a sweet, gentle dog."

"I'm sure she is. It's ... it's just me. I'm..."

He was going to apologize again. Before he could, Emma said, "Please, sit down. I won't be a minute."

He sat in one of the chairs and tapped his foot on the floor and tried to smile at her. "Thank you."

"I'll just be a minute. I'm very sorry about your daughter, Mr. Walls."Emma went into the doctor's office and opened the side door that led out to the yard. She was sure she would make an exception in this case, considering how devastated he was. She was right. Dr. Snow said she would see him in a few minutes.

Returning to the waiting room, Emma said, "The doctor will be pleased to see you this morning Mr. Walls, if you don't mind wait..." But the man was gone. Strange, Emma thought. She peered out the window that looked onto the street, but he was nowhere in sight.

"Not all that strange at all," Doctor Snow said when she came downstairs, the yellow tee-shirt and jeans replaced with a grey striped skirt and silk pale blue blouse. "People often change their minds about seeing the therapist they'd thought for a moment might help them. It's about the fear of giving up control," she told Emma. "We're not always comfortable trusting our private selves to others. Our innermost feelings. Or maybe he honestly believes no one can help him." And he could be right, she thought sadly.

She could only imagine how terrible it must be to lose a child. How he must be grieving.

"He has a fear of dogs," Emma said. "He told me he got bit as a child. Maybe he thought you would bring her inside anyway."

"Oh, of course I wouldn't have, Emma. Well, he's gone now. Did he leave a number where he can be reached?"

"No. We didn't get that far. I'm sorry, I should have..."

"No, no, Emma. You did exactly right, not pressing him. Well...he may call back."

She accepted the coffee Emma gave her with thanks and took it into her office, still trying to shake off the lingering feeling of someone standing on the sidewalk watching her this morning.

Sadie seen that someone and reacted as if that individual posed a danger. She liked people, generally. Melanie was sure she wouldn't mind someone just watching them playing fetch. Would she? But she had growled and barked, threatened the watcher, in protective mode. Whoever it was, went on their way.

By the time Emma rapped on the door to tell her her first appointment had arrived, she'd put the matter out of her mind. Before she did, it occurred to her that her watcher might very well have been Randall Walls. In fact, probably was Randall Walls. He must have stood observing her for a few minutes before he knocked on the door. Assessing her. Dogs can usually sense when someone doesn't like them. They can smell fear. And he'd said he had a fear of dogs. Yes, that would explain it.

A soft step came across her threshhold.

"Hi, Andrew. How are you?"

"Hi, Dr. Snow. Pretty good."

She was gratified to hear his voice so much stronger and confident since the last time she'd seen him. He sounded upbeat. He'd obviously been doing the inner work he needed to do, and it showed. This young man had been so bullied as a child that the aftermath had followed him into adulthood and was stopping him from living life to its full potential. They'd been making good progress before Melanie's accident and Melanie was glad he'd come back. Though she had a feeling he wouldn't need her too much longer and that made her feel good. Made her feel that she could still make a difference.

Chapter 16

Allison brought the video tape with her on her next appointment. "I took it to the police," she said, "but they said they couldn't do anything because they couldn't make out the license number and we couldn't be sure it was Ed. I guess he'll have to kill me first before they can do anything."

"Leave it with me, Allison. I have a friend who might be able to enhance it enough to bring up the licence number. At least we can give it a try. Some men think of women as a possession and they don't take well to having their property taken over. He's clearly desperate. Like I said, be careful." Forewarned is forearmed, came the old adage. She hoped it would prove out in this case.

"He won't be happy until I'm dead."

The happiness she'd heard in Allison's voice in their last session was all but gone, replaced by fear and anxiety. She was near tears.

"Don't say that. When you get some proof that he's violating the restraining order, and you will, they'll toss his butt in jail."

"For how long though? A couple of months? And what happens after that ...when he gets out?"

Melanie had no answer for that. "Let's just take it one step at a time, okay? And have faith."

Sadie crawled out from under the desk, and curled up by Allison's feet, as if to show support, "What a good girl you are," Allison said. "A fine friend." To Melanie, she said, "Maybe I should be like you and just forget men. Get a dog for a companion. Oh, darn, I'm sorry, I ... I didn't mean...."

"I know you didn't. It's okay. I know what you meant." She had to work a bit to keep the smile in her voice.

Later in the day, her determination to be as independent as possible reinforced, Melanie phoned the blind school to see if a person could train their pet to be a guide dog.

"Yes, it's possible," the woman on the line said. "Though it's a common misconception that a Guide Dog is essentially a well-trained pet. Nothing could be further from the truth. This is one of the most highly trained working animals you'll ever meet. On the other hand, like I said, it's not impossible, but I do recommend you get a trainer to work with you. I'll give you the number of a woman I know who used to be in the business of training guide dogs. She's retired now, but occasionally does some work locally, or offers her services as a consultant. I think you and your pet -- Sadie...?"

"Yes."

"Well, you and Sadie might just benefit from her expertise. The qualities you describe definitely make her an excellent candidate, although we do like to start training them earlier. Regardless, it won't come together overnight, Melanie, no matter how wonderful she is. It's a big commitment, requiring enormous patience on both your parts; a lot of hours of trial and error. Good luck, dear."

Melanie thanked her and ended the call. She had at first thought she wasn't that sort of person who would do well with a guide dog, that she didn't have the right temperament for it. But Sadie was changing her mind about that.

* * *

That night, Francie's husband, Norm Henderson called to invite her to Francie's birthday celebration; she'd be thirty-seven on May 16th, Saturday, which of course Melanie already knew. He'd made reservations at Angelina's for next Saturday night. "Dinner and a little dancing, good food," he said. "I've invited a few friends. The celebration would have a pretty big hole in it if you weren't there, Melanie. I know it would mean a lot to her if you'd come."

A dinner party was the last thing she was in the mood for but there was no question that she would be there to help celebrate Francie's birthday. She hardly needed coaxing. Francie was her best friend. "Of course I'll come, Norm. I'm looking forward to it."

After hanging up, she wondered if Matt would be interested in going with her. Norm would have invited other couples and she didn't like the idea of being odd woman out. Was Matt still seeing someone? Gretchen? Well, Gretchen could hardly be jealous of a blind woman, could she? Especially someone who was just an old friend of Matt's. Still, she didn't want him to feel obligated. It wouldn't be a real date, of course, just friends attending another friend's birthday celebration. She called the station and when he wasn't there, left a message. He called back within five minutes. She let the phone ring twice before answering while she worked up the nerve to ask him, and wondered why she was making such a big deal of it. She answered.

"Hi, Mel, what's up?"

"Hi. Uh, Norm, Francie's husband just called and invited me to a dinner party at Angelina's Saturday night. It's her birthday. I was wondering if you're not busy if you'd..."

"I'd love to be your escort," he cut in cheerfully. "What time shall I pick you up?" She hadn't expected it to be so easy; he'd actually sounded pleased that she'd asked him. Well, they were friends, weren't they? And she knew Matt liked her company. So why was she so surprised? But she didn't want him to feel awkward either.

"Around eight-thirty would be fine. Norm made the reservation for nine o'clock. Look, Matt, it's ... it's not really like a date, so please don't feel any pressure. Just friends helping to celebrate the birthday of a very good person who deserves a little fun."

"Not a date, huh. Well, no, of course not. But I'm thinking it's also been a while since you had a little fun. We'll dance the night away. We'll be eighteen again?" She heard the teasing in his voice.

"Thanks, Matt. I really appreciate this. But I'm doubtful I'll be doing any dancing. Look, I know I'm kind of leaning heavily on my friends these days, but..."

"Like the song says, "Lean on me." His soft, very sexy chuckle over the line caused a flutter in the pit of her stomach, or thereabouts. "See you Saturday night, Melanie."

Almost at once, she began mentally sorting through her closet as she considered what to wear. She decided on her little black number with the lacy sleeves. It suited her, and was also easy to find in the closet. She had a pretty pair of crystal drop earrings that would go fine. The heels on her black slingbacks weren't very high. Stop it! She told herself. You sound like a giddy teenager getting ready for the prom. What was the matter with her? She and Matt were friends and that was all they would ever be. She had Sadie for her life's companion, she thought sardonically, recalling Allison's stinging comment, however innocent. Anyway, Saturday night isn't about you. It's about Francie. Get over yourself. Although he did say they'd dance the night away. Like they were eighteen again. Was that even possible?

Lord, when had she gone from not wanting to go to the party at all to anticipating the evening with a fevered brain, all caught up in what she was going to wear. But Matt was right; she could use a little fun in her life. That was the way to look at it. There'd been nothing but talk of the murders for weeks now. A change of topic would do them all good and Francie deserved to have a great birthday, with all her friends in the best of moods.

Another thing to the good, she wouldn't have to worry about shopping for a gift for her. Alan had given Melanie a gold oakleaf pendant with a tiny diamond in the center last Valentine's D ay - nothing terribly expensive but very pretty. Francie had admired it on her. She put it in its small velvet bag and slipped it into her purse. Felt the edge of the video tape at the bottom. She'd promised Allison she'd ask her good friend to see if he could blow up the shot of the car enough to get the license number, and she would do that.

* * *

Randall Walls didn't make another appointment and occasionally Melanie wondered about him, wondered how he was getting on, but she was much too busy with other patients to dwell on him. Patients like Lacey McMann, for example. Lacey was having abandonment issues, and was terrified that her out-of-control jealousy was going to drive her husband away from her. The thing she most feared. Melanie thought her fears had some validity. He apparently had given her no reason to distrust him but fears are not always rational. It wasn't really about her husband, but about learning to trust again after being badly hurt. To take the risk of loving without reservation. Today Melanie suggested that Lacey imagine the worst scenerio possible, that her husband left her and even worse, took off with her best friend. "You'd be crushed," Melanie told her. "Really thrown for a while, a long while, but you'd get past it. It would take time, but you would."

"That's happened to Shania Twain," she said.

It took a moment to process the connection. "Right. And she's healing. For a long time she lost her confidence, even her lovely voice, but today she's singing better than ever. You would too. Actually, singing's not a bad metaphor for living your life with joy. You'd still have you, Lacey. And that's pretty major. You'd be okay."

She didn't know of course if that was true. Sometimes it wasn't. Sometimes people killed themselves because they couldn't bear the pain of such betrayal and rejection. Sometimes they even turned that wrath on the object of their affection. Although she saw no tendency to violence in Lacey. She was more apt to hurt herself though she didn't think that was going to happen either. That she was relating to a beautiful, talented woman like Shania Twain was a good sign. But it was no secret that therapists didn't have all the answers. Much depended on the patient. You can only do your best work, and hope it's enough.

Chapter 17

"You look amazing, Melanie," Matt said as they moved rhythmically over the highly polished dance floor. Melanie could feel the floor's smoothness under her slingbacks and hoped she wouldn't skid on it and embarrass herself and everyone else. Angelina's night club was packed on this Saturday night, but Norm had gotten them a good table near the band to accommodate four couples. Norm's sister, a petite dark-haired woman with a great sense of humor came with her husband, Stan, an accountant, a quiet man. When he did speak, there was a pleasant tone to his voice, an intelligence in what he said. There was another older couple she'd never met before from Norm's work. They added a lot of fun to the mix.

The faint smell of Matt's cologne - a clean, male scent - brought her back to the moment.

"Thanks, Matt," she said, "you're looking pretty sharp yourself."

He said nothing, just held her a little tighter. His hand was warm and firm at the small of her waist. "I remember how you look," she said into the crook of his shoulder, deliberately teasing him. "You smell great too." She needn't have worried about slipping and falling. She felt at ease in Matt's arms. He led her perfectly, as if they'd been dancing together for years.

The music was great, consisting mainly of old standards like Fly Me to the Moon, Don't Blame Me and other of her favorites. The female vocalist was presently singing a very mellow of At last, although it didn't quite come up to the wonderful Etta James' version, but still very nice. Only Celine Dion had recorded a version that equalled James', in her opinion. Melanie's mom was a big fan of the music of the era and Melanie could picture her singing those songs as she washed up the dishes or packed Melanie's lunch for school. When did the songs stop? she wondered. When did she know she was sick?

"Where did you go, Melanie?" Matt murmured in her ear.

"Right here," she said. "Just remembering how much my mother loved this great music. I've inherited her taste for it." She fit so well into Matt's arms, as if she'd always been here. How long have I been denying my attraction to him?

"You're a good dancer," Matt said. "Like a dream."

"Thanks. You're easy to follow."

He drew her closer and she gave herself up to the music, and the moment. Trusting him to lead her around the floor safely. He was right. She felt eighteen.

When she returned to the table, Matt's hand still at her waist, she felt slightly unsteady on her feet and she wasn't blaming it entirely on her blindness. As she sat down, Francie, seated to the left of her said softly in her ear, "You make a gorgeous couple."

"Thanks. But we're just friends."

"Right. Oh, oh."

"Alan's here."

"Oh? Where?"

"A couple of tables away, just to your right. He's with a blond. She's ugly."

Melanie couldn't help laughing, despite the myriad of emotion that flowed through her. "Right. She's probably got calluses on her heels." But the stab to the heart she expected, never came. Maybe the mildest twinge of hurt. Of discomfort. She supposed a bit of wounded pride as well. She loved Francie for respecting her enough to tell her he was here instead of deciding on the basis of whether or not she could handle it. That wasn't Francie. She was treating her in exactly the same way she always had.

"Matt can't take his eyes off you, Melanie. You really look hot in that dress. Oh, oh, Alan, just looked this way and he looks like he saw a ghost," Francie said. "He said something to the blond and she's gathering up her bag and wrap. They're leaving. Good riddance. They're ruining my birthday."

"They're really going? Well, good." Melanie sipped her wine. It was an Italian brand, not too sweet. Very good, in fact. At least Alan had some sense of shame. Enough to be uneasy in her presence anyway. Or whatever.

Norm chose the moment to whisk Francie onto the dancefloor. A moment later, Matt took her hand in his. The band had launched into a jazzy version of Blue Moon. "Shall we?" he said. "I want him to see what he's missing."

* * *

Melanie had given Matt Allison's video when he came to pick her up for the party and on Monday afternoon he phoned her in her office to tell her he was coming over.

"I think your patient is not going to have to worry about him bothering her for a long time," he said. "Not only did we get a good view of his license number... but I'll tell you the rest when I get there. Unless now is not a good time."

"No, it's fine."

Ten minutes later he was in her livingroom. "I think you need to sit down," he said. She sat down on the sofa. He joined her. She waited.

"Gosh, I wish you could see this, Mel. It would do your heart good."

"What? What are you taking about? Don't keep me in suspense, Matt."

295

"Okay. There are transfers of maroon paint on the bumper and right hand corner of his van, which is dark blue by the way. The transfers match the paint on your Honda perfectly."

Shock ran through her. "What? You're kidding."

"Nope. We've already picked him up."

"Ed Greer. Dear God, it never occurred to me it was him." He must have struck her car deliberately. She didn't believe in coincidence. "He planned it."

"More than likely. He says it was an accident, but I'm not buying. At best, it's a hit and run."

Melanie was having a hard time believing they'd actually caught the guy. But it made sense. Of course Ed Greer would hate her and he had a history of violence. He saw her as instrumental in Allison's leaving him. "You'd think he would have painted over the evidence on his van."

"Plain old arrogance," Matt said. "Didn't think anyone would suspect him. After all, you'd never even met him. Never occurred to Greer his ex would be his downfall." Matt appreciated the irony. "Or maybe he just left the paint there as a trophy to remind himself that he'd gotten even with you."

"There's no question in my mind, Matt, that it was deliberate. I left for the office pretty much the same time every day."

"Or it's possible he could just have happened to spot you that morning, recognized your car, and was overcome by rage. Possible. He wanted to hurt you, that much is true. But he's not telling and we can't prove it was deliberate. Either way, he's going to jail for a long time. Hit and run is an indictable offense."

"He had to have seen the flames in his rearview mirror and kept going anyway," she said thoughtfully. "He expected-- wanted me to die. God, he really did hate me, Matt. He blames me for Allison's leaving him. But he abused his wife. He beat her. Belittled her."

"He'd never see it that way, Mel. His kind always blames someone else for their troubles."

She knew it was true. She remembered Allison telling her that Ed said it was her fault when he hit her; she just got him so damn mad. If she'd just keep her mouth shut, do what she was told, they'd be fine. But she kept screwing up. "You're right, Matt. He used to tell her, 'You really know how to push my buttons, Allie'. She believed him. Believed it was her fault – for a very long time. She figured she must deserve whatever punishment he doled out. He was a worse creep than even she knew."

"You got that right. The second I looked at the blowup of the van," he said, "My eye went straight to maroon paint on the van's right bumper. For a moment, I thought I was seeing things. Wishful thinking, you know? Your dad and I had actually talked about how lucky that would be. So I didn't trust my own eyes for a minute or two there. But it didn't go away. And then I knew we had our guy."

"He was obsessed with getting revenge. But I thought it was directed solely at Allison. I was really worried about her safety. I'm so glad you got him Matt. You said you would. Thank you."

"I wish I could give you back your eyesight. I was going to say vision, but you have plenty of that."

"I wish you could too. You're an amazing detective but you're not God." She gave a small laugh that held no bitterness.

They sat quietly for a few moments. She was acutely aware of Matt's body next to hers and had a sensual memory of how it felt being in his arms, dancing, eyes closed. It almost seemed like a fantasy in the light of day.

As if reading her mind he said, "I had a great time Saturday night."

"I'm glad. It was nice. It was good of you to come with me."

"Good of me? Don't be silly. It was my pleasure. Totally. How about we try it on our own next Saturday night?"

Her heart was rollicking in her chest, her face warm as a bonfire. He was asking her out on a real date. Nothing to do with catching bad guys. "What about Gretchen?"

"Who?"

"Gretchen. She came with you to the office one time. Are you still seeing her?"

"Oh, that Gretchen. That was a long time ago, Mel. We had a couple of dates. She had an appointment with the orthodontist that day and we met up by accident. Anyway, nice girl, but no sparks. So how about Saturday night? Maybe you could wear that little black number again. God, you are so sexy in that. But then you're lovely in whatever..."

"Matt, you don't have to play the role of good Samaritan. I couldn't bear it if --we're friends; we can be honest with one another."

"Good Samaritan?! What are you talking about? I've been crazy about you for years. We couldn't date back when because I was your patient and it was somehow unethical. Or against the law or something. And then you were seeing someone else. And then-- I don't know-- but I love you, Melanie Snow. Do you think your being blind is going to change that?"

It did for Alan, she thought.

"I'm not him," he said softly, as if she'd spoken the words aloud, and heard Sadie 'whuff'. In agreement? Sadie had excellent judgment.

"You like having your belly rubbed, eh Sadie girl?" he said. "Ah, what a good girl you are." His voice rose a fraction and she knew he had turned to face her again. "How are things going with the trainer?"

He'd said he loved her. Did she imagine that?

"Good. Great. Her name is Joyce Reardon," she said, trying to shake the dizzying spin in her head, her fluttering heart. "She's spent a good part of her life training service dogs and she's impressed with Sadie. She said she thought her last owner must have spent a lot of time working with her. But I think Sadie is just naturally smart. I bought her a new harness; she knows she's working when she wears it. She doesn't seem to mind it at all. I didn't think I would do well with a guide dog, but I'm proving myself wrong about that. I think she'll be able to be my eyes one of these days."

"I'd like to share the honor with you, Sadie. If your mistress will have me."

Sadie let out a short bark and thumped her tail on the hardwood floor. Matt's phone trilled.   He answered. Short, clipped responses. When he hung up, he said, "Gotta run.   Remember   our   'peeping   tom' incident?"

"Yes, of course, I do. Her husband took her and the child to an out-of-town relative for safety."

"That's right. An aunt. Well, she's been remembering more details about what the perp looked like. She thinks she blocked it out in the beginning. Her husband is driving her back home now and they're going to meet me at the station."

"Oh, that's great, Matt. It could be him. The killer. An artist's composite might help to catch him. Someone could recognize him if the sketch is even close."

"That's the general idea. But we'll see. It also could be just an overactive imagination on Lana's part. She could be conjuring up his features in her mind because she wants to help. I'll know more after I talk to her. I'll call you."

She walked him to the front door. He turned and laid his hands gently on her shoulders. There was a strength in his touch that went beyond the mere physical. When she didn't move away (as she had on Saturday night when he brought her home because she was still confused about his true feelings) he kissed her. And the kiss traveled through her like a slow-building heat and left her light-headed and wanting more.

"I'll call you," he said again, hoarseness in his voice that told her she wasn't alone in her feelings. But he didn't let her go, and as he drew her ever closer to him, his need was obvious. It wasn't sympathy he was feeling at the moment, no question of that. He wanted her just as much as she wanted him. Knowing that filled her with both trepidation and joy.

When she was alone again, she filled the tub with warm, sudsy water and lay soaking in it and going over every detail of the past hour - the way his arms had felt around her, the way he smelled, that low sexy laugh, his voice, telling her he loved her. Then, out-of-the-blue, or maybe not so out-of-the-blue, that long ago patient interjected herself into her thoughts and she had a strong sense that it was an important clue in the murders. She wanted to call Matt back right then but restrained herself. The following morning he picked her up and they went to Timmy's for coffee and donuts. She was sure they were beginning to be regarded as regulars by the employees, possibly a curiosity. The cop and the blind woman. She didn't mind.

"So, what's up?" Matt asked.

"I'm not sure. First, how did it go with Lana Drew?"

"She's with the artist now. I won't know anything for awhile. So...tell me."

"It may be nothing. Have you ever heard of a man by the name of Peter Burke? He's a social worker and a professor at the University of Hull, in England. Or at least he was."

"Can't say I have. Why?"

"He wrote a book titled Brothers and Sisters of Disabled Children. Burke introduced the original concept of Disability by Association. I read it years ago. And I got to thinking about a patient of mine. A teenager. I hadn't been practicing long. She had a sister who was paraplegic and as a result, was having problems in school. Her sister was only five when the accident happened; they'd gone sliding and her sled struck a tree. It was a tragedy for the whole family, as you can imagine. Since her little sister's needs were more immediate than her own, she felt ignored, and abandoned. In contrast, she blamed herself because she hadn't taken better care of her sibling. She blamed herself for what happened. She also came to resent her. She resented having to be responsible for her at school, which affected her social life in a major way. In turn, this added to her guilt since she loved her little sister. This was one mixed-up, unhappy kid. This all may have nothing to do with your killer, but I thought it worth mentioning."

"Absolutely. So how did it all work out?"

"Great actually. The older sister is happily married last I heard. The younger girl attends university and is doing well. And is a doting aunt. I get an occasional card, Christmas, Easter. The family is close."

"And your point?"

"That situation by itself won't make someone a killer. But if there were other influences-- poor role models. Physical, mental, or sexual abuse-- it might have ended differently. So much depends on the dynamics of a child's life growing up. It might even have been his mother who was infirm in some way and he carried that burden and came to resent, even hate her."

"Interesting."

"Yes. And as I said, it may mean nothing. But if I'm right, he may not be stalking his victims because it gives him a sense of power, as I first thought -- but because he fears them."

"Fears them?"

"Yes. Could be it takes every ounce of courage he has to get that close to his victims before he strangles them. I can feel your skepticism, Matt, and I get it. But if he did murder someone close to him years ago, then it could be overwhelming guilt that's driving him to kill again and again."

Chapter 18

That night The Eraser found himself riding along the narrow road that ran past his old school with no thought of how he got there. He'd seen them going into Tim Horton's this morning when he was on his way to work and he hadn't been able to get her out of his mind. He dropped things at work and got his orders mixed up. It startled him to see her, sent a shock of fear through him. Why was she still alive? Why hadn't he killed her?

The bike's headlight cast a single swath of amber light along the pavement. He braked, again as if with no will of his own. He hadn't meant to come here. Why had he? Something drew him. But what? He'd hated every minute he had spent inside those old brick walls. Just thinking of this place was enough to make the bile rise in his throat, to choke him with a rage that went beyond mere anger. Yet here he was. A visitor into his past.

The chain-link fence enclosed the yard where the boys had played baseball. He could hear their yells and catcalls and mean laughter even now.

Darkness had fallen but he could see the school with no problem, just as it had always been, red brick, tall windows, now lighted by a bright moon in a star-strewn sky. He got out of the car and wandered close to the fence. A light gust of wind ruffled his hair as it had that day. As he stood there looking through the fence, his thoughts drifted down through the years, back to the day The Eraser came into being.

He'd been watching through the fence that day, watching as the boys lobbed the ball to one another. Hearing the 'thwack' with each solid catch. One of the bigger boys, Marv Hendricks had spotted him watching them and was coming over. At first, his heart had jumped and he felt nervous, palms sweaty on the handles of Emiline's wheelchair. He was thinking that maybe he was in for it, wouldn't be the first time, but then he saw that Marvin was grinning at him in a friendly way and he let himself relax a little. Marvin raised his cap and ran a hand through his mop of red hair. "You wanna take your retard sister home and play ball?" he asked gruffly. "We need another player. You got a glove, right?" He already had a deeper voice than any of the rest of them. The half-smile (smirk, he thought now) stayed on his face like he couldn't get rid of it if he wanted to.

The other boys were standing around on the field watching, waiting. Robbie Bosco was tapping his bat against his red sneaker, impatient, but interested in what was going on between Marv, Robbie's hero, and himself, 'The nurse', which is what they sometimes called him. Had he heard right? They were asking him to play ball with them? To be on their team? At first, he thought it was some kind of mean joke like so many others they'd played on him and he wasn't sure how to answer, when Marv growled, "Well, you wanna play or not?"

"Yeah," he murmurered. "Sh sure."

He pretended not to hear what he'd called Emiline, even though it made his face burn, made him hot with shame. Shame because it was the truth, but mainly because he hadn't defended her. It didn't matter though, not as much as it did that they wanted him in the game. Anyway, she WAS a retard.

He ran the whole way home, feet flying over the dirt road, pushing Emiline ahead of him, her wheelchair rocketing over boulders and ruts in the road. Emiline liked the speed and made a squealing sound that was almost a laugh. He laughed too; he was happy. He could have flown home and looked down on Evansdale's rooftops as he soared above them. He hadn't really begun to hate her yet. He loved his little sister, even felt sorry for her. But it made him mad too that he could never go anywhere or do anything without her. Made him mad that her head lolled like a broken doll's and she drooled on herself.

That she would dirty her pants and he had to change the saggy diaper. Sometimes the mess and the smell made him gag.

As he ran, images of himself as a hero flooded his mind, images like in a movie. He would save the day. He saw himself making the crucial catch, smack into his glove the ball went. A cheer went up among his teammates and in the stands. The other boys lifted him high on their shoulders across the field.

Nearing the house, the fantasy faded as he thought of other times he had tried to go off on his own. "Where do you think you're going?" his mother would snap at him. "You just take Emiline with you. It won't hurt you; I've had her all day. Give your mother a break, okay?"

But not today, momma, he pleaded inside his head. Not today. "Momma please, just for an hour," he pleaded for real. "The guys asked me to play..."

"Can that whining, okay? I can't hear my program. You just watch Emmie and never mind your damn complaining about it."

She was sitting on the old plaid sofa in front of the TV, watching one of her soaps. He stood looking at the back of her head, her frizzy dark hair, the smoke rising from her cigarette. He'd been shaking and hot standing there, wanting so much to wrap his hands around that scrawny neck and squeeze until her head flopped over and she was dead. But she was his mother and he was only thirteen, five years older than Emiline. Nothing he could do about anything. So he just walked out of the room and felt as though all his hopes of ever being just a normal kid were gone like so much dandelion fluff.

Lifting Emiline from her chair, he carried her into her bedroom and closed the door. Emiline gave him a wet grin. The stink rose off her. "Shitty pants," he said, and threw her on top of the bed, where she bounced and grinned wider. Her thin legs, encased in their brown ribbed stockings stretched out before her, her feet in their black laced shoes dangling over the edge of the bad. "ants," she croaked. "Dada." Every male was Dada. She didn't know any better.

His father was a truck driver, hardly ever around and when he was he never talked to him, mostly just mumbled his displeasure at all of them and tossed back another shot of Jack Daniels. He was a big man with thick greying hair; he was mean and sometimes smacked his mother around when he had a few too many. She would cower and try to protect her head with her hands, whimpering, "Don't Al...don't...please..."

It made him sick to hear her groveling before that big oaf, pleading with him not to hit her again, and at the same time he wished he was big enough to kill his father. If he'd had a gun, he would have. The old man blamed his mother for Emiline. "Didn't come

from my side of the damn family," he'd say.
"Neither did that wimp you bore."

"Not such a wimp, daddy," he said aloud as he turned his back on the school and got back on his bike. "I did what you didn't have the guts to do. I did what needed to be done."

If she would just stay dead, he thought. If she would just stay dead.

He thought of Melanie Snow. 'Pure as the driven snow'. Except that she wasn't. It was time.

Chapter 19

Just after nine o'clock that night Melanie's phone rang and the person on the other end of the line identified himself as Randall Walls. At first, the name didn't ring a bell, but then it did. He had come to the office that morning and left without seeing her. His little girl had died. She had thought about him now and then, wondered how he was. Not good, she thought now. He sounded terrible. His voice was raspy and broken. "Could you see me?" he asked, and there was pleading in his voice.

It wasn't possible. She wouldn't see anyone in the office when she was alone, and certainly not this late at night. "Not tonight, Randall, I'm sorry. I am glad you called though. I'll be glad to see you tomorrow, first thing. Will you come?"

His voice was heavy with defeat. "It'll be too late then."

"We can talk now, then. It's your little girl, isn't it? I can only imagine how much you must miss her. When we love someone..."

"No, I don't want to talk about it on the phone."

He sounded desperate, lost and Melanie was afraid for him.

"Give me your number. Please don't do anything foolish. You just need some help to get you through this, that's all. I'll send someone..." It occurred to her to ask him how he got her private number, but she decided not to. The internet made things so easy these days.   There was something familiar about his voice. She had heard it before. Where? she wondered.

He didn't answer. Instead, he said, "I'm sorry to have bothered you, Doctor Snow. I know it's late. I don't want to live anymore, not without ... Vickie. Goodbye..."

"No, Randall, please don't hang up. Talk to me. Don't do anything to hurt yourself. I'll call 911. Someone will come and..."

"No. It will be over by the time they get here. You were my last hope, Dr. Snow. I thought if I could just talk to you in person. You seem nice. A caring person. I've heard that you're a great therapist, and I thought...but it's okay. I understand if you can't do that. If you can't see me tonight. Goodbye."

"I'll see you," she blurted impulsively. "I'll see you. Come now. It's okay. Do you know the address?" He must, musn't he? He knows the phone number.

His voice broke with emotion. "Thank you. Thank you so much. The dog? I saw it in the yard when I was here before. It's a nice dog, I know, but... "

She remembered Emma telling her that he was afraid of dogs. That he'd been bitten as a child. He still sounded like a child, a frightened child.

"It's okay. She would never hurt you, but I'll leave her upstairs."

"I'll come to the front door?"

"No, my office, Randall. Go around back and ring the bell. I'll go down and open up." She had no intention of letting him or any other stranger into her home. She also didn't intend on being alone with Randall, as harmless as he probably was. She sifted through the mental list of those she could call to come. Calling her father could make waves with Doreen, though she had to admit she'd been very good since the accident, always considerate and warm. But no. She wanted to call Matt but even in casual dress, he looked like a cop and she didn't want Randall to feel she'd betrayed his confidence. She dialed Carl's number. They'd gotten quite close since the accident. "It's Melanie, Carl. Are you busy?"

"Just got off work, Princess," he said. "Do you need a drive somewhere? "

"No." She gave him a brief explanation of the situation. "I just don't want to be alone here with him. He came to the office before but left before I had a chance to talk to him. So I've never really met him. Although he seems perfectly fine, just -- upset." That was putting it mildly. She could still hear that soft-spoken, apologetic voice on the phone.

But she wasn't taking any chances. You never knew. "Could you just sit in the waiting room, pretend you're a patient?"

He chuckled. "Yeah, sure, I can do that. I'm a natural for the role."

"Ah, you're so sweet. Thanks. I'm going down and open up the office now. Come around back to the office entrance and ring the bell," she told him as she'd told Randall. "I appreciate this, Carl. I know it's an inconvenience."

"No, no inconvenience at all. I'll see you in ten minutes." She ended the call. She felt guilty, as if she were using Carl and she supposed she was. Of course, he would be inconvenienced. But she was trying not to over-burden any one person, but spreading the feeding and care of Melanie Snow around.

"You have to stay here, Sadie," she said, unlocking the door in the kitchen that led downstairs. Sadie barked her protest.

She hesitated. "Sorry, girl. He's afraid of dogs and we don't want to distress him more than he already is, do we? "

Not surprising he'd be ravaged with thoughts of death and dying right now. It was so hard to lose someone you loved. She remembered how devastated she'd been herself after her mother died. Beyond comforting. The pain grew less sharp over time, but she never stopped missing her. Death is so final. Just the knowing that it's the last time you'll ever see that person, hear them laugh, touch them. How much worse it must be to lose a child. She could understand how you might want to go too, to follow that beloved child into the beyond. Sometimes she had felt that way about her mother. Her father had told her that her mother was a star in the heavens, another angel watching over Melanie. But at twelve years old, Melanie didn't quite believe him. She had just wanted to be with her. She'd been so angry at God at the time, the angel story didn't quite work for her.

Behind the closed door at the top of the stairs, Sadie whined and barked. It wasn't like her to complain about being left behind. For an instant something instinctive in her implored her to go back and unlock the door and bring Sadie downstairs with her, but she shrugged off the warning voice. Carl would be here any minute now. It would be all right.

She'd chosen to wear a grey blouse and slacks, a long navy cardigan. Low-heeled grey patent-leather shoes and small pearl earrings completed the ensemble. Professional. Dressed to inspire confidence. At least that was the intention. Feeling an inner chill, she did up the buttons on the sweater.

When she reached the bottom step, she put out a hand to her left and flicked the wall button upward to 'on'. At once, the soft buzz of recessed fluorescent lighting sounded in both the waiting room and her office. The electrician had installed the on and off switch directly across from where the railing ended and where she now stood, so it was easy for her to locate. Melanie, of course, remained in darkness, but for the sliver of greyish-white in her right eye.

Chapter 20

Across town in an old Victorian house that had belonged to her grandmother and was now hers, Emma Wilkins sat in front of the TV, but her mind wasn't on the movie starring Spencer Tracy and Katherine Hepburn. Ordinarily, she enjoyed watching the old black and white movies that her grandmother had loved before she lost her sight, but tonight her mind kept drifting back to the man who came into the office that morning a couple of weeks ago wanting to speak with Dr. Snow and had fled by the time she got back. She'd been curious about him and later Googled the name of Randall Walls, but could find no one by that name living in the area. Nor had she been able to find any obituary for a child with the last name Walls, the daughter who had died. It didn't make sense and she wondered about it. There was no Randall Walls in the phone book either. Her findings, or lack thereof, got her thinking about how he looked - his strange red hair – too red for that pale complexion, too thick, especially in the back. She was positive now that it had been an ill-fitting wig he wore and a cheap one at that. Emma had a bad feeling in her stomach and wondered if she should call Dr. Snow and let her know her thoughts, but she also didn't want to alarm her employer unnecessarily, didn't want to be a nuisance. Enough that Emma had trouble getting to sleep herself lately without visiting her anxiety on Doctor Snow. But the edginess did not go away.

She wished her grandmother were here to talk to. Since her death, the old house seemed bigger, emptier. Emma missed her. When her parents split up and went their separate ways, finding new mates who didn't want her around, her grandmother had been there for her, opening her arms and her house to her granddaughter. She had saved her life. Emma yearned for her wisdom, and her warm smile, even if she hadn't been as brave in her blindness as the doctor. But then her grandma was in her eighties when she went blind and that had to make a difference. She was also of a different generation.

It must be so hard to be brave when you live in darkness. Maybe not so much if you were born blind, though that had to be hard too, but when it came upon you suddenly as it had with Doctor Snow. When you can only sense what's around you, not see people's faces when they look at you. She could understand why her grandmother hadn't wanted to leave this house to venture out into the world.

But Grandma would know what to do in this situation. She would have been able to advise her. She ran her fingers over the white doilies on the wide chair arms, crocheted by those loving arthritic hands with such diligence and patience.

Suddenly sensing she was no longer alone in the room, Emma looked up toward the portrait of her on her wall. As Emma looked into those eyes that seemed to be looking straight at her, her grandmother's essence poured through her body like warm rays from the sun. Her voice was clear as if she were right beside her: She heard it inside her head.

'Call her, Emma. She's in danger. Terrible danger.'

Chapter 21

When Sonny's mother heard the front door close, she went to the window and watched her son hop on his blue and silver bike and take off down the street as if he were racing to a fire. When he'd left the house, his hands were at his sides and he was looking straight ahead, like a sleepwalker. She spoke to him but he didn't answer. Not even a 'see you later'. She tried not to think about the dark intention she saw in his eyes.

He had his father's eyes. Grey, cold now like the sea in winter. They used to be warm and laughing when he was a child. She'd named him James after his father, but they'd called him Sonny because he was such a bright, happy little boy. Even when Emilene came along he remained happy and helpful. She went into a deep dark hole of depression, and the responsibility of his little sister fell almost entirely upon his small shoulders. She knew it wasn't fair but had been helpless to do anything about it. She could barely look at Emilene. She blamed herself for this hideous child God had visited upon them, this drooling, boneless thing, and it didn't help that Jim blamed her too. Maybe if Jim had given Sonny the time of day, things would have been different. But he didn't. Her marriage inevitably fell apart and she grew to hate Jim Pervis every bit as much as she'd once loved him.

Jim was a big man, good looking, with a way of making you feel that you were the most special woman on earth. But it was the back of his hand he gave her once the ring was on her finger. And then came Emiline.

She watched until Sonny disappeared around the corner onto Baines Avenue, then she turned away from the window and went upstairs; his room was located at the end of the hall. His door was locked as she knew it would be. "I need my privacy," he'd said when he put the new lock on the door. And she hadn't minded really. Young people need their privacy, she told herself. But she'd had disturbing suspicions about Sonny lately, uneasy thoughts that frightened her and made her feel ill when she dwelled on them too long. But she'd always had them. But now she knew she had to know the truth, whatever that truth turned out to be. So she swiped the key out of his jacket pocket one-night last week when he was out, God knows where and had a copy made.

The key was in the slot but she hesitated to turn it. She let out a long, slow breath, trying to gather her courage. Then she turned the key and let herself into the room. Into what she would later think of as 'the door into hell'.

Sonny hid his bike in some bushes and was crossing the street that ran behind the blind woman's house where the entrance to her office was when he saw the car pull into the drive and a man get out. He slowed his pace, at once beginning to fondle the scissors he always carried in his pants pocket, the ones he'd used to cut Dora Nabers' fingernails with and to cut off a snippet of her hair to take with him, as he had with them all. Not enough hair that anyone would notice. He liked to take them out of their hiding place and look at them sometimes, feel the texture of the hair between his thumb and forefinger. Remember the faces that went with them. Sometimes it made him weep. Other times he would just feel a cold fury drumming through his veins.

He thumbed the protective piece of plastic off the pointed ends of the scissors and ran a finger over the cool steel. She must have phoned a friend, like on that TV millionaire show, he thought, the one his mother always watched. Not likely there'd be another patient showing up at this time of night. Did she think he was stupid? He grinned to himself. Well, this friend wasn't going to save her.

"Hey," he yelled, friendly-like, using the hospitality voice he used in his work every day. The man stopped and turned around. A big man, not young. Something about him reminded him of his father. Maybe just his bigness, or the hair, greyish white in the moonlight. But he sensed no danger from the man as he always did with the man who sired him. Sonny waved and loped toward him, smiling in the way you'd smile at a friend you knew but whose name you couldn't quite recall.

* * *

When the soft knock sounded on the door, Melanie said tentatively, "Carl?"

"It's Randall Walls, Doctor Snow."

She stood there for the longest moment, trying to block out Sadie's plaintive whining from the top of the stairs, her furious scratching at the door. She'd never known her to be like this. Always, Sadie would lie patiently behind the door until Melanie opened it again.

She had her hand on the doorknob but didn't turn it right away. This is a mistake. Don't open it. But then she did open the door, even though her hand had become clammy on the knob. Even though every instinct warned against it. She had said she would see him, and how could she say no now? She couldn't. If she should find out tomorrow morning that he'd shot himself, or thrown himself over a bridge after she turned him away, she would never forgive herself. She couldn't just leave him standing out there anyway. She should have brought Sadie down with her, though, whether he was afraid of dogs or not. She could have kept her on a leash. She was going crazy up there, her whining turned to frantic barking.

"Hello, Doctor Snow."

Too late now. But there was nothing to worry about. After all, her Uncle Carl would show up any minute now. At least she'd had enough sense to call him. She wasn't a complete moron. But where was he? It must be at least fifteen minutes since she called him. She listened for the sound of his car, the crunch of wheels on the gravel drive. Come to think of it, she hadn't heard Randall drive up in a car, either. Had he walked? Outside her door, there was only silence, interrupted by the occasional whisper of a passing car.

"Hello, Randall." As she spoke the name, her phone burbled in her sweater pocket. She reached in and turned it off. "Sorry." She'd call them back, whoever it was. Randall Walls was her first concern, a patient in a desperate state of mind and deserving of her full attention.

"You must be feeling better, Randall. You sound much calmer than you did on the phone."

"That's because you agreed to see me, Doctor."

Had there been a trace of contempt in the word 'doctor'? No, she must have imagined it. Don't go getting paranoid, she admonished herself.

"Please, come into my office." Where are you, Uncle Carl?

* * *

He followed her into her inner office, closing the door behind him. Light oak office furniture, and pale blue walls, were meant to have a calming effect on her patients. Her framed degrees and diplomas hung on the wall to his left.

Sonny could barely believe he was sitting across the desk from her. That he had made it happen. It seemed almost surreal. He hadn't spoken with any of the others. Certainly never sat across from them like this before he killed them. Never talked to them. She had a nice voice, soft and sincere. She was pretty, too, with smooth, creamy skin. Only a tiny mole on her neck marred her complexion. Her eyes were very blue, like cornflowers. He remembered seeing her at the drugstore that day, trying on sunglasses, standing with her friend who was helping her to choose just the right pair. She should wear them all the time, he thought, even here in her office. Maybe especially here. He didn't like her looking at him. Her eyes made him uneasy. He had not thought of that. She had a way of looking at him almost as though she could see him, but he knew she couldn't. Emmie? Are you in there, Emmie? Yes, of course, she was. This woman had invited her in. Invited her in to torment him.

"Let me begin by saying I'm not sure I can be of any real help to you, Randall." She was leaning forward, her elbows on the desk, slender fingers making a pyramid beneath her chin. "What you're feeling is a natural result of your loss. I can't know your pain at losing your daughter, but I think I have some sense of what you're feeling. I'm very sorry."

"You've lost things too," he said.

"Yes, it's true. I have. Most people have. But I'm sure losing one's child is the ultimate suffering. A crushing sense of loss. It will take time, but gradually the sharpness of that pain will lessen. Although I know that doesn't seem possible right now. The sense of loss will never go away completely of course. Our children are not supposed to die before we do." She knew she was talking in cliches, but could think of no words that would lessen his grief. This was a journey he had to take alone.

"She was the light of my life, you know. My Princess. I miss her so much." Sitting here talking about her like this, it was as if it were true. The chair he sat in was padded, comfortable, the music soft and relaxing. He made himself look directly into those blue sightless eyes. He could lunge across the desk right now and strangle her to death if he chose, and no one could stop him. He could close those eyes forever. His fingers twitched, alive with eagerness to encircle that pale slender neck and squeeze. She wouldn't even have time to scream. Not that it would do her any good.

"How old was she?"

"Seven."

"So young. May I ask how she died?"

"Died? Oh. Men Meningitis."

"Such a terrible disease." He had hesitated. Why? "Well, Randall, you're going through a natural process of grieving right now. There's no way to circumvent that. Grief has its stages, but we are all different. Some of us stay in that dark hole of despair longer than others. Some people feel emotion more deeply than others. Your beautiful little girl is gone from you. Though not necessarily forever. If you have faith, then perhaps knowing she's in Heaven will bring you some comfort. People of strong faith seem to get through these tragedies better than others."

"I believe in the Lord."

"Good. That's good, Randall. Have you considered joining a group ¬- of other parents who have also experienced the loss of a child, and who know your pain? It can sometimes help..."

"No," he cut in. "I'm no joiner. That's not for me."

She nodded. She understood. It hadn't been for her either. They had suggested in the hospital that she join a group of people who had lost their sight. She had said no. They thought it was a strange attitude for someone who did therapy for a living. No one said that, but she could tell. Maybe they were right.

"You'll have to find a way to compartmentalize your pain so that you can get on with your life. And even that will seem to you like a betrayal of your child. We don't get over these things despite the adage 'Time heals all wounds'. It doesn't. We just learn to live with our losses. There's a gaping hole in your life now. But one day you will be able to find pleasure in thoughts of her time on this earth with you. Your memories will comfort you. No consolation now, I know. In the meantime, I have a few suggestions that may help. You might want to try a sleep aid. Valerian may help. Some patients swear by it. But it's a temporary aid. If it doesn't work for you, Randall, I can refer you to another doctor who may prescribe something stronger. But give Valerian a chance. It's an herb but quite effective."

"Okay."

"And try to force yourself to eat." She smiled at him to show him she understood.

But of course, she couldn't since she had no children of her own, Sonny thought, momentarily forgetting that he had never had a daughter, that he made her up. That little fact he put in some far corner of his mind. But he had made it his business to know about Melanie Snow. To know about them all. She thought she was so clever telling other people how to live their lives.

"Even if it's just a little," she said, innocent of the track her new patient's mind traversed. Of his deadly intention. Though she did have a vague sense of something not quite right about Randall Walls. "Milkshakes can be good," she said. "At least you'll get your nutrients. You don't want to let yourself become sick. And you need your strength right now, especially since you're feeling emotionally fragile. You might also want to supplement with a daily vitamin. And there are a couple of books you might find helpful too."

She gave him the titles but he was no longer listening.

Pat answers, he thought. Bullshit advice. Did she think she'd told him anything a person wouldn't know on their own? You didn't need a degree to spout all this crap.

"What was your daughter's name?"

"Em... Vickie."

The question caught him off guard and he almost said Emiline before he caught himself and said "Vickie". It was so easy to check stuff out on the internet these days. Not that she could, but she could ask her receptionist to search his name. Well, she wouldn't find him on the web. Funny how the name Vickie just popped into his mind. It was his grandmother's name, on his mother's side. She died when he was nine but he remembered her well. He liked going to her house. There was always a bowl of real fruit on her table and her kitchen smelled of apples. She always seemed glad to see him too. "Hey, Sonnyboy," she'd say, and ruffle his hair and laugh. And she wasn't afraid to speak her mind to his mother, either. And he knew she didn't like his father. The house on Neally Street had been torn long ago; he couldn't even visit the building anymore. Just a vacant lot there now.

"When did Vickie die?"

"Six months ago." Like the name Vickie, the answer just popped out of his mouth without conscious thought. Should he have said that? What did it matter? She wouldn't be telling anyone.

"Sometimes good honest work can help us get through the day. What kind of work do you do, Randall, if you don't mind my asking."

He shifted in the chair and said, "Odd jobs. Landscaping, basic maintenance. That sort of thing."

She nodded slowly. "I see." The small bell on her desk dinged. She pressed the button to off. "Sorry, Randall. Well, you sound like you're in much better spirits than when we spoke on the phone."

"Oh, I am. You're listening for something, Doctor Snow. Are you expecting someone?"

She hadn't known it was obvious. "Yes. Another patient," she lied.

"Suicidal, like me?"

"No." She heard the smile in his voice, and a small thrill of fear trickled down her spine. Something was wrong here. She wasn't imagining it. She could still hear Sadie whining upstairs, though the barking had stopped. "My dog needs to go out, Randall. I'll just bring her down and let her out in the yard if you don't mind. It'll only be a minute. Don't worry, I'll have her on a leash."

"I'm not worried. But I do mind, Doctor. You're not going anywhere."

Something cold and metallic touched her cheek then and she heard herself gasp. When he took it away, she touched her fingertips to her face and they came away wet and sticky. She smelled something metallic, a coppery smell. Blood.

Oh, God. Blood. She swallowed and told herself not to scream. She was sure it was the blade of a knife he had pressed against her cheek. And she suddenly knew what that meant, and her stomach flopped over like a fish in cold water. Uncle Carl. He'd stabbed Uncle Carl. It was all her fault; she'd called him here and told him she needed him. Called him to his death. Her eyes welled with tears of anger at herself. How could she have been so stupid, so careless? So damned determined to be independent that she'd risked both their lives. She deserved whatever happened to her, but Carl didn't. He was just a nice kind man who only wanted to help.

"Scissors come in handy for so many things," he said, speaking in a monotone, almost hypnotic voice.

Not a knife then. Scissors. She could still feel the wet stickiness on her cheek, her fingertips, drying on her skin. She must remain calm, and keep her wits about her. She would not allow herself to regress to that cowering thing that Alan had managed to reduce her to. She refused to go into that pathetic fetal position again even in her mind. No, not ever again. That didn't mean that she wasn't frightened, because she was. She was terrified. But she wouldn't let him see her fear. "Let us just talk a little more, Randall. That's what you wanted, isn't it? For us to talk?"

"Name's Jimmy - Jimmy Purvis, but everyone calls me Sonny. You can call me Sonny if you like. Sure. We can talk. Are you really blind? I saw you with your white cane when you were leaving the hospital. Then later at the drugstore with your friend. You look like you can see. Is Emiline with you?"

His voice had taken on the cadence and pitch of a child. A young boy. Emiline? That was the name he had begun to say before he changed it to Vickie. There was no Vickie, she realized.

"I'm sorry," she said. "I don't know anyone by that name."

"You're lying. She's my little sister. She hides in the defectives."

"Defectives?" The women he murders. "You think she - possesses their bodies?" Our bodies.

"No. Emiline would never do that. She just enters the defectives softly and watches me through their eyes."

Her mind was a clamor of noise making it almost impossible to think. He was mad, by all standards.

"Unobtrusively," she said, for want of something to say. It was important to keep him talking, that much she knew. While he was talking, she was still alive.

"Yes. That's the right word. Unobtrusively. I read a lot, you know. I'm not dumb. But you let her in, Dr. Snow. She can't enter her hosts unless she's invited."

"I didn't invite her, Randall. You must believe that. She's not in me."

Melanie had no weapon with which to defend herself, only her limited knowledge of the human psyche and her intuition. Would it be enough?

Allison had told her she had an all-knowing aura about her now. "Like you can see into a person's soul as well as her mind." The look of the clairvoyant. She hoped she was right.

"You killed those women. Those women whom you saw as flawed. They did nothing to deserve what happened to them."

"I'm serving the Lord. They were mistakes. I erased them. I handed them up to Him."

Her mouth and throat had gone dry. She would try a different tactic. Her heart was thumping so hard in her chest that she thought it might just burst. The reality of her situation was clear. She was sitting here across the desk from a crazed killer she couldn't even see. And no one knew. Except for Carl. And he was... no, don't go there. Keep him talking. She could press the emergency button on her phone. Yes, of course. She could -- would, do that. At the moment, however, both hands were on her desk, folded together, resting on the hardwood top. The phone was in her pocket. The pocket lay heavy on her thigh. Talk. Ask him something.

"Is Emiline watching you now, Rand...Sonny?"

"You know she is. Don't play head games with me, Doctor Snow. Don't think you're so clever I don't know that's what you're doing. You're stalling. Trying to stop the inevitable. Your death. But I'll answer your question anyway: Yes, she is. And you know she is. When I look in your eyes it's like you can see me. But you can't, can you? Only Emiline can see me."

Don't answer. Don't reassure him. She unfolded her hands, and let the left index finger curl beneath her chin. A listening, sympathetic pose.

Her right hand crept away from the desk and down toward her sweater pocket.

She assessed her chances of escape, which were poor at best. There was no way past him. The only other door was at her back, leading outside to the yard, and it was bolted. The small brass clock with its timer sat on the desk, near her left hand. The timer was off now.

"You never had a daughter, did you?"

"Ah, you figured it out." He went back to speaking in that chanting way, as though he'd gone far away from her in his mind. "I had a sister once though," he said, repeating what he'd already told her. He'd forgotten so quickly. "She was a defective. Couldn't walk, talk...even sit up straight."

"|I see." She swallowed. "And you took care of her."

He didn't answer.

"What happened to her?" She questioned softly, already sensing the answer, not needing to hear the words spoken aloud. When he didn't reply right away, she stilled her hand, let it lie in her lap, so as not to forewarn him with any sudden movement.

"I killed her. I put a pillow over her face and I held it there until she stopped jerking and her hands and feet stopped moving."

Horror crept over Melanie. Gooseflesh rose on her arms, despite the sweater. Oh, God. She was in serious trouble here.

His expressionless tone suddenly turned animated, defensive. "She was a retard. A stupid retard. That's what Marvin called her."

"Marvin?"

"Yes."

As if she should know who Marvin was. But in the way he'd said it, she intuited that it was someone from his boyhood. What kind of childhood that was, she was just beginning to get a handle on.

"Now I am The Eraser. I am ridding the world of defectives. That's the bargain I made with God. But she won't stay dead."

"You're talking about your sister. The God I believe in wouldn't ask you to kill his children, Randall. And we are all his children.

He said nothing.

"What happened after Emiline died?" she asked.

"They buried her. Joke. ha ha. Nothing happened, Doctor. My mother told the police she died of her condition. She simply stopped breathing. They believed her. Everyone did."

"But you knew better. Do you think your mother knew what happened to her?"

"Maybe. Yes, I think momma knew I killed Emiline. She never said though."

"I see." Melanie's mind raced frantically, trying to think of a way out of her dire situation, but nothing came.

"She wasn't sad that Emiline was gone. She pretended to be, but I knew she wasn't. But she -- Emiline -- won't stay dead," he said again. "She's in you now, staring out at me through your blind eyes. You can't see. But she can. She can. And you're letting her do that."

"You're wrong about that. She isn't in me, Sonny. I promise. She's in you. Only in you. Inside your mind." Her fingers inched off her lap, toward her sweater pocket, to the phone.

Melanie was gaining some understanding of his psychosis. The answer rose in her mind like words she might enter in a journal. Or speak into a tape recorder:

The patient is haunted by the sister he murdered. He sees her in every woman with any kind of impairment, whether intellectual or physical and strangles them to death. And he's rationalized his deeds by telling himself that he's doing it for God.

So simple, yet so complex.

"Why did you come to see me that first time?" she asked.

"You know why. I - I needed to see if she was in you. I needed to know for sure."

"I don't think that's the reason, Sonny. Well, maybe there was an element of that. But I think the main reason is that you wanted me to help you stop the killing. I don't think you want to hurt anyone else. I can help you with that. I will help you stop." Please let this work, she prayed silently. Because she believed it to be true. At least in some part of himself, he wants to stop.

"Tell me about Emiline," she said, casually removing her left hand from her chin.

"Tell you what? I told you. She was a retard."

Melanie swallowed. "But you're not the one who called her that, are you? You loved Emiline. Someone else called her that ugly, cruel name. It made you mad. You didn't mean to hurt her. How old were you?"

"Thirteen." His voice became soft, reflective. Keep him talking, she told herself, clinging to the hope that if he was engaged in conversation, she might yet save herself. Might still change his mind about killing her. She slipped her hand into her sweater pocket. Slowly. Carefully.

Just as her fingertips touched the hard edge of her phone, his hand clamped around her wrist like a steel trap and she screamed. He had stood up and was hovering over her, darkening the portion of her right eye that let in light. His breath on her face was warm and foul.

"Give me the phone, Dr. Snow. And don't press any buttons to call anyone, because I'll know if you do and I'll kill you. And then I'll slit the throat of that damned yapping thing upstairs."

Sadie was barking furiously again, and she hadn't even noticed. The barking had become part of the background noise of this nightmarish scene that was playing out with herself in the role of a potential murder victim. Like the faint hum of traffic out on the street, like the ticking clock by her left hand.

Chapter 22

Helen Pervis stood on the small oval mat in the doorway and looked around her son's room. It was neat and tidy as a girl's. Sonny had always been a neat freak. His bed was made up, the grey quilt drawn tight as a hospital bed. The only thing on the dresser top was a small dish with some change in it and a wooden tie rack that someone at work had given him for Christmas. He never wore ties though she knew he had a bunch of them hanging in the closet. The ceiling fan was whirring softly, and she pulled the cord, turning it off. What did he care about the electric bill? He didn't have to pay for it.

She went through the ill-fitting dresser drawers, pulling them out, one after the other, hearing them scrape and squeal, closing them again Nothing, just underclothes, tee-shirts, a couple of white caps he wore for his work. Next, she checked the walk-in closet. His clothes hung on plastic hangers, mainly jeans and shirts, but all clean and pressed. He did his own laundry. She switched on the bare light bulb at the back of the closet, then stood on a chair he kept by the bed with his alarm clock on it and checked the shelf. She found a broken radio and an old microscope she'd bought him one Christmas. Earmuffs. An old baseball glove that used to belong to his father, the leather worn and dry, taking on the shape of his hand. She'd almost forgotten that Jim used to play ball. A long time ago. It was at the back of the shelf that she found the blue tin cookie can with Santas painted on it. She removed the lid. Inside, were six tiny bunches of hair, each bound with a white twist tie, like tiny bundles of kindling. She felt a sense of vertigo and holding onto the back of the chair, carefully stepped down off the chair.

Helen examined the swatches of hair one by one, each a different shade. Her eye returned to the caramel-colored one and lingered there – the exact shade of Emiline's hair. She felt its silky texture between her fingers and her eyes brimmed over with tears. She put the cover back on the tin, climbed back up on the chair, and put the can back. As she did, she noticed the scrapbook with its dark green covers, further back on the shelf.

She carried the scrapbook to the bed and sat down. The bed squeaked as if a small animal were trapped in the springs. She turned the cover. Moved to the first page, and heaved a painful sigh. Went on to the next page. And the next. He'd clipped and saved every write-up from the killings of those women. They went clear back to five years ago. Two other women were murdered in a small town outside Toronto where they'd lived before moving to Evansdale; she had only a vague memory of the killings. Though her skin tingled and her heart raced with the horror of what he'd done, she wasn't altogether surprised. Somewhere deep inside, she had always known. She just hadn't wanted to face it.

Helen didn't get the newspaper so Sonny must have bought them on his own. Or more likely took them from the hospital cafeteria, newspapers customers had left behind. She turned out the closet light, smoothed the wrinkles from the blanket where she had sat down, and went back downstairs. She stared at the black phone on the living room wall for a long time, mulling over whether to call the police. Maybe she would talk to Sonny first. Though she knew she wouldn`t. There was nothing to say. Helen sat down on the sofa, lit up a Matinee Light cigarette, and turned on the TV.

An artist's composite filled the screen and she could only sit and stare at what she knew was a sketch of her son's face.

The newsman with his serious face was saying: '...the man in this sketch was reported as peering in the window of a west side resident. The resident has an obvious physical challenge and police believe the suspect is the same man who murdered two local women this past spring - Dora Nabers and J..."

Mid-word, she clicked the off button on the remote and the screen went black. Like his heart, she thought. He has Jim Purvis' black heart.

She refused to listen to the faint voice that told her it was her own indifferent heart that killed Emiline and turned her bright, cheerful little boy into a crazed killer. She was a good mother. She'd always been a good mother.

Even her own admitted truth was turned away.

Chapter 23

"Give me the phone," he demanded. His hand still gripped her wrist like a steel vice, causing her hand to tingle and throb.

"Yes," she breathed. She stood slowly. "All right. I'll give it to you." She brought the phone slowly out of her pocket. In the instant he let go of her wrist to take it, her left hand closed around the small brass clock on her desk, and feeling the heft of it, she swung it with all the force of a discus thrower in the direction of where she gauged his head to be. She was rewarded with a satisfying crack as the clock hit him full-on. He let out a curse and the phone went flying. He cursed again and staggered backward, the chair scraping the floor as he grabbed onto it. She heard him hit the floor, taking the chair with him. Without hesitation, she gripped the edge of the desk with both hands and upturned it, heard it strike flesh, then bang to the floor. Hearing his mumbling behind her, she made for the door, slammed open the bolt with the heel of her hand, and stumbled out into the backyard.

Her heart was racing like the triphammer she'd heard outside the hospital window the day she was leaving. Her mouth was dry as the ground beneath her feet. Which way to go? It would be dark out now, not that it made any difference to Melanie. She thought of hiding in the doghouse, curling up at the very back, but that would be the height of foolishness. He would know at once where she was and she would be trapped there. Instead, she made an awkward half-run toward the far end of the yard, her left hand trailing along the side of the building for guidance, her right hand flailing back and forth like a windshield wiper before her, instinctively testing for obstacles in her path. If she could just get the gate open and escape out onto the sidewalk, someone might see her waving and screaming and help her.

* * *

The ten o'clock news ran the artist's sketch of the man who had peered in Lana Drew's window as she was preparing for bed. Francie and Norman Henderson were watching TV. There was a clip of the Drew couple being interviewed. Norm gave a small chuckle. "Damn," he said, "if I didn't know better I'd swear that guy is a dead ringer for the kid who works in the cafeteria. Sonny, yeah, that's what they call him. Nice young man, soft-spoken. Always pleasant. Funny, isn't it? We always think we know someone who looks..."

"Oh, my God," Francie interrupted, dashing to the TV screen to peer closer at the sketch. "No, Norm, you're right. I've seen him in the cafeteria, too. And that's not the only place I saw him either. He was at Shoppers one day when I was in there with Melanie. She was trying on sunglasses. I'm sure it was him. He was standing at the pharmacy counter and he was staring at her. He turned away when he saw me looking at him."

"She's blind. People look."

"No. She didn't have her cane, and she doesn't look blind at first glance. Anyway, it's the way he was looking at her. There was anger in his eyes. But I could see fear in them too."

"If it was the killer, why would he be afraid of her? That doesn't even make sense. Francie, Honey, these composites seldom turn out to be someone we've seen ..."

"I know. But there are exceptions, and I think this is one. Even if we're wrong, Norm, we have to phone the police."

"If we're wrong, we could put this kid through a lot of hell. Do you have any idea how many people are calling the cops right now with other people's names they think are look-a-likes?" Norm said. "People always think they know..."

The image disappeared from the screen and the newsman was on to something else.

But Francie was already on the phone.

Melanie had the gate open when she felt his hand grab the back of her blouse. Her own hands flailed at empty air as he yanked her backward, sending her feet out from under her and landing her hard on her back on the ground. The ground was hard and cold beneath her. Terror seizing her, she imagined she saw a star-studded sky. She tried to get back up but he was on top of her, his hands around her throat and she couldn't breathe. She clawed the back of his hand and he yelped and released his hold. "Bitch," he cried, striking her hard across the face. The slap echoed inside her head, making it swim. *Don't pass out. Don't. Or you'll die.* His hand gone from her throat, the other loosened, she was able to gasp in air.

Remember Allison. Remember what she said. You have that all-knowing look about you. Like one of those mediums.

Like a clairvoyant? Melanie had asked her. She was teasing. But there was no teasing now. Make him believe. It's your only chance.

The terror slipped away and a strange calm took its place as she began to speak. "Sonny, it's me, Emiline." She made her voice childlike, plaintive in an eerie chanting way, intuiting that it was how Sonny heard Emiline in the dark of night when he couldn't sleep. Even in his waking moments. Even in broad daylight.

"You can't get rid of me by killing people. I'll never leave you. You're my big brother. I'm a part of you, now. I'm inside your head, just like Doctor Snow said. But I love you, Sonny. I've always loved you even when I couldn't say the words. I forgive you, Sonny. I forgive you. I know it wasn't your fault."

She felt him freeze above her, his entire body going perfectly still.

It was in her DNA to help people where she could, in the very fiber of her being. But right now, the law of survival was stronger, and she wanted more than anything for Sonny to believe it was Emiline speaking to him, through her. Why wouldn't he? He already believed she watched him through the eyes of those he killed. And planned to kill. Her life depended on her convincing him that Emiline had forgiven him. That the haunting - the torment - would finally stop. Please let it work.

He went silent for a long moment. Then he laughed, his body relaxing. A terrible, chilling laugh. "Good one, Dr. Snow. Almost had me there for a minute. But you're not as smart as you think you are."

The hope of escape seemed futile as his hands reached for her throat again, despair taking its place. She was helpless to stop his hands curling or his thumbs pressing into the soft flesh of her throat. Tears filled her eyes as she struggled beneath him to try to free herself. But it was no use. He was so strong. So much stronger than she was.

Then, from somewhere came the memory sense of the scissors in his pocket; he'd used them to kill her Uncle Carl. Even now, she could still feel their cold blades against her cheek, the sticky wetness from Carl's blood now dried and surely smeared on her face.

Willing herself to remain conscious, she forced her hands away from his, even while they were squeezing the very breath from her. Her hand fumbled and groped toward his jacket pocket, bright lights flashing before her eyes, lungs straining, screaming for breath. She felt the heft of the scissors inside the nylon fabric, reached inside the pocket, and gripped their handles. On the edge of unconsciousness, unable to take any clear aim, she just stabbed and stabbed until the blades found flesh, and then she stabbed again.

He grunted above her, his breath hot on her face. Just before she was about to lose consciousness, his hands left her throat and he rolled off her, staggered to his feet as she gulped in precious oxygen. Having no idea what would happen next, but grateful for the reprieve, she half-expected to feel the scissors' blades thrust into her body in retaliation. Except, unlike her, he would be able to see where he was aiming. Having nothing left to fight with, she waited. When she heard the creaking of the gate opening

and the sound of his unsteady footsteps
walking away, she felt only faint surprise.
Was she dreaming?

The sirens in the distance seemed like
part of the dream.

And then Sadie was licking at her face.

Chapter 24

Matt was sitting in the folding chair beside Melanie's hospital bed. The nurse had just removed the thermometer from under her tongue.

"Sadie took a sniff of his blood on the ground and after making sure you were okay," he said, "she shot out of that gate like a bullet. We just had to follow her in the car, the full six blocks. When we got there she was just lying down in front of his building, panting and looking up at us out of those liquid brown eyes. It was the most amazing thing, Mel. She followed the droplets of blood from where you got him in the side with the scissors. Not enough to kill him, just shallow punctures, but he bled a lot. He also had a good-sized egg on his head where you hit him with the clock."

"I wish I could have helped him."

"I know you do."

Emma had been in earlier and told her she had tried repeatedly to call her on the phone and when she couldn't get her, she called the police. At about the same time, Francie was also on the phone with the police and was able to give a first name and his place of employment.

"Maybe you did help him," Matt said. "Maybe there was no other answer for Sonny Pervis. If he didn't get the death penalty, he would have spent the rest of his life in prison. Anyway, Sadie was amazing. So were you. I don't think I would have wanted to go on if you were no longer in the world, Mel."

He smoothed back her hair with his gentle hand, and smiled at her, his warm, brandy-colored eyes, soft with tenderness. With love.

Melanie could see him, though just out of her right eye and the vision was blurry. Not so much that she couldn't see the fine lines at the corners of his eyes, his full sensual mouth. His strong jaw that right now needed a shave. No one had ever looked so handsome to her. But then he always had, even when he sat across from her as her patient all those years ago. And she had dared not admit her feelings for him, even to herself.

That she had even limited vision, was like a miracle. It was when they were carrying her in here on the stretcher that she saw the high ceiling rushing past. The young Chinese intern who was wheeling her down the corridor, his white coat so bright. She hadn't imagined she'd seen a starry sky last night as she'd thought. It was real.

Doctor Howell said she might regain complete vision in that eye, but as yet had no explanation for the reversal. There would be more tests, and she'd wear glasses now.

There had been deterioration in the left eye and that one wasn't coming back. No chance. That was fine with her. She was more than grateful to have regained even partial sight. And of course, felt very lucky to be alive at all and not Sonny's next victim. Francie said she was like a cat with nine lives. She had seven left, she said. Melanie wouldn't bet on it.

When the police arrived at Sonny's house, they found Sadie lying in front of his front door, panting. Sonny's bike leaned against the building where he'd left it. Inside, they found Sonny's (Jimmy Pervis') mother sprawled on the kitchen floor. She'd been strangled. They found Sonny in his bedroom closet. He had hanged himself by knotting several ties together.

"There was a light on at the back of the closet," Matt said. "As soon as I walked into the room I saw his shadow thrown across the bedroom floor. Not a pretty sight."

"Oh, God. So sad." Her voice was still hoarse from the near-strangling, but better than last night. Just a little sore, some bruising but she'd be okay.

"I tried to make him believe that Emiline forgave him," she said. "I think he might have believed it finally. But he couldn't forgive himself," she said. "Or his mother."

"Hi, sweetie," said a man's voice from the doorway.

"Uncle Carl," she said, beaming at the sight of the man she had feared was dead. He was wearing a maroon robe and his arm was in a sling. Sonny had tried for his heart but missed it by inches, thank God. He scuffed into the room in his slippers.

"How are you feeling?" Melanie asked.

"Just a little worse for wear and abuse." Melanie heard the double meaning in the joke, or maybe it was just in his smile. A certain sadness there. "And I know just by looking at you that you're going to be just fine. I'll be heading home this afternoon. Albert's coming to get me. Won't be driving a cab for a bit, but, heck, I can use a vacation. Just wanted to drop by and say hi before I leave."

Matt shook his good hand and said he'd be back to see her later. The doctor wanted her to stay in the hospital another day or two just to be on the safe side. She was anxious to go home but wouldn't make a fuss.

Last night when her father and Doreen had come to visit, her father had hugged Carl and said he was glad he was going to be okay and thanked him for being there for his daughter. To Melanie's surprise, when Carl rose to leave, her dad spoke up and he'd walk him back to his room, leaving her alone with her stepmother.

Doreen took her hand. "Melanie, I'm so sorry for what you've had to endure, but I'm so happy you can see – even a little."

"Thanks, Doreen. Me too."

She thought about the woman her father had loved for so many years now. She was

354

older now. No longer the young woman that Melanie had resented for so long. But Doreen had made her father less lonely and cared for him. Put up with his foolishness. Her father wasn't an easy man to live with, she knew that. He was stubborn, set in his ways, though not as much as she'd thought considering he was walking Carl back to his room. He'd even hugged him. He'd grown. Maybe they all had.

"Melanie, I'm so sorry for all the years I..."

"It's all water under the bridge, Dee-Dee," she said, using her father's pet name for his wife, thinking how important forgiveness was. Even more so for the person doing the forgiving. It freed you to move on in your life. "I wasn't any picnic either. Maybe we can all move on from here, in a better way."

And they would.

The End

Bibliography

When the Curtain Fell: Anthologized in Crimeucopia The Cosy Nostra - Murderous Ink Press - UK 2021

Dark Reunion: Originally published in Investigating Women

Freeing Henry: First Published Crimeucopia The Lady Thrillers Murderous Press Ink. 2021 UK

A Long Dark Road: First published Crimeucopia We'll Be Right Back--After This! Murderous Press Ink 2022 UK

I Hitched A Ride Into Hell: First published Books We Love 2013

Tragic Spawn: First published Books We Love 2015

**_Joan Hall Hovey novels also
published by BWL Publishing Inc._**

Listen to the Shadows
Chill Waters
Nowhere to Hide
Night Corridor
Defective
The Abduction of Mary Rose
The Deepest Dark
And Then He Was Gone

As well as penning Award-winning suspense novels Joan Hall Hovey's articles and short stories have appeared in such diverse publications as The Reader, Atlantic Advocate, The Toronto Star, Mystery Scene, True Confessions, Home Life magazine, Seek and various other magazines and newspapers. Her short story, "Dark Reunion" was selected for the Anthology, Investigating Women, published by Simon & Pierre.

Joan lives in St. John, New Brunswick, Canada.

www.ingramcontent.com/pod-product-compliance
Lightning Source LLC
Chambersburg PA
CBHW070048120726
47909CB00002B/318